Planning on Prince Charming

LIZZIE SHANE

Copyright © 2015 Lizzie Shane

All rights reserved.

This is a work of fiction. Names, characters, places, brands, media and incidents are either the product of the author's imagination or are used fictitiously. Any resemblance to actual events or persons, living or dead, is entirely coincidental.

ISBN: 1516906721
ISBN-13: 978-1516906727

DEDICATION

This book is dedicated to BFFs, the ones you can talk to about anything who get you through everything.
You know who you are.

With special thanks to
Melinda Horn & her BFF Lea Eldridge.

CHAPTER ONE

Sidney Dewitt was a coward.

On any other night she might have been ashamed of that, but after two mini-bar vodkas she was rapidly coming to terms with her cowardice and was well on her way to acceptance.

Sure, if she refused to appear on *Marrying Mister Perfect* now her business wouldn't get any of that lovely free publicity to catapult them to an elite place among wedding planners, she would never meet the man who might very well be the man of her dreams, and her mother would invariably shake her head and mutter disapprovingly about her lack of follow-through.

And then there was the bajillion dollar breach of contract suit the producers could bring against her.

But surely that was better than parading around on national television in a cocktail dress that made her look like a stuffed sausage.

Auditioning with her best friend for *Marrying Mister Perfect* had been a dare. Being chauffeured down to LA for the follow-up interviews and screen tests had been too good an opportunity to pass up—an actual look inside one of her all-time favorite television shows.

She'd never thought they would actually *pick* her.

When she'd gotten the call, her friends had screamed loud enough that the producer on the other end of the line assumed she was screaming right along, but instead of excitement, all she felt was her internal panic level being revved up to Def Con One.

She'd told herself it was just jitters. Nerves. Perfectly natural. How many nervous brides had she talked down over the years? If anyone knew how terrifying leaping into love could be, it was a wedding planner.

She'd kept telling herself it was normal to be nervous. As her friends were helping her shop and pack for the show, she'd pretended she liked being called Cinderella as they dubbed themselves her fairy godmothers. She'd played the part.

But now it was the night before the show was scheduled to begin filming, the night before the romantic adventure of a lifetime, and Sidney was facing facts.

She was a coward.

How had she thought for even a second that she could go on national television and compete with twenty-nine insanely gorgeous women to actually get the guy? The one thing she'd always been good at was being invisible—which was an asset at weddings where she could fade into the background—but she'd seen enough seasons of *Marrying Mister Perfect* to know the invisible girls went home the first night.

The show favored bold women with big personalities. She knew that and she'd thought she could do it—take a risk, jump in with both feet, be daring—but reality had set in as soon as the door to her hotel room shut.

The producers had taken her cell phone and tablet. No more contact with the outside world would be allowed until she was kicked off the show. Which meant no more Parvati and Victoria goading and teasing her into bravery. No more late night strategy sessions where

Parvati told her to follow her heart and Victoria told her to guard it—and made her vow to stay away from the alcohol lest she become famous as the girl who puked on Mister Perfect's shoes on national television.

Just hours alone in a room with her fears.

She couldn't do it.

The show would have to go on with only twenty-nine Suitorettes vying for Mr. Perfect's heart.

She might get sued for breach of contract, but what was a lifetime of debt? She wasn't brave. She wasn't daring. She wasn't Cinderella. She was more comfortable as the fairy godmother herself—making bridal dreams come true with a wave of her magic wand.

But now she was supposed to be the princess and it felt odd, a glass slipper that didn't come close to fitting.

It didn't help that she still wasn't one hundred percent sure who Prince Charming was going to be.

The show always closely guarded the identity of Mister Perfect until filming began, but it had to be Daniel. He seemed so genuine. So sweet and real. If it was Daniel, maybe she could do it.

Maybe even she could be Cinderella this time. Meet her Prince Charming, who would take one look at her and know she was the one. The television show would become a record of their romance...which would also boost Once Upon a Bride into the national spotlight and give them the kind of success that even her mother couldn't scoff at.

The business would flourish and she would finally have a ring on her finger and a fiancé who looked at her as if he couldn't believe his luck... the way the best grooms always looked at their brides. It would be a dream come true.

If it was him.

If only she could be sure. Mister Perfect had to be staying in this same hotel. Sequestered in his room just like all the Suitorettes. If she could just catch a glimpse of him...

It was against all the rules. She could be kicked off the show for leaving her room, let alone trying to make contact with Mister Perfect before the cameras were rolling.

But would that really be so terrible?

Just one little peek could ease all her fears... and if she was caught, maybe it was the universe telling her she wasn't meant to be on national television, hiding from the cameras and cringing every time she thought about them adding ten pounds.

Sidney grabbed one more mini-bar dose of clear liquid courage without looking at the label. She coughed as the kick of gin rather than vodka slammed into the back of her throat, but it did the job. Warmth and a fleeting sense of certainty ran through her veins. One way or the other, fate was going to answer her tonight.

Tucking her room key into the pocket of her yoga pants, Sidney reached for the door handle. Quick. Decisive. One way or another.

Josh Pendleton, beloved television personality and World's Biggest Hypocrite, was on a mission to get roaring drunk.

Tomorrow he would resume his duties peddling the illusion of love to the gullible masses, but tonight his marriage was officially, legally over and he figured if ever a man deserved oblivion, he did. Unfortunately, oblivion was slow to arrive and he was out of ice.

Hence his ancillary mission to replenish the bucket.

It was an insult to good scotch to water it down, but since the bottle of six-year old scotch room service had delivered so he could toast the end of his six-year marriage was a distinctly crappy vintage with notes of cardboard and a subtle hint of mold, it needed all the dilution it could get to make it palatable.

Hence the paramount importance of ice.

People really should say *hence* more often.

Josh gripped the freshly filled ice bucket with one hand, the other braced on the wall to keep him from going off course as he made his way back to his room. Or what he hoped was his room. The halls were twisty and it was getting harder to keep the details straight... except for the ones he would just as soon forget.

Like the fact that tomorrow he would resume his hosting duties for the new season of *Marrying Mister Perfect*, guiding another poor bastard toward true love, reality TV style.

A job he'd once loved.

A job he'd only landed because he was a shining example of happily married life.

A job he was going to lose in a heartbeat when his bosses found out about the divorce.

Divorce.

It ought to be a four letter word.

His hand slipped off the wall as he hit the corner and he stumbled, catching himself and correcting course.

The corridors were empty—no surprise there. The show had bought out the Beverly Hills boutique hotel for the night before filming began. All of the Suitorettes were in residence, packing on the beauty sleep in preparation for tomorrow when they would be herded over to the Suitorette mansion and paraded before

Mister Perfect on camera for the first time.

A handful of crew members were also staying at the hotel—mostly to make sure the girls stayed safely locked in their rooms and didn't accidentally make contact with one another before their sanctioned on-camera meetings.

Miranda—the show's executive producer— had insisted that Josh take one of the spare rooms at the hotel so he would be within an easy commute to the mansions in the morning and in her control, rather than risking the traffic he might encounter driving himself in from his Malibu beach house to the pair of back-to-back Beverly Hills estates where the show filmed.

Josh had acquiesced without an argument. It had saved him having to explain that he no longer owned the Malibu beach house and was now living in a block of depressing divorcee-filled apartments in Studio City.

The longer he could go without Miranda discovering he was no longer a paragon of wedded-bliss, the better the chance he might actually keep his job for one last season.

It had been a good gig, *Marrying Mister Perfect*, he thought with nostalgic fondness, even if he was the World's Biggest Hypocrite for selling love on national television.

The hours could be insane—especially during the marathon Elimination Ceremonies that lasted past dawn—but the work was easy. And there was never a dull moment in the world of reality television. Every season had its own scandals and tears, but it was also awe inspiring, in a way, to see each new batch of romantic hopefuls arrive at the Suitorette Mansion, ready to throw themselves headlong onto the pyre of love, praying the fates and reality television gods would be in their favor.

Poor saps.

Most of them would go home heartbroken, sobbing their eyes out for the cameras, and even the winners didn't have an impressive track record of making it all the way to the altar.

And even if they did, what chance did anyone have of going the distance these days?

Divorced.

Josh staggered to a stop, bracing his weight on the door in front of him and squinting blearily at the number. Had he been in 312? Or 321? Why did everything have to be so damn complicated?

He fumbled with his key. Down the hall, a door opened and closed. He swung toward the sound, and the world blurred, his vision taking a moment to catch up to the movement. He had only the vague impression of a blonde blur before something soft and warm slammed into him and he went down like a redwood, ice flying.

His arms closed instead around feminine curves as he landed on his back with a grunt—and those feminine curves landed on top of him in a tangle of limbs. A feminine yelp filled his ears as ice rained down around them.

"Holy crap. You're Josh Pendleton. I flattened Josh Pendleton."

His alcohol-blurred vision cleared and he found himself staring into the most striking eyes he'd ever seen. Teal. Her eyes were freaking *teal*.

She squirmed, wriggling off him, and the blood in his body made a detour away from his brain as her delectable curves rubbed everywhere. "I'm so sorry. I wasn't looking. Are you all right?"

She touched his arm and he snapped out of his

momentary stupor, muttering an apology and stumbling to his feet. It was only when they were both upright and he was relatively steady that he realized he still had a three-quarters full ice bucket tucked under one arm.

"The ice survived unscathed. I think I'll live. How about you?"

"No injuries to report."

Pink lips twitched in a smile and dim recognition flickered in the inebriated recesses of his mind. Something associated with the show. Makeup artist perhaps?

"I know you."

Her grin broadened. "Well, we haven't been properly introduced, but I am up on the auction block this season. Sidney. Sidney Dewitt."

Distracted by the way the sheer, pale green fabric of her threadbare Tinkerbell T-shirt clung to her slight curves in a way that was surprisingly erotic for such a modest style, it took a moment for her words to register through his liquor-slogged thoughts.

This season.

A Suitorette. Crap. She was one of the *Marrying Mister Perfect* Suitorettes. One of the thirty extremely eligible young ladies who would be vying for Mister Perfect as he made the journey to true love, reality style.

She was here for Daniel. The lucky bastard. And therefore officially off limits.

She thrust out her hand and he took it automatically, shaking without conscious direction from his brain. "Josh Pendleton."

She smiled and he felt his IQ drop ten points. Jesus, she was gorgeous when she smiled. "I know who you are. One of my best friends wants to move to Utah with you and become your second wife."

I'd have to have a first wife for that. He dropped the hand he was still shaking, bitterness streaking through him at the thought. "You aren't supposed to be out of your room," he informed her, doing his best to sound stern, rather than drunk off his ever-loving ass. "You're gonna get yourself kicked off the show." Her gaze slid guiltily to the side and he frowned. "Are you *trying* to get kicked off?"

"I just wanted to see who Mister Perfect is," she said, but she wouldn't meet his eyes. "Would they really kick me off the show just for being in the hallway?"

"Yes." Just like they would fire his ass for standing here talking to her. The producers loved their rules and they didn't make exceptions. "Ever since Season Three when we were nearly two Suitorettes short thanks to food poisoning, they keep spare Suitorettes on hand just in case." Hell, they probably had a spare host waiting in the wings. Miranda was nothing if not prepared.

"Could *you* tell me if it's Daniel?" The Suitorette—Sidney—wheedled. "Then I'll go back to my room like a good girl and no one will ever know the difference."

A muted bing from around the corner interrupted his reply—and shot chills through his blood.

The elevator.

The show had bought out the hotel and all the girls were supposed to be tucked away in their rooms. The elevator could only hold one of the producers or production assistants. And here he was, drunk off his ass in the hall with a Suitorette.

A jolt of adrenaline crashed through his system to clear his thoughts as voices carried around the corner—one of them feminine and cracking with authority.

Miranda Pierce.

The executive producer of *Marrying Mister Perfect*

was a dragon in skirt suits, with a sleek, edgy haircut and a terrifying efficiency that didn't negotiate or accept less than perfection.

"Shit."

He could talk his way out of this. All he had to do was tell the truth. He'd gone for ice and she'd run into him. He could throw the Suitorette under the bus and walk away from this with his job intact—at least temporarily. But she would be booted from the show so fast her head would spin.

Her teal eyes flared with panic as she heard the voices too. And damn if his instinct to save the damsel in distress didn't kick in like never before.

Acting on instinct more than thought, he grabbed her arm and tucked her between his body and the door of 312 so she wouldn't be as obviously visible if Miranda came around the corner. He waved his keycard in front of the sensor, hoping he wasn't actually staying in 321. If this wasn't his room they were so screwed, but after only a second's hesitation the door beeped and popped open. *Hallelujah.*

Together they stumbled inside, Josh snapping the door shut behind him with his foot. He held his breath, listening against the door for some indication that he'd been seen smuggling a Suitorette into his room.

Shit. What had he been thinking?

"Was that...?" the girl whispered.

"Miranda," he confirmed direly.

"What happens if they find us together?"

"I get fired and you get kicked off the show. And the tabloids run the story for weeks."

Teal eyes widened. "I can't go out there."

"No," he agreed, without hesitation.

"So we're..."

"Stuck here."

To his left, the abandoned half-bottle of six-year-old scotch taunted him from the wet bar.

To the right, a light illuminated the bed like a spotlight, casting a glow over the massive expanse, piled high with pillows and an overstuffed comforter.

And in between stood the picture of temptation in pink yoga pants and a freaking Tinkerbell T-shirt.

If Miranda came to check on him, there was no way he'd be able to explain this away now. This day just kept getting better and better.

CHAPTER TWO

Sidney had gone looking for Mister Perfect and found Josh Pendleton.

She tried not to read too much into that. Sure, they were trapped together in his hotel room, but nothing could happen. He was famous for being happily married, for crying out loud—not to mention a million miles out of her league. And she was going to meet the man of her dreams tomorrow.

Maybe. Provided it was Daniel.

But in the mean time she was trapped with one of *Us Weekly's* 100 Hunkiest Hollywood Hotties in his hotel room.

The room was posh. Luxurious. Easily double the size of her own, with a sitting area, a wet bar and a giant gift basket overflowing from the small coffee table. Stepping deeper into the room, she turned in a circle in the center of the sitting area. "Your room is nicer than mine."

"Well, I'm the talent," he said with just enough faux arrogance to be self-deprecating.

She felt her lips curving in a smile as he crossed to the wet bar—which looked like it could host a rock band for a week without needing to be restocked—and put the ice she'd nearly knocked out of his arms on the bar, next to a half-empty bottle of something golden.

Normally she would feel uncomfortable, alone with such a disturbingly attractive man. Chiseled features and the kind of toned body that was more commonly associated with action stars—the man was lethal. But her tongue wasn't tying itself into the usual awkward knots. Maybe it was the fact that he was so clearly off-limits. Or maybe it was the three mini-bar bottles of liquid courage. Or maybe it was the familiarity of the warm, understanding brown eyes that had gazed sympathetically at countless Suitors and Suitorettes over the many seasons of *Marrying Mister Perfect* as they had their countless hearts broken.

Whatever the reason, she wasn't nervous with him.

"Would they really fire you?" she asked as he filled a pair of glasses with ice water.

"In a heartbeat. Thou shalt not screw around with the Suitorettes is commandment one."

"But nothing happened." She rounded the couch and came over to accept one of the glasses from him. "And you're so popular. I bet there are thousands of viewers who tune in just to see you each week." Not that she would ever admit to being one of them. "There are fan sites devoted to you."

"And whoever they replace me with will be younger, have more rabid fans and draw an even bigger audience. Welcome to Hollywood."

"Such a cynic. I had no idea."

"I mask it well."

"You'd have to." He was so charming every week on *Marrying Mister Perfect*. So upbeat as he encouraged the contestants to follow their hearts and leap headfirst into love. She'd always thought they had that in common—the foolish romantic optimism—but if this was how he really was...something sad panged in her chest. "You're shattering my illusions here."

He grimaced, downing his water. "Never meet your heroes. It will only disappoint you."

She studied him. *The* Josh Pendleton. "I guess you were a kind of hero."

He cringed. "Don't say that."

"Why not? I used to watch you on *Brainiac*."

"Ah, so you were the one," he said dryly.

The short-lived quiz show had never made it to prime time, but she remembered his quick-witted banter with the contestants, the way he'd always made her laugh. "How does a quiz show host become the host of Marrying Mister Perfect?"

Josh shrugged. "Right place, right time, right wife."

When the last word left his mouth, something heavy entered his eyes.

Sidney was good at talking down nervous grooms and jittery brides. Like the version of Josh Pendleton who hosted *Marrying Mister Perfect*, she excelled at pointing her charges toward love. But she'd had the odd couple call it quits too. It happened. Sometimes their happily-ever-after lay elsewhere.

There was always an air about those couples, when they finally called it a day. A misery that held a finality that always made her heart hurt. Often mixed with resignation and a guilty relief.

Josh had that.

Something had happened to him. And she'd bet her next commission it had to do with his wife. "Rough night?"

He shrugged, downing his water and then grimacing as if he wished it were something stronger. "You're interrupting my bender."

"I can see that."

He frowned down at his hands, then began yanking at something on his left hand. His wedding ring.

Josh tugged at the gold band, cursing as it caught on his knuckle. He struggled with it, taking a better grip and it came loose with a jerk. The back of his hand smacked his glass, sending it flying to shatter against the base of the bar, glass raining down to cover the floor.

"Shit. Your feet."

Sidney looked down. She hadn't bothered with shoes when she made her ill-advised escape attempt and belatedly realized she was standing barefoot in a carpet minefield of glass shards. She barely had time to register the fact and set down her own glass before strong arms caught her behind her knees and swept her away from the mess.

Or at least tried to.

Josh realized his mistake approximately five seconds after trying to do the gallant thing. Carrying the barefoot Suitorette away from the debris would have been chivalrous... if he hadn't been too tipsy to make it through the maneuver with his balance intact.

He staggered as he tried to straighten with her in his arms. Knowing he was going down, one way or another, he managed to aim his collapse toward the nearest sofa and all but tossed Sidney onto it before crash landing onto the adjacent ottoman.

She smothered a laugh with one hand. "Your heroism is a little rusty."

"I'm not supposed to be your hero," he grumbled, giving vertical another try—and coming up with more success.

"Don't worry, Sir Galahad. I'm not planning to fall in

love with you," she said, laughter still lingering in her voice. "I know better than that."

He crossed to the bar, spread a towel over the glass to mark the spot and toed off his shoes—which doubtless had glass clinging to the soles. Deciding sobriety was overrated, Josh filled a spare glass with ice and collected the crappy scotch as well as her water glass before returning to claim the other half of the couch where the barefoot blonde was curled up.

"Can I have one of those?" she asked, tipping her mostly empty water glass toward the bottle. "I promised my best friends I'd get hammered tonight."

"Strange promise." He tipped scotch on top of the mostly melted ice cubes in her glass.

"Strategy," she explained. "I swore I wouldn't be the girl who gets drunk and stumbles around the mansion babbling about how ready she is for love to every cameraman who will listen before throwing up on Mister Perfect's shoes. I figure if I'm hung over I won't even want to *think* about having a drink to take the edge off and that will guarantee I'm sober when we meet."

"Smart," he acknowledged, taking a draught of the unpalatable scotch and finding it much smoother now that he was halfway through the bottle.

She lifted her own glass and drank, her face contorting as she swallowed. She coughed, wheezing. "Wow. That's terrible."

"Yes, it is," Josh agreed, raising his glass to clink it against hers before draining half of it.

She watched him with a sort of concerned awe, and then bravely went back for another sip, choking less the second time. "And why exactly are we punishing ourselves?" she asked, frowning dubiously at the alcohol calling itself scotch.

He shrugged. "Sentimental value."

"Ah."

It had seemed a fitting way to toast the end of his six year marriage. With a shitty bottle of six-year-old scotch.

He loved good scotch, but before long crap like this was likely to be all he could afford. Between his wife's very enthusiastic lawyer, their lack of pre-nup, and the fact that he was likely to lose his job as soon as the higher ups at the network realized he was no longer the perfect portrait of domestic bliss they'd hired to be the host of *Marrying Mister Perfect*—and that was if they didn't find out about the Suitorette in his hotel room—he'd be lucky if he could afford to drown his sorrows in Wild Turkey by this time next year.

Might as well get used to the cheap stuff. Josh downed the subpar scotch in a single swallow and reached for the bottle to refill his glass, watching as the amber liquid painted lovingly over the cubes.

He braced himself for an interrogation, but Sidney fell silent, sipping contemplatively. The minutes stretched out and they drank in comfortable silence. When her glass emptied, he refilled both of them, pleased his hands were steady enough to accomplish the task without spilling a drop.

Maybe make a career as a bartender when he was booted as host for *MMP*. The skill sets were similar.

Good listener when people were having emotional breakdowns? Check. Keep everyone around you with a full drink in their hand because that was where the money was? You bet. And *Marrying Mister Perfect* had certainly prepared him for dealing with drunken cat fights.

Now that he thought about it, he was really just an overpaid bartender with good hair.

He raked a hand through the thick brown mess. At least he still had his hair. Marissa could take his retirement fund and the house in Malibu, but he was still number ninety seven on *Us Weekly's* 100 Hunkiest Hollywood Hotties. So there.

Josh handed Sidney her glass and clinked it with his own, silently toasting the absent arbiters of hunkiness at *Us Weekly*.

"This is so surreal," Sidney murmured, rubbing a hand over her stomach. "I'm drinking terrible scotch with Josh Pendleton and tomorrow I meet Mister Perfect. Somebody pinch me."

"If it's such a dream, why were you trying to get kicked off the show?"

She looked at him, but there was something evasive in her eyes. "What makes you so certain I was?"

He arched a brow and her resistance crumpled.

"I'm not used to being Cinderella. When I'm playing the Fairy Godmother, I'm amazing, but cast me as the princess and I don't have the first idea what to do with myself."

Something jogged loose in his brain. "You're the wedding planner, aren't you?"

"That's me."

"You know, you and I have the same job." Maybe he could do *that* when he was fired for matrimonial failure.

"How do you figure that?"

"We both watch other people get paired off, knowing all the while that most of them aren't going to make it."

She shook her head, still smiling. "I always believe they're going to make it."

He almost laughed. "Naïve."

"Cynical," she accused without heat.

"So why come on the show if you don't want to be

Cinderella?"

"It isn't a question of want. Just because I don't know how to be the princess doesn't mean I don't want my own happy ending. Something just always seems to go wrong translating the dream to reality when it comes to my own love life."

"Maybe it will work out this time."

"Thank you for saying that. Even though I know you're too cynical to believe it for a second."

"What do I know? Maybe you and Daniel can fall in love in the middle of a three ring circus."

She went still, then rose with studied nonchalance and crossed to the bar to get more ice. "You don't believe in the show?"

"I'm not one to judge."

"Who better than you? You've seen dozens of hopeful Suitorettes come and go. Every season another batch of us."

"And most of you leave in tears." At the disappointment on her face, he back-pedaled as he took the ice from her and refilled his own glass. "Don't mind me. I'm just the World's Biggest Hypocrite. The man who peddles love for a paycheck until the seasons start blurring together even though I've sworn off love and marriage and the entire damn mess."

"Do you want to talk about it?"

"About the blurry seasons?"

She held up her hand and he squinted. Gold glittered, a shiny band hooked over the tip of her index finger.

His wedding ring. He'd forgotten it on the bar in the rush to get her away from the shattered glass.

He'd need to wear it tomorrow. Another season of *Marrying Mister Perfect* started filming in the morning and he needed to still be Josh Pendleton, Happily Married Host, when the cameras started rolling, but tonight it had felt like the fucking thing was cutting off circulation to his finger and he would lose the digit if he didn't get it off.

Now it hung on the end of her finger, an incriminating wide gold band.

Her teal eyes were somehow sympathetic without being pitying. He'd have to see if he could copy that look. It would come in handy in his line of work.

He took his ring, setting it on the coffee table, and met those eyes—seriously, who had teal eyes? For a moment the world around them seemed to fade out of focus. She was beautiful—not just pretty, but there was a quality about her, an openness and a sweetness. At least until the show corrupted it.

Suitorette. Off-limits, jackass.

She was about to go on a reality show looking for love on national television. *His* reality show. At least until they fired him.

He followed her gaze to the ring. And then he said it. Said the words out loud for the first time since he'd told his parents. "I'm getting divorced."

Only there was no getting. He was. It was final. As of three o'clock this afternoon. Marissa was officially free to run into the arms of the man she'd been screwing behind his back for the last year and half.

"I'm sorry," she murmured.

He shouldn't have told her about the divorce, he realized belatedly. If she told his bosses he was screwed. But it wasn't just the alcohol that had loosened his tongue. There was something about her. She was too easy to talk to, this long, leggy blonde with the impossible eyes.

"You can still believe in happily ever afters," Sidney said softly.

"Yeah?" Josh tore his gaze off the ring, lifting his drink. "How does that work?"

She shrugged. "You just do. Every broken heart is another step in the road to your happily ever after."

"Wow, you're like a Hallmark card. No wonder the producers cast you."

She laughed softly, hiding her mouth behind the tumbler as she took another sip.

"You didn't say why you were coming on the show, but I'm guessing you're one of the True Love girls. Did you watch last season? Is he your soul mate, only he doesn't know it yet?"

"You don't have to make fun of me. I know how ridiculous the show is," she said, though there was a stubborn hope in her eyes. "I never really expected to get picked. I auditioned on a dare and then suddenly I'm here. Meeting him tomorrow. And I know the odds are ridiculous, so every time someone asked me why I was doing it I would say it was for the *experience* or because I wanted to launch Once Upon a Bride onto the national stage, but the truth is I want to be the princess for a change—and I can't believe I'm admitting that to you."

"I'm trustworthy."

"You think I'm crazy. But I watched last season and you can't tell me that Marcy and Craig didn't find real love on the show."

"You're right. But they were the exceptions, not the rule."

"But it's possible. And even if it's only a possibility, don't you owe it to yourself to give your heart every chance at happiness? For a chance at something real?"

"Reality television might not be the best place to look

for that."

"Even if it's Daniel?"

A startling gong of something that could have been jealousy echoed in his brain. "You're so certain Daniel is perfect?"

"That is the name of the show. *Marrying Mister Perfect*. I'm not the one anointing him."

Josh's grip tightened on his glass. Daniel was a nice guy. A little cliché. The kind of guy who did things because he'd been told he should rather than because he had any personal desire to do them. He'd be perfect because he followed instructions well, but was he right for Sidney? Who shone with her belief in love?

"I wasn't supposed to tell you it was him."

"We're hiding in your hotel room drinking the worst scotch on the planet. I think we've pretty much abandoned what we're supposed to do."

He smiled—and realized he was staring at her mouth.

He didn't want her going on the show. He didn't want it to spoil her. *He* wanted her.

Which sent a warning alarm echoing in his brain.

Josh rocked back into the far corner of the cushions, taking a deep breath of air that didn't carry a light floral scent. What the fuck was wrong with him?

The glass of scotch was heavy in his hand.

Oh. Right. That.

"Josh?" Her teal gaze snared him again.

They had to be contacts.

But his body didn't care. The air seemed to crackle around them, a lightning storm waiting to happen, pulsing with inevitability. Every inch of his nervous system was waking up and reporting for duty. She looked at him with mischief and promise in those teal

depths and his better judgment went on hiatus.
He was going to kiss a Suitorette.

CHAPTER THREE

She was possessed. It was the only explanation.

This wasn't her. Sidney had never been this girl before. She didn't break curfew. She didn't drink scotch—which was frankly gross. And she had certainly never flirted with the host of a major network television show.

She read about adventures. She planned them for other girls. But this wasn't *her*.

She'd come to *Marrying Mister Perfect* with a plan. Get the guy, grow her business, live happily ever after. None of which included making gooey eyes at one of *Us Weekly*'s 100 Hunkiest Hollywood Hotties.

Even if he was single.

That didn't make him available. Not to her. But the way he was looking at her...

Almost like he might kiss her.

Holy Moses. Josh *Freaking* Pendleton was looking at her like he might kiss her.

This wasn't her life. She'd been lifted right out of her body and dropped into the shoes of someone a thousand times more glamorous than her.

She wanted to pinch herself—

But then his gaze skated off to the side and he cleared his throat roughly, rising from the couch. "Miranda's probably gone by now."

PLANNING ON PRINCE CHARMING

With those words, reality returned with a thud. This wasn't her Prince Charming. Even if he was single—which would give Parvati heart palpitations. Sidney stood as well. "Right. Of course."

Yes, if she was honest she'd sort of had a crush on Josh Pendleton ever since she'd first seen him hosting the *Brainiac* quiz show ten years ago—but she was meeting Mister Perfect tomorrow, she certainly hadn't *planned* to fall into the arms of another man tonight.

Or be awkwardly lifted into them.

This strange electric feeling in her blood wasn't attraction. It was just a reaction to meeting her first bona fide celebrity. If he seemed to glow with the force of his personality—well, that was probably just what celebrities did.

She trailed after him to the door, waiting as he opened it and peeked outside before closing it again and giving her a nod. "All clear."

"Thanks." She moved to stand close to him in the small space near the door. She might never be this close to Josh Pendleton again.

His hair was thick chestnut, messier than she'd ever seen it on television, when it was always neatly trimmed and gelled into position. It made him seem more approachable somehow, that disordered mop. Touchable.

A hint of wryness shadowed his eyes, something just a little bit cynical that he'd never revealed to the cameras. It gave him an edge—and made him more real. This wasn't Josh Pendleton the host. This was Josh Pendleton the man.

And what a man.

"I'm sorry about your divorce."

He shrugged, looking away. "It happens."

"Not always," she said with quiet emphasis. It was suddenly irrationally important to her that he realize the entire institution of marriage wasn't a lost cause because his had ended. "Sometimes love finds you when you're least expecting it."

He studied her then, his gaze so intent she could almost feel it tracing her features. "This show is going to eat you alive," he murmured low.

"Maybe," she said. "But I bet I come out the other side believing in love just as wholeheartedly."

His expression turned quizzical. "Why?"

"A girl has to believe in something. Why not love?"

"Because it hurts like a bitch when it ends."

"But what if it doesn't end? What if the next guy will be the one that goes the distance and I might have missed my destiny if I was too scared to take that chance?"

"You've been watching too much *Marrying Mister Perfect*."

"Listening to all the things *you* say every week on the show, you mean?"

His dark eyes gleamed wryly. "What can I say? I'm a peddler of false dreams."

"Have you always been this cynical or is it a product of your divorce?" His relaxed face tightened and she lifted a hand. "Never mind. Don't answer that." She'd rather believe he was speaking from pain rather than core-deep cynicism. "It was nice to meet you, Josh Pendleton."

It was the most natural thing in the world, going up on her toes to kiss him. One hand rested gently on his chest as her lips brushed his.

It could have been innocent. It could have been a sweet, inconsequential goodbye kiss.

It wasn't.

His head angled, his lips parted, and suddenly he was kissing her back with the taste of scotch on his lips, and she melted against him, lost in the searing rightness of the kiss.

It ought to feel wrong. He hadn't kissed any woman other than Marissa in over seven years. He shouldn't even remember how, but damned if it wasn't all coming back to him. And damned if he didn't like it. Probably far more than he should.

She was sweet and soft and smelled heavenly. Daniel didn't know what he was in for.

Daniel.

Josh pulled away, his good sense returning in a rush as soon as he wasn't kissing her anymore.

She was there for Mister Perfect. And his job was to smooth their path to love. He couldn't want her. Not without losing the job that was the only thing left of the life he'd worked toward for years.

"You should go."

Wide teal eyes gazed back at him. "I should?"

"It's late. We both need to get some sleep. Busy day tomorrow. You're meeting the man of your dreams." And that man wasn't him.

Questions darkened her eyes. "Josh, I—"

"Good luck this season," he said, more forcefully than necessary, as if emphasis would make his wish more sincere. "I'm sure you'll go far. Mister Perfect will love you."

"Thank you," she murmured softly.

He opened the door, checking the hall one last time. Finding it empty, he urged her through the doorway.

"Good night, Sidney."

"Are you ready to meet Mister Perfect?"

Sidney forced a smile, hoping it looked even remotely genuine as the segment producer chirped excitedly about fate and romance and that all-important first impression with the man she would spend the rest of her life with.

All she could think—over and over—was *I kissed Josh Pendleton*. But she had to keep her eyes on the prize. She couldn't let last night's stupidity destroy her dream. Parvati would be thrilled that she'd laid one on the hottest host on TV, but that was as far as it could go.

Sidney had spent all morning mentally preparing herself for her fairy tale romance, psyching herself up for love with the help of the show's producers and therapists... but *Marrying Mister Perfect* didn't feel like a fairy tale.

It just felt staged.

She tried to stay positive, but it was hard to find anything romantic about waiting for hours in uncomfortable heels as Mister Perfect slowly made his way through the various set-ups around the mansion, meeting the Suitorettes one by one. There was no sense of destiny approaching. Just looming boredom.

And the sense that she was being indoctrinated into a cult.

If she hadn't already been determined to find love, the enthusiastic—and constant—reminders by various producers to *lead with her heart open* and *embrace the journey to love* and *consider the possibility that she was about to meet her husband* would have brainwashed her into doing just that.

No wonder the Suitorettes were usually chugging cocktails on night one. If the regular first date jitters weren't bad enough, they had to deal with the competition aspect as well as the constant pressure to feel insta-love from the producers. It was enough to drive anyone to drink.

But Sidney clung to her soda water, no matter how many times a production assistant offered to fetch her a glass of champagne. She was determined to be sober when she first appeared on prime time.

Though even without the help of alcohol, she might throw up on his shoes. The waiting was not doing good things for her stomach. Of course that might have been the aftereffects of the putrid scotch as well.

The producers would probably love it if she tossed her cookies. She'd be in every highlight reel for the entire freaking season.

"Just a few more minutes," the segment producer who had been assigned to babysit her enthused. "One more girl to go and then it's your turn."

Sidney shifted her bouquet to one hand, adjusting the veil that was perched precariously atop her updo. Each of the Suitorettes had been assigned a different setting, supposedly designed to show off her unique talents—musicians played music, chefs cooked, athletes demonstrated their prowess and models displayed their shapely selves. It was a time-honored gimmick-fest, and Sidney, as wedding planner, was, of course, this year's bride.

The dress Victoria and Parvati had helped her pick out was cocktail length and ice blue, but the lace overlay gave it enough of a bridal feel that the producers were in raptures. They'd even set up a sort of altar in the gazebo where she was waiting.

Unfortunately, the strange autumn heat wave had yet to let up and Sidney had resorted to fanning herself with her bouquet in an effort to keep from being the Sweaty Suitorette when Mister Perfect finally made an appearance. It was downright sweltering out here.

She tried not to think about the camera lens only a few feet away—and the ten pounds it would add.

Not exactly how she'd envisioned meeting the man of her dreams when she'd agreed to come on the show.

"All set?"

Sidney whirled toward the familiar voice, her heart pounding triple time as Josh stepped out of the shadows and into the professionally lit gazebo. Her hands clenched hard around the stems of the bouquet. She'd already known he looked amazing in a suit, with every hair styled into place, but somehow he was even more heart-stopping now that she knew what he looked like when he was a little rumpled.

"Hi." God, why did she sound so breathless?

She hadn't seen him since he'd thrown her out of his room the night before. She'd made it back to her own room undetected and so far no one had even hinted that they knew she'd snuck out.

Sidney wished she could tell Josh that they'd gotten away with it unscathed, but more than anything, she wished she could talk to him about the kiss. She shouldn't have kissed him—he'd made that clear when he'd all but thrown her out—and she needed to smooth things over, get back to normal with him, tell him it had just been the scotch kissing him, but the cameraman, segment producer and audio tech were all watching, absorbing every word—and probably filming it for all she knew.

"I just wanted to make sure you were all set," Josh

said, the words seeming filled with a thousand possible meanings as he held eye-contact.

Was he checking up on her? Checking to make sure she hadn't been kicked off the show because of last night's adventures? Checking to make sure she hadn't made a run for it? Or was there some other meaning she was missing entirely?

"Good to go." The words rushed out on an exhale.

"Good. Good." He nodded to himself. "You've got a good set-up here."

"I do?" She reached up self-consciously to check the veil. It was a massive monstrosity of a thing. Huge to the point of tackiness.

Marrying Mister Perfect wasn't really known for their subtlety.

"The gazebo's good. You know you're a favorite if they put you in here." Josh smiled reassuringly. "You have nothing to worry about. He's going to love you."

Sidney had to remind herself which *he* they were talking about.

Mister Perfect. Daniel. Man of her dreams. Right.

"Thanks. I just keep telling myself to think of *The Veil*. It's my new mantra."

Josh cocked his head quizzically and she explained, "*The Veil* magazine. There's a list they put out every year. A Who's Who of Wedding Planners. If you get on there, you're set for life. But it's more than just a list. It's a tangible marker of success."

"And that matters."

"I'm a Dewitt."

He arched a brow questioningly.

"In my family, you don't do anything unless you're The Best. My father is Titus Dewitt—"

"Holy crap."

"Exactly. My mother is the president of one of the largest pharmaceutical companies in the world. My brother started his own business when he was seventeen, sold it for millions when he was twenty-three and started another last year just for fun. And I plan parties for a living."

He shrugged. "I play matchmaker on national television. We've all gotta do something."

"Yeah, but I have to be The Best. Hence the *Veil* list."

He smiled. "More people should say *hence*."

Something warm and sweet unfurled in her chest at his smile, but when she would have spoken, he lifted a finger, his eyes going distant as he listened to an exchange through his earpiece. "He's on his way. Just relax. Be yourself and he won't be able to resist you."

"Thanks." A flush heated her face that had little to do with the sweltering weather. Then Josh was gone, vanishing into the night beyond the reach of the industrial grade lighting.

Seconds later, another man stepped into the bright lights of the gazebo, grinning from ear to ear and trailing a pair of mobile camera crews.

"What have we here?" he asked, his charm on highbeam as he took in the altar, veil and bouquet.

Daniel the Teacher. He'd been the odds on favorite to win it all last season, but Marcy had shocked the world by picking Craig instead, leaving Daniel unattached and ripe for the picking as the next Mister Perfect. She'd thought it would be him. She'd been thrilled by the idea. She'd *wanted* it to be him.

So why was she just standing there like an idiot staring at him while the cameras captured her tongue-tied idiocy?

"I'm a wedding planner. Sidney," she blurted—and

thank God her tongue came unstuck.

The next few minutes were a blur. She didn't know what she said or what he said back. She made him laugh—a deep, warm, appealing sound—but then he was promising to speak more with her later before disappearing back out in the night, surrounded by the whirling orbits of his mobile camera crews.

The whole thing couldn't have taken more than a minute and a half.

Sidney stared after him.

"Was that it?"

The segment producer—who never had given Sidney her name—beamed at her. "You did great. Now we'll just move you back up to the house for the welcome toast and the first challenge. Come along."

Sidney tugged off the veil and set it on the altar along with the bouquet. She trailed along like an obedient child until they reached the Suitorette Mansion that would be her home for the next several weeks—or as long as Daniel decided to keep her.

It was surreal, that uncertainty, that lack of control. Her entire life suspended on his whim.

She entered the living room—one of many in the mansion—where the rest of the Suitorettes were gathering. It was her first chance to size up the competition—and meet the women she'd be living with.

Blondes, brunettes, redheads. Women of every ethnicity and type, they covered the spectrum, except for the fact that they were all, every last one, intimidatingly beautiful.

And thin.

They showed off their sleek figures with the confidence of women who never gave a second thought to the camera's extra ten pounds.

The first challenge would begin soon. Some ridiculously impossible or embarrassing task designed to reveal their true characters to Daniel—and entertain the drama-hungry masses at home. Sidney had been one of those eager viewers for too long not to know the drill.

Many of the women were already laughing together in clusters of three or four—or sizing one another up with barely concealed predatory stares. Sidney sidled up to the nearest wall, tugging at her skirt and trying to avoid being in the line of fire for the majority of the cameras, painfully self-conscious. A couple feet down the wall, a waifish redhead hovered, anxiously apart.

A yank of empathy had Sidney leaning toward her and murmuring, "The worst is over, right? We've all made whatever first impression we're going to make. I'm just glad I didn't lose my lunch all over his shoes."

The redhead turned to her with palpable relief. "Oh, thank God. I was sure I was going to be sick, but everyone looks so confident and together, I thought I was the only one." She thrust out her hand, the long elegant fingers tipped in pastel polish. "I'm Caitlyn. Piano teacher."

"Sidney. Wedding planner."

"Nice to meet you, Sidney."

"You too." Sidney had always thought the stories of Suitorettes forming life-long friendships with other women who were competing for the affections of the same man were ridiculous, but as soon as she shook Caitlyn's hand, she felt a weight lift off her.

She wasn't in this alone. All the insanity. The cult-like indoctrination. The surreal blur of her first conversation—she'd never be able to adequately explain it to anyone back home. Not even Parvati and Victoria. But Caitlyn was in the trenches with her. For better or worse.

A cheer went up at the far side of the room, announcing the arrival of Mister Perfect. Sidney steeled her nerves. She'd known it wasn't all going to be fairy tale dates. She just had to get through this to earn her happy ending. "Let the games begin."

She was in this to win—and not to moon over Josh Pendleton. No matter how he kissed.

CHAPTER FOUR

"Josh Pendleton, you're an imbecile."

Josh opened his eyes, moving just his pupils and keeping the rest of his face completely motionless as the makeup artist smeared the necessary pastes and products over his skin to make him look natural on camera. His boss glowered on the threshold of his dressing room like an angry goddess.

"Nice to see you too, Miranda," he said to the executive producer looming in the doorway when Eunice stopped dabbing at him and stepped back to survey her work.

"Give us a minute, Eunice," Miranda commanded, her expression not lightening in the slightest.

Eunice quickly gathered her things and ducked out of the room—but that gave him a solid twenty seconds to wonder which of his indiscretions Miranda had discovered and whether he'd be allowed to finish out the season before he was fired. Was it the divorce? Sidney's kiss?

"Did you really think we wouldn't find out?" Miranda asked as soon as the door closed behind the makeup artist—giving him no freaking clue what it was she had apparently found out.

But regardless of what they'd discovered, the answer was the same. "Not really." If there was gossip, *Marrying*

Mister Perfect would uncover it. "But I thought I'd see how long I could maintain the head-in-the-sand approach."

"You're a celebrity, you moron," Miranda said with her usual tact. "And divorces are public record. Did you think entertainment reporters would just give you a pass because you're such a nice guy? Or do you have a better reason why I had to learn about your marital problems from an online gossip magazine?"

"Denial?"

"Cute," she snapped. Then she grimaced. "Sorry about your divorce though. She always seemed like a nice girl. Though I'm sure she was an evil cow and I'm one hundred percent on your side." She continued to glare at him, though he knew her words were sincere—Miranda's sympathy just usually came attached to mild irritation. "You could have told me, you know. We have you running around extolling the glories of marriage. I could have cut in footage from another season if you weren't up to it."

"So I'm not fired?"

"For not telling me about your divorce? I'm annoyed to learn about it from a fucking online rag, but I don't think I'm allowed to fire you for irritating me."

"You told me when Elton hired me that I was only getting the job because I was happily married."

"Did I? That's a stupid reason to give anyone a job. And you believed me?"

"It seemed plausible after the last host…"

"Got caught in bed with three of the girls playing Suitorette roulette? Yeah. Don't do that. In fact, you probably want to be even more careful than before that nothing that could even remotely be construed as flirting goes on between you and the girls, but as long as you toe the line on that front no one cares that your vile wife got her walking papers."

Sidney flashed through his brain, along with the vivid memory of the kiss, but Josh ruthlessly suppressed the image. Probably best not to tell Miranda about that. "I thought you liked my wife."

"I'm being supportive," Miranda snapped. "We're friends. And friends don't let friends learn about important news items from crappy gossip rags, especially when we want to carefully spin the stories to our own narrative. Am I clear?"

"Crystal. I promise next time I get divorced, you'll be the first one I tell."

"Good. Now go be charming and calm Daniel down. He needs more gravitas for the second Elimination Ceremony tonight—and to look a little less like a kid in a big-breasted candy store. The home viewers hate it when Mister Perfect isn't respectful of the hearts he's breaking."

"He'll have gravitas. Don't worry. This isn't my first rodeo."

Miranda frowned. "Speaking of rodeos, I need to check on the set-ups for the cowgirl date."

A soft knock on his dressing room door preceded one of the story producers popping her head inside. "Miranda? It's Sidney."

Josh's heart rate quadrupled. "Sidney?"

"Did she tell him?" Miranda asked the producer.

"No."

"Tell who what?" Josh asked, trying to keep the note of panic out of his voice.

Miranda thanked the producer and turned back to Josh as the woman retreated back to the editing bays. "Damn it."

"Problem?" Josh swallowed when the word came out a croak.

Distracted, Miranda grimaced. "She's holding back. Her story makes her a lock for a sympathy ring, but if she doesn't tell him before the Elimination Ceremony we can't coach him into keeping her."

"Her story?" Encouraging the Suitorettes to exploit their personal tragedies was standard operating procedure on *Marrying Mister Perfect*, but Josh hadn't been aware Sidney had a tragedy to exploit.

"A girl like her should be a front runner by now," Miranda complained, barely paying attention to Josh, "but she's barely said two words to him. Or about him. We barely have any useable confessional footage. She's even avoiding the cameras. None of us can figure out what's up with her."

Maybe she's distracted by the fact that she made out with the host before filming began.

"I'll need you to talk to her about opening up to Daniel. The usual drill. I'll get it set up and let you know when we need you to work your magic."

"Are you sure I'm the right person to talk to her?"

That got Miranda's attention. She never liked the word no—or even the implication of it. "Is there a reason why you think you can't talk her into opening up to Daniel?"

"No. Of course not."

"Then we're fine." She turned toward the door. "Be good, Pendleton."

"Aren't I always?"

The EP didn't answer, already halfway down the hall, moving off to avert another catastrophe.

So the divorce was public knowledge.

And Sidney had a secret and wasn't invested in the

process.

It could have been much worse. And if they ever found out about him kissing Sidney in his hotel room, it would be. But there was no reason for them to ever know. Nothing had happened and nothing was going to happen. She was a Suitorette. End of story.

He hadn't had a chance to talk to her about that night, but he thought she was clear that there could never be anything between them. Maybe he needed to be more clear.

Even if she hadn't been a Suitorette, nothing would have happened. Josh Pendleton didn't believe in happily-ever-after anymore.

The soles of her sneakers smacked against the hard-packed dirt path in a steady, hypnotic rhythm, the repetitive thump-thump-thump taking her brain to that quiet place where all her troubles receded into the distance. Running had always been the one thing that never failed to make all her stress melt away—at least temporarily—and over the last two weeks Sidney had found herself running *a lot*.

There wasn't much to do at the Suitorette Mansion as she waited for her turn to date Daniel, but the paths that ran around the perimeter of the estate were always open.

Books, magazines, computers, televisions—all of them had been taken away from the Suitorettes in an attempt to encourage them to interact with one another, and give the cameras more juicy confrontations when boredom erupted into petty arguments. Most of the girls spent their days lounging around the pool, doing yoga and gossiping—but Sidney was attempting to avoid being caught on national television in a bikini at all costs.

So she hid in the music room with Caitlyn and she ran.

Two weeks. They'd barely begun, but already it felt like a lifetime.

She missed her friends. She missed her life. She missed having something productive to do with her days. Sidney had never been good at being idle, but active moments at *Marrying Mister Perfect* were few and far between.

There were other Suitorettes who were thriving. They cavorted for the cameras and for Daniel, worked on their tans and their yoga poses, and gossiped about celebrities and each other. They argued passionately about who had the most genuine connection with Daniel and threw down over who was there for the Right Reasons.

And Sidney bit her tongue.

Because she didn't have a genuine connection with Daniel and she wasn't sure she was there for the Right Reasons anymore.

She'd seen him a grand total of four times in the last two weeks. And three of those times had been at Elimination Ceremonies when he was slipping a little gold band on her finger as a symbol of his desire to continue their journey toward love and commitment.

Sidney had been one of the unlucky girls who didn't get a date with Daniel at all during the first week, but he'd kept her around at the Second Elimination Ceremony anyway. She'd been rewarded for her patience with a private date the second week—and it had been fun. Just not life-altering. Daniel was a nice guy. On paper he was exactly what she wanted, ticking all the boxes, but the more the other girls went on about *connections* the more she realized she just didn't feel one.

At least not the instant one the producers seemed to want her to feel. Or rather, not with the man they wanted her to feel it for.

Other girls were already starting to drop the L word and she couldn't stop thinking about someone else.

Someone she should *not* still be thinking about. Especially because Josh Pendleton seemed to be going out of his way to avoid her. He wouldn't even *look* at her during the Elimination Ceremonies he officiated.

The truth was that while she really liked Daniel, it was Josh she couldn't wait to see. Josh who made her heart race and had her counting down the hours until the next Elimination Ceremony.

She wished she could feel that way for Daniel.

And that she didn't have the tiny niggling voice in the back of her head telling her that Daniel looked at her like a trophy.

Her perspective was warped. That was all it was. She had a stupid crush on the host—a feeling that was obviously not mutual—and it was interfering with her ability to fall madly in love with the man she was supposed to be falling madly in love with.

Even now she felt that irresistible sizzle in her blood when she thought of Josh Pendleton—every cynical, muscular, surly inch of him beneath his flawless host façade. But when she thought of Daniel...nothing. He was a nice enough guy, but he might as well have been her brother for all the romantic zing she felt when she was with him.

Not like the other girls seemed to feel.

A branch snapped and Sidney looked toward the sound, slowing her stride. Another few seconds and she would have been a dozen feet farther down the path and may have missed it entirely, but her timing was perfect to see the bushes rustle as a figure emerged from the brush.

A very familiar figure wearing only a bikini top and tiny denim cut-off shorts.

"Elena." Sidney stopped on the path a few feet away.

Dark eyes turned toward hers, wide and startled. Her hair stuck out at odd angles—as if a man had been fisting his hands in it. "Sidney. What are you doing out here?"

"I could ask you the same thing." Though by her rumpled appearance, she could easily guess.

Elena was this season's siren. The sexy Latina oozed seduction from every pore and never missed an opportunity to flaunt her assets for the cameras—or to taunt the other contestants with her superior connection with Daniel. She made no secret of the fact that she had Daniel's hormones on a tight leash, seeming to revel in the villainess role and leaving a trail of resentment wherever she went. Sidney had pegged her as one of the girls who was only looking for her fifteen minutes of fame, but there were no cameras out here to capture her exploits. And as she smoothed down her tangled hair, something almost guilty flashed across her face.

Had Elena and Daniel had a private rendezvous? Or could she have been sneaking off to meet someone else? An illicit affair with a cameraman perhaps?

"Are you sneaking around with a crew member?" Sidney blurted. With her feelings for Josh Pendleton, she was hardly one to judge, but she might ask for tips on how to get away with it.

"Of course not." Elena drew herself up to her full height—which was still a good six inches shorter than Sidney. Superiority suffused her face, washing away any traces of guilt that might have lingered. "I was just visiting Daniel."

"*You* climbed the wall?" She'd heard of Suitors and Suitorettes scaling the wall between the two estates over the many seasons of *Marrying Mister Perfect* and *Romancing Miss Right*, but she hadn't pegged Elena for the rock-climbing type. It reeked of desperation, whereas Elena seemed more like the goddess of sex who sat back and let men flock to *her*. But if Elena could do it, Sidney could too. And Daniel wasn't the only gorgeous man residing on the other side of that wall. "How?"

"If I tell you, do you promise not to tell all the other girls you saw me?"

Sidney frowned, confused. "I thought you would want them to know. You seem to like lording your connection with Daniel over them."

Elena shrugged, but her face wasn't nearly as unconcerned as the gesture, her eyes too intent. "It was obvious from the beginning that the girls were going to see me as a threat no matter what I did and playing the villainess role gets me more screen time, but I really did come here for him."

"But Mister Perfect never picks the villainess in the end."

Elena shot her one of her patented *are you really that thick?* looks that had so endeared her to the rest of the house. "He picks the woman he wants the most. And you can bet your ass there's no way I would put up with being tarred as the catty villain bitch if I wasn't one hundred percent certain he'll be giving *me* the final ring. But I'll put up with it until I get my guy. Now do you want to know how to get to his mansion or not?"

"You would tell the competition?"

Elena snorted. "No offense, chica, but no one here is

my competition."

And that attitude is why everyone adores you. "I want to know. And I won't tell anyone I saw you if you don't tell anyone I'm going over."

"Deal." Elena waved toward the bushes behind her. "There's a door connecting the two estates back there. About ten yards in."

"You mean all these seasons when Suitors and Suitorettes climbed the wall they could have just walked through the door?"

Elena shrugged. "I think *climbing the wall* is a metaphor. The producers don't want us breaking our necks."

"So you just waltz on over there to see him whenever you like while the rest of us are begging for scraps of his attention?"

The Latina goddess arched a brow, utterly unperturbed by Sidney's veiled accusation. "If you want to see him, take the initiative to figure out how to do it. I'm not going to feel ashamed for doing what it takes to keep his focus on me. And I don't just waltz over whenever. Sometimes it's locked."

"That hardly seems fair."

"All's fair in love and *Marrying Mister Perfect*," Elena said dryly. "Just keep it to yourself. If all the girls find out about it, we'll all be locked out." She smiled, the look somehow both catty and sweet. "Have fun, Sidney. But go easy on Daniel. He's exhausted." With that parting shot, Elena turned back toward the mansion and sauntered off, hips swinging.

Leaving Sidney alone with the temptation of the door.

She could keep running. Play it by the book. Go back to the mansion and wait around for the next chance to see Daniel and the next Elimination Ceremony when Josh would make an appearance.

Or she could take initiative to see the man she wanted, like Elena said. Find out where she stood with him without the cameras on them.

Sidney stepped into the brush.

CHAPTER FIVE

Josh was not in the habit of taking strolls around the grounds. He liked the noise and chaos of the crew area in the basement of the Mister Perfect mansion. He could count on one hand the number of times over the years the frenetic pace of crew activity had gotten to him and he'd needed to step outside for some fresh air.

So it was pure dumb luck—or unholy coincidence—that he happened to be walking to clear his head near the back wall when the access door to the Suitorette Mansion swung open and a blond in a bright purple hoodie and hot pink running pants burst through, nearly taking him out in the process.

"Whoa." He caught her arm, steadying her when she stopped too abruptly to avoid colliding with him. Teal eyes gazed up at him and his lips curled up in reflex. "Sidney Dewitt. We have to stop meeting like this."

Her smile echoed his. "Maybe the universe is trying to tell us something."

Yeah, like abandon hope all ye who enter here. He dropped her arm, putting distance between them. "Are you sneaking over to see Daniel? I know the producers were hoping you guys would steal some alone time today. He's up at the house resting up for the Elimination Ceremony tonight. Give me five minutes and I can get a camera crew on you—"

"Actually, I was hoping to see you."

Danger, Will Robinson! "Go back." He couldn't be alone with her. He would lose his job. But hurt barely had time to flicker to light in her eyes before a second thought tripped over the first.

He could fix this.

He couldn't talk to her bluntly on camera, couldn't give her the hard facts with America watching, but if he could set her straight about That Night now, he could undo any damage he'd done. "Hang on." He caught her wrist, glancing around them to get his bearings on the expansive property. They weren't far from the Old Grotto. "Are you wired for sound?"

Sidney shook her head. "They don't make me wear a mic pack when I run. It's too bulky and throws off my stride."

"Good." He nodded. "Come with me."

He tugged her along behind him, leading her away from the main area to the far northwest corner of the property, where a set they hadn't used in years was gathering dust among the overgrown plants. Sidney's jaw dropped as soon as she recognized where they were.

"I haven't seen this spot in years," she marveled, reaching out to touch one of the curved stone benches.

"We haven't used it in the last five seasons," Josh explained. "Too over the top."

Which for *Marrying Mister Perfect* was really saying something.

An oasis in the middle of overgrown foliage, the Old Grotto looked like a cross between a sultan's palace and a Greek temple. Low stone benches and half-finished columns surrounded a shallow pool which bore a distinct resemblance to a part of the female anatomy.

"It is something." Sidney eyed the emptied pool.

"The producers keep talking about remodeling it, but it never seems to happen."

She perched on one of the stone benches and Josh thrust his hands deep into his pockets. "Look, Sidney, I know we didn't really have a chance to talk about that night. Things happened that shouldn't have. I'd had a lot of scotch and I'm not sure what all I said, but you're here for Daniel. We both know that. Anything else is impossible, but I can't help thinking you aren't fully investing in the process because of me. I'd just hate to see you lose out on this opportunity because you imprinted on me that night like a baby duck."

Sidney released a startled laugh. "As flattering as the baby duck assessment is, there might be more to it than that. Both my lack of interest in him and the fact that I like you. I might just like you, Josh."

"You don't even know me."

"I like what I do know."

"From watching me on television? Do you really want to give up your shot at something real with Daniel because you're infatuated with my celebrity? I've seen it before. You build up this golden ideal of who I am in your head, but that isn't me. No one sees who you really are when you're famous. They only see what you can do for them and who they want you to be."

"Such a cynic. I'm sure your family and friends don't see you that way."

"Yeah, but they knew me before I was anything." It was part of why he'd clung to his marriage to Marissa long after they both knew it was a lost cause. She'd wanted him before he was TV's Josh Pendleton. He might never have that again.

Sidney cocked her head at him. "I bet you were always something."

He frowned. "How did we get on this topic? We're supposed to be talking about you and Daniel. Miranda wants me to talk to you before the Elimination Ceremony tonight about opening up to him."

"I'm not so sure Daniel wants to be let in."

"Of course he does."

"You're so certain of that? Can you honestly tell me you never get the impression he's just nodding and smiling and waiting until it's his turn to talk when he's with us?"

"Hate to burst your bubble, sweetheart, but all men do that."

"*You* listen to me."

"Yeah, well, you won't stop talking. I don't have a choice."

"Very funny." She leaned forward on the edge of the bench. "I know he's the one I'm supposed to want, but do you really think he actually has feelings for any of us? He loves being Mister Perfect, but I don't think that's the same thing as actually being interested in any of us. Let alone *loving* us."

"It's early. Give your feelings time to develop. If you just let him closer—"

"It's hard to get close when he's busy putting you up on a pedestal. He wants the trophy girl. The one he can show off as tangible evidence that he won at life. We're the prize. I feel like if I showed him any human frailty he would send me home. If he even noticed."

"Give the guy a little credit."

"I guess being objectified is flattering in a way. I'm not used to men thinking I'm too pretty to have a personality. I'm more accustomed to being the invisible girl."

"I find that hard to believe." He took a seat opposite

her, bracing his forearms on his knees.

"You'd be surprised." She stood then, pacing around the grotto. "Miranda wants me to tell him my story. Ride my past to next week—but if I take the sympathy ring, all that will prove is that Daniel doesn't want to be the dick who dumped a girl right after she told him something that made her vulnerable. It won't mean he actually cares about me or feels any sort of connection with me."

"I didn't know you had a sob story to tell."

"I used to be heavy." She said the words sharp and fast, without hesitation, though he could tell they weren't easy for her. "Which isn't a tragedy, but the producers are treating it like it's my deep dark secret that I lost 85 pounds before I auditioned for the show."

"Did you lose the weight just for the show?"

"No, it wasn't for him or anything like that. I struggled with my weight my entire life and then a few years ago I started running. I wasn't doing it to lose weight. I'd pretty much given up on being thin by that point. But running cleared out my head and calmed me down and it sort of became an obsession. I always avoided scales, so it wasn't until my clothes started fitting strangely that I even realized I was losing weight. Then I started being more careful about what I ate and I don't know. I guess my metabolism shifted. And voila." She waved a hand at her lean runner's build.

"And you don't want to tell Daniel that?"

"I don't trust him to react the right way." She shoved her hands into the pockets of her hoodie, circling the pool. "I'm still that girl in my head. When I go shopping, I still automatically go toward the plus sizes. I still hate having my picture taken."

"That's why you shy away from the cameras."

Sidney grimaced. "They do add ten pounds."

Her nervousness, her shyness—so much more made sense when he realized she didn't see herself as others did. He'd type-cast her as the bubbly California blonde without a care in the world, but that wasn't Sidney.

"There's this voice in my brain telling me I'm being silly," she went on. "Saying I'm thin now and I'm pretty now, but the rest of me calls that voice a liar. And I *hate* compliments. From anyone."

"Compliments?" Josh often got sick of the sycophantic praise that Hollywood seemed to run on, but he didn't think that was what Sidney meant.

"When you're the chubby girl, people say things like *oh, what pretty eyes you have*, and I always felt like it was a little patronizing. Like there was this little *for a fat girl* attached to the words. Even being complimented on how smart I was felt like it was the consolation prize for the fact that I wasn't pretty and thin. My track coach in high school told me during tryouts that I was pretty light on my feet for a big girl. He was amazed I could get over the hurdles. I'd always loved running, but after that I never wanted to go back. It took me years to start running again and when I did the weight fell off and everyone started giving me gushy compliments without the fat girl qualifiers and I started to resent it."

"Your track coach sounds like an ass."

"He meant it as a compliment. And it wasn't just him. People always judge you on how you look. I know I'm not different inside, but people treat me differently and it's hard not to resent it. Like when you said the only people you trust to really love you are the ones who knew you before you were famous?"

"I'm not sure I put it that way—"

"I want someone who would love me even if I was

eighty-five pounds heavier. And we're both being ridiculous. Because everyone wants to be famous and thin. But it still feels unfair that we don't get to test our lovers to see if they really do love *us* or just the people we present to the world now. I never would have gotten on this show before I lost the weight and even if I had I wouldn't have made it past the first Elimination Ceremony, but I still wish I knew if he would have picked me even if I wasn't thin."

"He might have. I don't think he's as shallow as you're painting him."

"I'll never know. Just like you'll never know if your celebrity is the only thing attracting me to you."

He was *not* going to get sucked into another conversation about her attraction to him. "You need to give Daniel a chance. He might surprise you. Just be real with him. You might be the most real person we've ever had on this show."

"With *you*. It's different with him. Besides, I'm not sure he wants real."

"Give him some credit. Show him what you show me and he'll love you. He won't be able to help it."

CHAPTER SIX

Show him what you show me and he'll love you. He won't be able to help it

Those words seemed to echo in her brain like a song on repeat as she dressed and put on her makeup for the Elimination Ceremony. She wasn't sure why they stuck so firmly in her brain, every detail engraved down to the look in his eyes and the pitch of his voice—like the moment somehow formed the basis of her existence.

Was it because he was right? Did she need to show Daniel who she really was? Josh had accused her of imprinting on him like a baby duck and not giving Daniel a chance. Had she really done that? She'd painted him as shallow and self-involved in her mind, but was she doing him a disservice? Was she ruining her own happy ending by dismissing Prince Charming as a frog?

Only one way to find out.

Sidney threaded her way through the pre-Elimination party. The other girls were all in the habit of being aggressive, but this was the first time she'd gone hunting.

She found him in front of the outdoor fireplace, curled up beneath a faux bearskin throw with Elena as she purred sweet nothings into his ear.

"Daniel, I was wondering if I could steal you away."

His head snapped up, a guilty flush rising to his

cheeks. "Of course!"

Sidney carefully averted her gaze as he disentangled himself from Elena's clutches and straightened his clothes—making a conscious effort not to think about what Elena had been doing to him beneath that blanket. Daniel took Sidney's hand, threading their fingers together, and led her away from the scene of the crime, toward the gazebo where fairy lights twinkled. The altar from the first night was long gone, but the padded benches were still there and Daniel led her to one, settling down and automatically cheating out toward the cameramen who were circling to get the best angles.

Sidney smoothed her skirt, barely resisting the urge to hunch away from the cameras.

Daniel took her hands, gazing straight into her eyes. If nothing else, he was good at eye-contact. "You look beautiful tonight."

"Thank you." She squirmed, then realized he'd given her the perfect opening. "I've never been very good with compliments."

"Gorgeous girl like you?" he grinned. "I'd think you'd be bored of them by now."

"Actually, I, uh, I didn't used to look like this."

He dimpled at her, little boy charming. "Plastic surgery?" he joked.

"I was... bigger. Growing up. A lot bigger."

He lifted one hand to trace her cheek, his gaze as besotted as ever. "And you're so beautiful now. You may have had an ugly duckling phase, but now you're my beautiful swan. We all had to go through struggles to get here—like Marcy breaking my heart—but now I know that all that happened for a reason. So I could be here in this moment. With you." He leaned in and she had to fight the urge to pull away from him as he went in for a kiss.

He was a perfectly adequate kisser, but her spine felt like it was being pulled in two—all her instincts shoving her back as she forced herself to lean toward him through sheer willpower.

Josh had listened, but Daniel couldn't get past the listening fast enough. He just wanted to give a speech about how he accepted her and then kiss her... without ever making her feel accepted.

Comparing Marcy dumping him to a lifetime of battling her weight and her poor self-image... she couldn't help thinking he'd diminished what she said. Or just used it to pivot the subject back to him as quickly as possible.

His tongue invaded her mouth and Sidney pulled back—her instincts winning the battle. Daniel smiled seductively and stroked her cheek. Crap. He was going to kiss her again.

And double crap that her reaction to him kissing her again was crap. That couldn't be a good sign.

"Oh, Daniel..."

Tiffani's cooing call preceded her around the corner—and a spike of relief jabbed hard into Sidney, letting her breathe again like an emergency procedure to open her airway.

"Duty calls." Daniel winked and Sidney forced an understanding smile.

He rose and Tiffani latched onto his arm, already simpering about something she just had to show him. Sidney watched them go, certain she would later hear Tiffani gush about their intense connection. The camera men filed after the pair in a perfectly choreographed dance, but one of the producers hung back, crouching in front of Sidney.

"Would you like to do an interview now? Tell us how it felt to talk to Daniel about your past while it's still fresh? We can get you set up in one of the confessionals right away."

"No, I'm good. Thanks."

Somehow she didn't think the producers wanted to hear that she'd been annoyed by Daniel's reaction and mildly repulsed by his kiss.

The producer smiled understandingly and patted her knee. "We'll make sure we get you in there before the Elimination Ceremony."

"Great."

Maybe by then she would have thought of something camera appropriate to say.

"Caitlyn, do you accept this ring as a symbol of my affection and commitment to this journey?"

"I do."

Josh watched as Daniel slipped the gold band onto Caitlyn's slim finger and kissed her cheek. On his left hand, his own wedding ring chafed at his finger. His divorce may be public, but the Suitorettes were kept so isolated they wouldn't know about it for weeks and to avoid distractions from the journey the producers had asked him to keep wearing his ring until they wrapped filming.

Caitlyn stepped off the platform where Daniel stood in front of a modified altar and returned to the line-up of beautiful women Daniel was picking between for the Elimination Ceremony. Samantha, Elena, and Tiffani already had rings on their fingers, with a half dozen more little gold bands on the altar waiting to be given out.

Josh had always liked the Suitorettes—even the ones who were only there for their fifteen seconds of fame. It was easy to dismiss the Suitorettes. Easy to diminish what they did, putting themselves out there in the most extreme way for a chance at true love. It was easy to discount them as naïve or shallow—as he'd been inclined to do when he was hammered the other night—but there was bravery in making yourself vulnerable on national television. He had to admire them.

Josh had befriended hundreds of gorgeous, accomplished ladies over the years, but never, not once, had he ever felt this slight, simmering edge of agitation during an Elimination Ceremony.

He wasn't jealous. The idea was ridiculous.

But every time Daniel picked up another ring, Josh's hackles went up until he called a name that wasn't Sidney's. Only then did Josh's tension ease.

He had a job to do. He couldn't be glowering every time Daniel looked Sidney's way. He couldn't be thinking that she deserved better than Mister Perfect.

He'd dodged a bullet with his divorce, but he couldn't afford even a whisper of impropriety with a Suitorette or he'd be another Hollywood has-been on the unemployment line.

It was a stupid infatuation. A rebound. She'd been in the right place at the right time and his subconscious had latched onto her when he'd needed someone to take his mind off Marissa. That was all this was.

He could beat it.

"Sidney."

The muscles in his shoulders knotted abruptly beneath his tailored suit. Sidney emerged from the line-up, her heels clicking on the polished hardwood floor as she crossed the room and climbed the platform to stand in front of Daniel. He held the ceremonial ring with both hands, raising it to chest-height as he stared deeply into Sidney's eyes.

"Sidney, do you accept this ring as a symbol of my affection and commitment to this journey?"

If he hadn't been staring at her, he would have missed it. Unfortunately, everyone was staring at her. So everyone saw her flick her gaze slightly to the side and make eye-contact with Josh. He nodded, just a subtle tuck of his chin, and her gaze returned to Daniel.

"Yes. I do."

Josh released a breath he hadn't realized he was holding as Daniel reached for Sidney's hand to slide on the ring. He wasn't sure what had just happened. A Suitorette had never looked to him for confirmation during an Elimination Ceremony before. When Sidney turned to return to the line-up, Josh let his gaze track around the room, watching for any sign that everyone else had noticed the momentary lapse, but the crew members all acted as if it was business as usual.

Until his gaze collided with Miranda's, the EP watching him with a question beetling her brow.

Shit. Of course the last person he'd wanted to notice had noticed.

Josh gave her a nod — as if he'd only been doing what she'd instructed him to do, encouraging Sidney to open up to Daniel. Her frown held for a moment longer. Then Daniel called the next name and she turned her attention back to the ceremony at hand. Josh released another breath. He was going to asphyxiate if this kept up.

Of its own volition, his attention returned to the line of Suitorettes. And the blonde in the blue dress.

She didn't look any happier about the ring on her finger than he was about the one on his.

Had she talked to Daniel? He wanted to ask one of the producers, but he couldn't show an unusual interest in her. He'd given her an on-camera pep talk earlier, going through the usual script about opening up and letting love in, but it had felt staged and stilted. And that was how things had to be between them. Even if he knew she was real in a way so few people were in this world.

She couldn't matter. He couldn't want her. He was just a broken guy looking for glue to put him back together where none existed.

Miranda's voice sounded through his earpiece, prompting him to wrap things up as Daniel slipped the final ring onto Brittany's finger. Josh stepped forward, saying the usual things, going through the usual motions—all without glancing once in Sidney's direction. Professionalism. That was the name of the game.

When he finished his standard speech—which the viewers at home could probably recite without him by now—he nodded to Daniel and the ladies, refusing to let his gaze linger on anyone in particular, then turned and strode out toward the terrace as a trio of production interns rushed forward with trays full of champagne for the post-Elimination party.

He didn't look back.

CHAPTER SEVEN

Brahms rolled off the piano like a tidal wave of sound as Sidney rested her forehead against the window, staring across the grounds to where just the roofline of the Mister Perfect mansion was visible through the trees. Caitlyn had said she was a piano teacher. What she had failed to mention was that she was also a world famous former child prodigy concert pianist. Only the best for Mister Perfect.

Caitlyn was beyond brilliant—and since music was how she de-stressed and *Marrying Mister Perfect* was nothing if not a constant stress factory, Sidney had been treated to a lot of free concerts in the last three weeks.

She would miss the music. And Caitlyn.

Ever since the last Elimination Ceremony, a decision had been solidifying in her mind. She'd never had much respect for the girls who left before they were kicked off by Mister Perfect. Sabotaging their chance at love, not respecting the opportunity they'd been given, protecting their dignity at the expense of their romantic forever. But now, from inside the bubble, everything looked different.

Maybe leaving was the romantic thing to do.

She could stay. The exotic travel dates would be beginning soon. She could use Daniel as her passport to Asia or South America or wherever the show was taking them this season. She could bide her time until he was done weeding out the crazy fame-hungry girls and got down to the business of selecting the ones he had the most feelings for...

But the truth was she still believed in the show too much to do that. The idea of even one girl who had genuine feelings for Daniel going home because Sidney was taking up space out of a selfish desire to see Rome went against every romantic bone in her body.

The rolling tide of Brahms crashed to a close and Sidney turned away from the window, applauding as Caitlyn lifted her hands from the keys. The redhead grinned, an easy comfortable smile that was never in evidence when the cameras were in sight.

There were hidden cameras in this room, as there were in every room of the house except the bathrooms, but at least without the blinking red lights they could pretend they weren't being filmed. While the other girls were fighting for their fifteen minutes of fame, she and Caitlyn had bemoaned the lack of privacy.

They'd bonded over that—and their overbearing mothers and childhoods ruled by etiquette rather than affection. Sidney really would miss her. And worry about her. Part of her was tempted to stay just so her friend wouldn't be alone.

"Are you happy here, Caitlyn?"

"I'm not *un*happy." Caitlyn ran through fingerings, little snatches of music erupting in staccato bursts from the instrument. "And I believe it'll get better. This part of the show is what we put up with for the chance at something amazing. Why? Are you unhappy?"

"I don't know," Sidney admitted. "I guess I thought it would be more... *romantic.*"

She'd counted on a connection with Daniel, counted

on that early-relationship excitement and infatuation to carry her through the stressful parts early in the show until real feelings could develop, but without those giddy feelings... waiting around for weeks on end, hiding in the music room with Caitlyn, running laps around the estate and entertaining herself as best she could as she waited to see whether Prince Charming would deign to grace her with his presence that week... it was hardly how she'd envisioned her fairy tale.

Catching Caitlyn's skeptical look, she grimaced. "I know it's stupid to think reality television could be romantic. I knew everything was staged and planned. But I've watched the show a thousand times and I've seen the girls who get that look in their eyes when they see Mister Perfect. You can't fake that—or maybe some of them can, but not all. Some girls really do fall for him and I thought, why can't I be one of those? I knew that the television aspect of it would be weird and crazy, but I watched Marcy and Craig last season. Both of them admitted they weren't really looking for love, but they were so perfect for each other they couldn't resist destiny. And I guess I thought—stupidly romantic though it may be—that Daniel could be my destiny."

"But you don't think that now?" Caitlyn asked. She picked out an ascending, questioning riff on the piano.

"I don't know. Other girls are talking about love and forever, but I feel like I've barely even met him."

She wasn't even sure she *liked* him. Let alone wanted to fall in love with him.

They'd barely spoken on their last date. The producers had arranged for them to go to a beer garden where Sidney and five other Suitorettes had dressed up in German barmaid outfits and trotted around the stage doing a little dance, embarrassing themselves on command for the show.

Daniel had hooted and applauded louder than the rest of the audience, eating up the fact that six beautiful women were making fools of themselves for him. After the performance, the producers had scheduled time for Daniel to have a beer with each Suitorette in an intimate one-on-one setting—but since Sidney was the last Suitorette on the agenda and Daniel hadn't limited himself to just one beer during each one-on-one, he was drunk enough by the time he got to her that his conversation was limited to slurred praise of her appearance and sloppy attempts to steal a kiss.

As he'd planted a hoppy kiss on her mouth, she couldn't help remembering the lingering taste of bad scotch on Josh's lips and the scent of his expensive cologne.

"Don't worry about how his relationships with the other girls are progressing," Caitlyn advised. "You'll just make yourself crazy. Focus on what you have with him."

What if we don't have anything? "What about your relationship with him?" Sidney asked. "Do you care about him?"

Caitlyn flushed and looked down at her hands. "I don't know. When I'm with him, it's easy to get caught up in the moment."

Sidney studied that blush. Caitlyn was enamored, no denying it. Sidney could stay—but what if her staying meant Caitlyn went home? Caitlyn who was a thousand times sweeter than she was—and beautiful and brilliant and talented and deserved her own fairy tale ending.

Caitlyn, who blushed when she thought about Daniel.

Even as Sidney was trying not to blush every time

she thought about Josh.

"I never get caught up in the moment with Daniel," she admitted. "Things are only getting more awkward with him. The last time he kissed me, I pictured someone else."

"Oh." Caitlyn's hands left the piano. "Who?"

As much as she wanted to tell Caitlyn about everything that had happened with Josh, cameras were everywhere and if she confided in her friend he could lose his job. "It isn't important."

"You aren't... are you thinking of...leaving?"

"I don't know. Maybe I'm just in the way of someone else's happy ending here."

She'd never expected that going home would be the romantic thing to do, but if she really believed in love maybe it was time.

Maybe it was ridiculous to expect that she would feel infatuation at first sight for Daniel, ridiculous to put this pressure on her emotions, but when the other girls were falling head over heels and she was just idling along at friendship—on a good day—it was hard to rationalize staying.

And all too easy to make up her mind to go.

Even Elena—the self-proclaimed villainess of the season—seemed to feel more for him than she did. She actually *wanted* to get the guy. Whereas Sidney couldn't even remember why she was here.

If it was meant to be, wouldn't something be holding her here?

Josh's face flashed in her mind.

She got caught up in the moment with *him*—but was that just her letting lust screw her out of a shot at real love? Or could there really be something there? Was it possible he felt the same way?

He'd said that if she behaved with Daniel the way she behaved with him that Daniel wouldn't be able to help loving her. Had that been just a nice thing to say or had he been trying to tell her something?

"Stay one more week," Caitlyn coaxed. "You owe it to yourself to be sure. Make sure you get some alone time with him. And maybe talk about how you're feeling. I bet he'll tell you he wants you to stay."

"Maybe." But it wasn't Daniel she was thinking of.

The door was locked.

Elena had said it wasn't always open, but Sidney hadn't even considered what she would do if she couldn't sneak over to see Josh until she was pushing ineffectually at the locked door between the two estates.

"Crap."

How was she supposed to find out if he was secretly in love with her now?

She could stay a few days longer, keep trying the door, but now that she'd thought of leaving the show, the idea had taken root in her mind and refused to give up its hold. When she pictured her future, there was only one man she envisioned and it wasn't Mister Perfect.

He couldn't be with her when she was a Suitorette, so maybe it was time for her to be brave and make the big romantic gesture of walking away from the show for him. Maybe he was waiting for her to give him that sign.

What would Cinderella do?

A giddy confidence bubbled like champagne in her blood at the thought of telling Josh how she felt.

Maybe Sidney wasn't such a coward after all.

CHAPTER EIGHT

"Josh, we need you at the Suitorette Mansion. Exit interview."

He looked up from the fan mail he'd been answering, frowning at the intern in his dressing room doorway. "Now?"

It was four o'clock in the afternoon and the next Elimination Ceremony wasn't until tomorrow night. It wasn't unheard of for a Suitorette to decide to call it quits, but usually she waited until a particularly dramatic moment to maximize screen time. Mid-afternoon departures on uneventful days were anathema to reality television drama.

"ASAP." The intern—Cadence, if he remembered correctly—shifted impatiently from foot to foot with the urgency of someone who knew Miranda would chew her ass if she didn't get Josh on set in the next thirty seconds. "She's already done the confessional and talked to Daniel. Pulled him aside when he was dropping Samantha off at the Suitorette Mansion after the Grand Canyon date."

Josh stood, taking quick stock of his appearance and unbuttoning his wrinkled shirt to change it out for the crisply pressed lavender button-down his wardrobe consultant had left hanging beside the mirror. "Who is it?"

"Sidney."

Shit. He bobbled the hanger, but years of experience kept his expression impassive as it clattered to the countertop. "Sidney?" Thank God his voice stayed steady. "Miss Happily-Ever-After herself? I thought she was in it for the long haul."

"You're telling me. I had twenty bucks on her to make final three."

"Don't let Miranda hear you betting on the results. That's a firing offense."

Cadence paled. "I didn't... Trent was starting a pool—"

"Relax. I won't tell the dragon lady." Josh finished buttoning up and straightened his collar. "But if Trent's still taking bets, tell him I've got a C-note on Samantha, Elena, and Caitlyn for the trifecta."

He tossed her one last reassuring grin and strode out of his dressing room and up the stairs of the Mister Perfect Mansion. He climbed out of the basement lair where the crew had their onsite offices as well as rooms to crash out when the hours were too crazy to allow time to go home to sleep. Several of the producers practically lived at the mansion during filming, but thankfully Josh's role as the "talent" gave him a slightly more humane schedule.

Usually by this time of day, his work was done— except for Elimination nights. He was only still on set this afternoon because Daniel had another date this evening and Josh was waiting to film the pre-date chat before he headed home for the day.

Pure dumb luck he was on hand for the exit interview.

Sidney.

Shit.

He'd fucked up her fairy tale. She'd been glowing with enthusiasm about the whole process that night when they'd talked in his room. A woman clearly in love with love. He'd thought she would at least make it to the first Meet-the-In-Laws date. But then he'd somehow imprinted on her and she was calling it quits.

He liked her. Of course he liked her, she was very likable—but that was where it ended. If she thought he was a better bet than Daniel in the happy-ever-after lottery, she was wildly delusional. Josh was a man going through the motions of life, subsisting on charm—and no one noticed because charm was all anyone saw when they looked at him. Sidney needed to wake up and realize that it took more than charm to make a happy ending. He was living proof of that.

Josh moved quickly along the path that connected the two properties, past the security check-points and through the elaborate landscaping toward the massive Suitorette Mansion. One of the cast handlers caught his eye and waved him toward the front drive.

He rounded the house and saw her, a lean, leggy blonde, already standing on the granite pavers with a single symbolic suitcase resting at her side. The rest of her luggage was doubtless being collected by the crew and packed off-camera into the back of the SUV that would take her home.

She really was leaving. The thought hit him strangely, seeming to squeeze his chest.

Miranda caught sight of him and waved him over as a team of sound, hair and makeup people descended on him to clip on his mic, poke a receiver in his ear, and make him camera-ready from the neck up.

"Just the basics," Miranda said with her usual brisk efficiency. "We have good footage from her talk with

Daniel—she just isn't feeling a connection, she doesn't want to get in the way of someone else's happy ending—the usual jazz. But her confessional footage is really minimal and I don't want this to seem like it came completely out of the blue. So let's make sure we've covered all the bases. You know the drill. Get all the sound bites you can. You ready to roll?"

"Aren't I always?" he lied, smooth, charming and fake.

Josh turned toward the woman waiting on the driveway.

He'd done his share of exit interviews over the years. The vast majority of them were with girls fresh off a very public and humiliating rejection. Nearly all of them had been sobbing—even several of those who had chosen to leave of their own volition—but Sidney was all elegant composure as she stood, shoulders squared, slim and proud on the granite pavers, with her straight blonde hair in a long loose fall down her back.

Josh approached, his most understanding camera smile in place. "I hear you've decided to leave us."

The producers had her facing the house, but she turned toward him at the sound of his voice, lifting those teal eyes to his face. Something in his chest went tight, but he ruthlessly suppressed the feeling. Whatever it was. He didn't need to be feeling *anything* for the Suitorettes except professionalism.

That unwanted feeling sparked another—relief. He couldn't be the guy who had inappropriate feelings for a Suitorette, and if she was gone, he wouldn't be.

He thought he'd done a good job of masking it. Even Miranda—who seemed to have a sixth sense about all things scandalous or romantic—hadn't given him so much as a suspicious look since the last Elimination

Ceremony.

Now Sidney looked up at him with something unreadable in her eyes. "It seemed like it was time."

"I know it can be hard here, but are you sure this is what you want? These opportunities don't come along every day."

"I think it's the right thing to do," she answered. The camera operators moved fluidly around them, framing up the best shots. "I think the other girls have more genuine connections with Daniel. He doesn't have the first idea who I am—"

"So give him time to get to know you—"

"I'm not sure he wants to. And being here, being part of this process, has really taught me to listen to my instincts..." Her gaze probed his and he suddenly realized what it was he was seeing in her eyes. Hope.

Shit. "Sidney..."

"If I'm honest I think I've realized that my heart is leading me in another direction."

Dread punched into the back of his heart, making his chest hurt. He didn't want to hurt her, but he couldn't care. Not for her. Even if he hadn't been beyond hope romantically—his heart officially closed for business— she was a Suitorette. End of story.

"I planned on coming here and falling in love, but you can't plan who you want," she went on. "I think maybe I was meant to come here, but not for Daniel—"

"I just want you to be one hundred percent certain you're making the right decision," he interrupted before she could make any declarations that would kill his career. He firmed his jaw. Merciless. That was the only way he'd get through this with his future intact. "You have Daniel here and he's open to love. He's ready for it. He's looking for it. If you stay here, you can still give it a shot with him. But if you go... I just don't want you to regret chasing some dream guy when that guy doesn't want you back." He held her gaze meaningfully. "Some guy who feels *nothing* for you."

"Nothing," she echoed—the hope in her eyes going into rigor mortis.

He'd expected disappointment to fall over her features, but it was still hard to watch it happen. "Think about this Sidney. Daniel—"

"No," she said, conviction ringing in the word. "I still think I should go. If I believe in this show, I have to. I don't feel connected to Daniel, but I do feel stronger." She firmed her chin, but her eyes were glistening now, her composure held onto by a death grip. "Coming on this show, facing my fears of what people will think of me and proving to myself that I really do believe I deserve a chance to be the bride someday, rather than the perennial wedding planner—this was incredibly liberating and I'm grateful to you for your part in that. This is the bravest thing I've ever done. Even if I didn't get the guy."

Her gaze held his and he knew without a shadow of a doubt that Daniel wasn't the guy she was talking about. His brain filled up with words he couldn't say. Words to make her stay.

Voices buzzed in his earpiece and the SUV pulled around the corner to stop in front of Sidney. The driver collected her symbolic bag and tossed it in the back with the rest of her luggage.

"I'll see you at the reunion special, Josh Pendleton." She climbed inside the SUV, where one of the show's producers would be waiting to film her departure interview—and try to wring a few tears out for the cameras.

Josh stood staring after the SUV as it pulled away. One of the sound techs stripped him of his mic and earpiece. The rest of the crew scurried back inside, off to catch the next emotional breakdown, Sidney already forgotten.

And still he frowned after her, regret, relief and frustration twining around one another in his gut. Miranda came to stand beside him, her arms folded over her tablet as she gazed after Sidney down the driveway. She waited until the rest of the crew had cleared the area before turning to him.

"What the fuck is wrong with you?"

Josh jerked, startled by the swift attack. "What do you mean?"

"Did you seriously just tell one of our Suitorettes that no one would love her except Daniel so she should stay?"

"No. Of course not."

"Really? Because it sounded a lot like that."

"I just wanted to make sure she'd really considered what she was giving up by leaving."

"She looked closer to tears saying goodbye to you than she ever got with Daniel. Next time let's try something other than implying that Mister Perfect is the only emotionally available man in America and she will die alone if she leaves, mmkay?"

Miranda strode off, sharp heels clacking on the pavers. Josh rammed his hands deep into his pockets and turned back toward the Mister Perfect mansion.

He'd been a jerk. That was true. But it had been the right thing to do.

Sidney had a crush on him. That was all it was. She was a romantic. She probably got crushes all the time. She'd get over it. All the faster now that he'd put a stop to her daydreaming.

He had to think of his career—not the hurt that seemed to echo in her eyes. Not the guilt that was burning in his gut.

His job was all he had right now. That and a pile of alimony payments. It was his entire freaking identity. If he lost that, he wouldn't know who he was anymore.

And even if she hadn't been a Suitorette...

Even if he had felt something for her, he was a bad bet. Better she find that out now. Better for them both.

CHAPTER NINE

Nothing.

It was such a horrible, demoralizing word.

Her brain couldn't seem to make sense of it. Not with the way his eyes would track her whenever they were in the same room together. It certainly hadn't felt like nothing to her—but was their *connection* all in her head? Had she been brainwashed to look for love everywhere by the show? Had she let a stupid one-sided infatuation ruin her best chance at the life she wanted? Was she really that terrible at reading signals?

Josh had told her flat out to give Daniel another chance. And for a fraction of a second, a little voice inside her head had said it was because Josh wanted her to stay. Then reality had intruded with that word.

Nothing.

The familiar streets of her hometown flowed sedately by outside the window, but she barely saw them as one of the show's drivers slowed to a complete stop at each and every stop sign. She'd been eager to get home for the last two days, sitting in her hotel room as the producers subjected her to an endless string of postmortem interviews and therapy sessions. She hadn't been able to wait to see Eden, California and Once Upon a Bride again, but now that she was here she almost wished the driver would slow his glacial pace even more.

She'd been calm and collected through the entire feeling-sharing marathon. It was only now, rolling along the upscale-kitsch Main Street of her hometown, that she started to have the first flicker of nerves.

She wasn't sure she was ready to face her friends and rehash it all.

The show had made her sign confidentiality agreements, but she trusted Victoria and Parvati to keep their mouths shut. She just had no idea how they would react to the knowledge that she'd left of her own accord.

For once seeing Once Upon a Bride filled her with uncertainty rather than pride. The wide display windows were a bridal fantasy, which in the next few weeks would become a tasteful holiday wedding display. Everything about the store, from the sweep of the awning to the cursive etching on the glass door, screamed elegance and taste.

The car slowed in front of the store and Sidney snapped out of her haze. "Could you go around to the back?" she asked the driver.

"Of course, miss."

As the car pulled into the parking lot behind the shop, Sidney peered down Main Street toward Parvati's coffee shop, wondering how long she had before word reached her friend that she was home.

Eden, California might be a small town, but it had become a favored hideaway for the rich in the last three decades—with more yacht clubs and country clubs per capita than any other town west of the Mississippi.

The adorable Main Street was perched in the hills above the Pacific Coast Highway, looking down over the massively expensive beachfront properties and four select yacht clubs—all of which made absolutely killer wedding locales. The hills were peppered with wineries and country clubs, for the brides who didn't want sand getting caught in their lace veils.

It was a wedding planner's paradise and together Victoria and Sidney had built Once Upon a Bride into *the* place for the elite bride to come to plan her romantic Eden wedding, whether she was a local princess or the sorority sister of a girl who once was a bridesmaid in a destination wedding on Eden's perfect white beaches.

They lived and died on word of mouth—which was part of why Sidney had gone on the show. But now, standing on the sidewalk in front of Once Upon a Bride, she couldn't help recalling the other side of the word-of-mouth coin.

Gossip.

Eden might be a luxury retreat, but it was still a small town and like all small towns it ran on gossip. She probably had fifteen minutes before word got out to her mother that she was back.

If she hurried, she might just have time to haul all her bags up to the attic apartment she kept above Once Upon a Bride before Hurricane Marguerite descended. Though maybe she was lucky and her mother would be out of town on business. She could only hope.

Victoria and her daughter shared the larger second floor apartment, but at this time of day Lorelei would be in school and Tori was undoubtedly inside Once Upon a Bride—unless she was off coordinating a tasting or a fitting for a bride-to-be.

It was cowardly, but Sidney hoped Tori was out. Suddenly she didn't want to face her best friend—or anyone else who had known how starry-eyed she'd been before leaving for the show.

She wanted to resume her life as if nothing had

happened—nothing to see here, folks—but she had a feeling she was more likely to be attacked by a giant squid while standing on Eden's Main Street than she was to get that wish.

"Would you like some help getting your things inside, miss?" the driver asked as he held her door for her.

Sidney gave him her most well-bred smile, already feeling her mother's rules of behavior closing around her like an iron maiden. "No, thank you, I can manage." She wanted her last connection with the show severed as quickly as possible—and he probably wouldn't understand why she was planning to sneak stealthily up the stairs to avoid her best friend.

She tipped him and waited until he'd driven off, leaving her and her five suitcases beside the back entrance to Once Upon a Bride. Tori's car was in the parking lot, but she would be in the office or with a bride and wouldn't hear Sidney creep in.

The back door screeched as she pulled it open and Sidney cringed.

"Hello?" Tori's voice carried down the back hallway from the main display room.

A momentary cowardly impulse almost kept her quiet, but Victoria was as much a sister as a business partner. "It's just me."

"Sidney?" Tori came flying around the corner from the front room. "You're back!"

Victoria was usually the composed one. Calm, organized and controlled in every situation. Sidney could play to the brides' dreams, but Victoria kept them focused, calm and on budget. But there was nothing calm or focused about her now. She ran down the hall, throwing her arms around Sidney in the doorway and squeezing hard. "God, I missed you. We weren't expecting you for weeks! Is it Meet-the-In-Laws time already?"

Sidney pulled back, feeling her first flicker of regret at leaving early. "Actually, the Meet-the-In-Laws dates are still a few weeks away."

"Don't tell me he let you go already. Couldn't he see how awesome you are?" Victoria's ivy green eyes, a striking contrast to her café au lait skin, filled with sympathy and understanding. "Forget about him. If he didn't know a good thing when it was right in front of him, he was a poor excuse for perfect. What kind of idiot doesn't know he's supposed to keep you until at least the In-Law dates when you could show him the business and set us up for life?"

Sidney knew Victoria was just trying to lighten the mood, probably make her feel better after what she thought was a rejection, but all she felt was a stab of guilt that walking away from *Marrying Mister Perfect* might hurt the business and by extension Tori and Lorelei.

"Actually, he, ah, he didn't let me go."

"They're giving you a break? I didn't think they did that. Oh God, is your family okay?"

"Everyone's fine. I just—" Sidney swallowed—she hadn't expected this part to be so hard. "I have to tell you something, but you can't tell anyone. Not even Lorelei."

"Sid, you're freaking me out."

"I left."

Victoria took a step back. "What?"

"I didn't feel a connection to him."

"But—our plan." Victoria visibly fought to keep the disappointment off her face and failed. "We were going to make the *Veil* list. Lorelei was going to have a college fund. I don't understand."

Guilt swamped her. "It wasn't like I thought it would be." And suddenly all the reasons that had seemed so logical when she was isolated inside the Suitorette Mansion didn't seem like enough.

Bells jangled as the front door of Once Upon a Bride opened and closed. "Sid?" Parvati's voice preceded her appearance in the back hall. "It *is* you! Tammy James saw a strange car pull around back here and was trying to convince me that it had to be you, but I said it couldn't be because you weren't due back for weeks." Parv's babble carried her all the way up to Sidney. She wrapped her in a hug before Sidney could get in a word edgewise. "What are you doing back so soon?"

"She quit."

Parvati pulled back, making no effort to mask her own disappointment. "Oh no! Was he a sleaze?"

Another wave of guilt crashed over her. "No, he was nice enough. There just wasn't anything there."

Parv frowned, visibly confused. "*Nice*. As in code for spineless?"

"No. As in a nice guy. Maybe a little shallow and self-absorbed, but it's hard not to be when everyone is telling you you're Mister Perfect and competing for your attention."

"So he didn't break your heart?"

"Daniel didn't come close to my heart."

"So that's it?" Parv frowned. "You just left? You hate the girls who just leave. You're always saying they expect love to be a walk in the park and relationships are work. Was he a jerk off camera?"

"He was exactly the same on camera and off." *But he wasn't Josh.* "It just wasn't there. Sometimes there's no chemistry."

"That's it? No chemistry?" Tori asked incredulously. "This from the woman who's always saying chemistry isn't as important as affection and compatibility?"

"And what do I know about it? Since when have I been in a serious relationship?"

"Tori," Parv said softly, reining her in.

Victoria's frown stayed etched between her brows, but she waved toward Sidney's bags, stacked on the ground behind her. "Do you want some help with those? I have a bride coming in at two. We can't just stand here blocking the back entrance all day."

The mood was tense and silent as they gathered up her bags and huffed them up three flights to the attic apartment. Victoria left immediately, returning downstairs to await her bride, but Parvati lingered as Sidney gazed around the familiar space.

Part of her had really thought she would be getting ready to move out of the cozy little apartment when she got back—moving in with Mister Perfect en route to living happily ever after.

"Lorelei's been looking after your plants," Parv commented from the doorway.

Sidney nodded absently, her eyes automatically going to the ficus in the corner. She'd always been able to talk to Parvati and Victoria, but now she couldn't find the words.

For the last two days, she'd been waiting for the regret to hit. She ignored the pressure in the back of her throat whenever she thought about Josh's rejection, expecting an anvil of regret to crush everything else when she realized she'd really done it. She'd walked away from Mister Perfect and her shot at love—not to mention any chance at making the *Veil* list and earning her mother's respect. But the regret never came.

Until now.

"I'm sorry I disappointed everyone."

"Hey." Parvati pushed away from the door and walked over to wrap her arms around Sidney in a side-hug. "You didn't disappoint anyone."

"No. I did. I screwed up. But you have no idea how hard it is to think straight when the only people you can talk to are the ones who are trapped inside the same echo chamber with you. At the time I thought it was empowering—leaving on my own. Defying the conventions of the show that say I have to wait until he kicks me off. Proving that I believe in love, in the process, and that it has to go both ways. I was *proud* of myself."

"I'm sure it was the right call. And Victoria will come around. You just surprised us is all."

"I'll make it up to her," Sidney said, making the words a promise. "We'll find some other way to hit the *Veil* list."

Three sharp raps sounded on her door and Sidney felt her spine snap straight in reflex. She knew that knock.

She moved to open the door. "Hello, Mother."

"So it's true. You are back."

Parvati edged around her, making her escape. "I should be getting back to the café. I'll see you later, Sid. Welcome home." She nodded to Sidney's mother. "Mrs. Dewitt."

"Parvati."

As Parvati retreated quickly down the stairs, Sidney opened the door wider. "Would you like to come in?"

"I can't stay. I have meetings in New York in the morning."

"Ah."

Marguerite Dewitt's gaze—the same unusual blue as her daughter's—raked her from head to toe. "You're looking thin."

Sidney felt her spine grow a little more rigid. "Thank you."

"Did he break it off with you?" Another mother might have been concerned. Marguerite just wanted the facts. And to know how disappointed she needed to be in Sidney's performance.

"I'm afraid I can't discuss it. Confidentiality."

Her mother nodded, as if she'd confirmed it. "At least it's over." She'd never made any pretense of supporting Sidney's decision to go on the show. The words *vulgar display* had practically become her catch phrase.

Sidney forced a smile. "I'll be home for Thanksgiving this way."

"But we aren't celebrating this year. Your father has meetings in Switzerland and your brother has to work over the holiday. Very high profile client. He's been swamped ever since his company got that fantastic write-up in Variety. Did you see the article?"

"I must have missed it. We didn't get Variety at the Suitorette mansion."

"The best personal protection money can buy—and that's a quote. The *best*. Your father was so proud. I had my doubts when your brother wanted to start a bodyguard service for celebrities, but I should have known Max would make a success of it."

Of course he had. Max was the golden child who could do no wrong. It was Sidney who drifted through life never quite measuring up, following her heart instead of her head. Not like the true Dewitts did.

Her mother tugged her gloves back on. "I'll leave you to get settled then."

Sidney thanked her and wished her a good flight, leaning in for an air-kiss.

She couldn't say she was disappointed about Thanksgiving. You had to be surprised to be disappointed. She'd celebrate with Victoria and Lorelei—and it would be a better Thanksgiving than she'd ever get with her family.

Provided Victoria had forgiven her by then.

She'd gotten caught up in playing Cinderella and forgotten that she had other reasons for going on the show. She'd squandered her chance to put Once Upon a Bride on the map, but she was going to make it up to Tori. Whatever it took.

She would make it happen. Like a Dewitt.

And when she was contractually allowed to date again, she would do that too. No sense wallowing in the memory of a man who thought *nothing* of her.

Screw that princess nonsense. She was going to be the queen of her own story.

CHAPTER TEN

Sidney ambushed Victoria as soon as she emerged from her apartment the next morning.

"I have a plan."

Victoria froze at the foot of the stairs, blinking sleepily at the sight of Sidney seated at the consultation table in the middle of Once Upon a Bride's main room before dawn. "Does the plan involve going to Parv's for a latte?"

Sidney sprang up from her chair, grabbing her notes and a to-go cup filled with Parvati's genius, thrusting the latter at Tori. "It's a three-pronged plan."

Victoria took the cup. "Have you slept?"

"Sleep is for the weak. And I am a goddess. Or a queen. I haven't decided which."

Tori eyed the cup dubiously. "How many of these have you had?"

"I'm sorry I bailed on the show and screwed up our chance to get all that free exposure."

Sleep cleared from Tori's expression as she frowned. "I'm sorry for how I reacted yesterday."

"No, you were right. We had a plan and I lost sight of it, but I'm focused now and we can still make that list. Hence the plan." A memory of Josh's wry smile as he told her more people should say *hence* tried to rise up, but she smothered it. She was focused. She was determined. She was a Dewitt, damn it.

"And there are prongs?" Victoria sipped the latte.

"Three prongs. Prong One—Broader exposure. We're going to need to start going to more bridal expos. Word of mouth got us started, but if we want to be the best, we need to be a household name in wedding planning. Prong Two—Exclusivity. We need to raise our prices. Being the best means catering to the best clients. Max didn't just start a security service, he started a specialized celebrity bodyguard service catering to the elite of Hollywood. So we need to find our elite and cater to them. Landing a celebrity wedding is priority one."

"I thought priority one was broader exposure?"

"Prong, not priority. And then there's prong three: Excellence. Our clients won't mind paying more because we will provide the absolute best wedding planning service money can buy—which will be the easy part because we're already doing that."

"How are we going to get broad exposure if no one can afford us?"

"Broader exposure isn't about more clients. It's about reputation. We want everyone to want us, even if they can't afford us. We'll be the fifteen carat pink diamond wedding experience. The one every little girl dreams of but only the select few can actually afford."

Victoria sank down at the consultation table, eyeing the scraps of paper Sidney had scribbled on during her night of frantic planning. "I'm not disagreeing—I think your plan could probably work—but are you sure this is the direction we want to take the business? When we started Once Upon a Bride, we talked about helping every bride—no matter her budget—get her perfect fairy tale wedding."

"And we will! But we can't do that if we can't afford to do business. You want to be able to afford to send Lore to a good school, right? We've barely been making ends meet, but when we hit the *Veil* list we won't have to worry about next month's rent anymore. We can still take on a pro-bono wedding every now and then, but this will set us up for life. Set Lorelei up for college."

Sidney knew she was playing to Victoria's weaknesses—Tori's mother was a single mom as well. She'd made a living as a housekeeper for Eden's elite, but she had never been able to afford the Ivy-covered education other Eden kids got. Lorelei was smart enough to get into those schools, but they still had to pay for them somehow.

Victoria grimaced. "So how do we land a celebrity wedding?"

Sidney smiled. "It's all about who you know. I'll call Max. Find out if any of his clients are looking like they might be tying the knot. And I may not have made it to the finish line, but I still have the entire *Marrying Mister Perfect* franchise at my disposal. I'll contact Miranda Pierce and see if any of the Suitors or Suitorettes from past seasons are looking to get hitched. We'll find a bride. It may take a few months, but it's going to work."

Victoria looked over the papers on the consultation table. "I guess it's a plan."

The star-filled Tahitian sky was annoyingly romantic. Josh gazed up at it from the balcony of his hotel room and wondered if room service had any crappy bottles of six-year-old scotch. He was in the mood to wallow in self-pity.

Shooting had officially wrapped. At sunset Mister

Perfect had gotten down on one knee, his Suitorette of choice had blushingly said yes, and Miranda was in raptures over the possibility of televising the upcoming nuptials. Josh, on the other hand, was biting his tongue on the constant urge to caution both Daniel and his fiancé to take their time and make sure they were really sure.

Tonight the happy couple was ensconced in the resort's finest suite, wallowing in their romantic euphoria. But tomorrow it was back to the real world. They would all fly back to the States, where the editors were already frantically piecing together the first episodes. Daniel and Josh would do numerous public appearances to promote the new season, but for the most part his work was done.

When he'd first gotten this gig, he'd loved this part. He hadn't been able to wait to fly home to Marissa, bringing her gifts and stories from all the places the show had taken him. Sliding back into his home life. When he got home after those first few seasons, they would stay in bed together for days, wrapped in each other. He'd stupidly thought it would always be that way.

And now he was flying home to a depressingly empty one-bedroom apartment in Studio City. And realizing that the home life he'd always slid back into when he got back to the States was hers, not his.

A brisk knock sounded on his bedroom door. Josh turned away from the irritatingly lovely night sky, crossing his suite to answer.

Miranda barely waited until the door cracked open to begin speaking. "Change of schedule tomorrow. We're putting Caitlyn and Elena on the first flight and pushing you and Daniel back to the later nonstop."

"Great. So I get to sleep in."

"Not exactly. We're going to use the time to pre-tape some promo segments. Teasers we can use when the last couple episodes are about to air. Then when we get back to LA, we'll need you at the mansions to pick up a few transitions and explanations for the places where the raw footage is weak. Shouldn't take more than a day or two."

"Fine. Is that all?"

Miranda pursed her lips, clutching her ever-present tablet to her chest. "I need you to be cheerful, Josh."

"Excuse me?"

"I know you're going through a rough time, but we've been looking over the footage we have so far and you've been a little dour this season. That episode with Sidney is a perfect example."

A swift kick of regret hit him at the mention of her name, but he hid his reaction. "I hardly think—"

"You're depressing," Miranda cut him off bluntly. "And the host of *Marrying Mister Perfect* can't be depressing. We're going to reshoot the parts where you let your game face slip, but I need you at one hundred percent. The network has already told me to focus group your viability as host."

"Are you kidding? I thought you didn't hire me because I was married."

"We didn't. But a grumpy divorced host may test differently with our audience than a happy-go-lucky schmuck with a ring on his finger. The network wants to make sure you're still appealing to our target demographics."

"No."

Miranda frowned. "This isn't the sort of thing you can say no to, Josh."

"You can't do this. I'm the host of *Marrying Mister Perfect*."

"For now you are. But you need to find a way to be optimistic about love again, if you want to stay on as our host. We aren't selling divorce. We're selling true love—even if the way we go about it sometimes is genuinely screwed up." Miranda tipped her head, studying him. "You might want to consider dating when we get back to LA."

He recoiled at the idea.

"Find a way to fit the image, Josh. Or there won't be anything I can do to help you."

Happy. Cheerful. Optimistic about love. He needed to be a romantic idiot again. No more wallowing. He was over this.

He just had to figure out how he was supposed to believe in the show when all he could think about was how often their Suitors and Suitorettes got hurt. And how this season he'd had a direct hand in hurting one.

"Do you think he loves her?"

Miranda's attention had already wandered back to her tablet, but now she looked up, frowning. "What?"

"Daniel. Do you think he's in love with Caitlyn or is she just his prize for winning at life?"

"He proposed to her. She said yes. They want to get married on the reunion special. Don't look a gift engagement in the mouth. The ratings are going to be insane if we can get an actual on-air wedding out of this."

"But are they going to be happy together?"

"Josh, what is this?" she snapped, impatient.

"Do you still believe in the show?" he asked her. Because he knew he hadn't been the only one who thought they were doing good work for the last few years. It was only recently, he'd begun to see the other side. "Do you really think we're helping people find love or are we just exploiting their hopes and dreams—twisting them around until they wind up heartbroken and crying for our cameras? Are we really trying to match people up or are we just giving them a platform to hurt one another on national television?"

The way he'd hurt Sidney.

Maybe that was the difference. This season, for the first time, it had been him breaking a heart. *He* had hurt her. The guilt had always been there, waiting, but he'd never felt it until a direct hit pierced his bubble of obliviousness, letting all the rest in.

"Are we doing more harm than good?"

Miranda folded her arms, glaring up at him. "I don't know where this little crisis of faith is coming from, but you need to get your head out of your ass before you have to be the face of the show next week with all the major publicity outlets. I get enough of this questioning-the-morality-of-what-we-do bullshit from Bennett and I don't need it from you too."

Bennett Lang was Miranda's on-again-off-again flame—and by the sound of things lately, they'd been more off than on. "Maybe he's got a point."

"And maybe you need to think about whether you want to have a job next season." Miranda put up a hand when he would have spoken. "Look. We're all tired. It's been a long season. More stressful than most. And I think we could all use some time off to get our heads on straight. Just remember who pays your salary."

And how much alimony you owe went unspoken, but Josh heard it loud and clear.

He'd believed in the show once and unless he wanted to go into debt in a hurry, he needed to remember how that felt—or at least act like he did.

CHAPTER ELEVEN

"I'm so sorry, Sidney. You did such a great job. The wedding would have been just beautiful—" Allison, the would-have-been bride, dissolved into tears and Sidney reached for the box of tissues they kept on hand. They always hoped there would only be happy tears in Once Upon a Bride, but lately their luck hadn't been so good.

"Don't apologize, Allie. These things happen."

The holidays were always hard on couples trying to blend their families and this year they had taken their toll. Allison was their third bride to call off a wedding this week.

Love was most definitely *not* in the air.

Twenty minutes later, after Allison's tears had been dried and she'd sent the bride on her way with one last hug, Sidney pulled out her tablet and began the Sisyphean task of cancelling all the plans that had been put in place for the Valentine's Day wedding.

Allison's parents wouldn't get any of their deposits back—including the one they'd paid to Once Upon a Bride—but after the groom's father had gotten drunk and called the bride's mother a socialist before knocking over the menorah and lighting a family heirloom tapestry on fire, they were prepared to lose the deposits.

Wedding dress. Cake. Venue. Band. Caterer. It was never a short list when a wedding called it quits, but it was part of the business.

If only it wasn't such a large part these days.

Sidney's plan was failing.

Or perhaps failing was too strong a word, but her three-pronged plan had, so far, been a complete non-starter. There were no bridal expos scheduled until January, her brother Max didn't know a single celebrity who was on the cusp of engagement, and even their normal holiday wedding business was so sluggish this year they'd been reduced to planning office Christmas parties.

She could only hope there was a rash of engagements on Christmas and New Year's Eve to stir up business, or they wouldn't last long enough for her three-pronged plan to take effect.

She'd put in half a dozen calls to Miranda Pierce's office, but the show had only just wrapped filming somewhere exotic so she tried not to read anything into the fact that the producer hadn't gotten back to her.

She tried calling Caitlyn, eager to get whatever gossip her friend was allowed to share about what had gone down at the show after she left, but Caitlyn was dodging her calls. Had she made it all the way to the end? Was she nursing a broken heart? Sidney was dying to talk about the show with *someone*, but Caitlyn's voicemail wasn't helping. And every time she thought about bringing it up with Parv or Tori she just felt guilty again, reminded that she had let them down.

The show would begin airing in under two weeks. She had no idea how much she'd be featured in the opening episode. She'd talked about Once Upon a Bride in all of her pre-taped interviews, but not all the girls were included in the Meet the Suitorette featurettes. Business could be booming by this time next month... or it could be more of the same, scrimping to get by.

When she finished the online cancelation for her favorite florist, Sidney grabbed her cell phone, determined to give Miranda Pierce one more try. Telephone stalking would be worth it if she could land a *Marrying Mister Perfect* wedding. She owed it to Tori to swallow her pride. Tori who had believed in her enough to go into business with her when even her parents hadn't been willing to invest in Once Upon a Bride.

Sidney was accustomed to getting the run around from one of Miranda's many assistants, but this time she was only placed on hold for a moment before Miranda Pierce's no-nonsense greeting sounded in her ear.

"Sidney. This is unexpected."

She immediately launched into her pitch, selling Miranda on Once Upon a Bride the same way she would any hesitant mother-of-the-bride, but Miranda cut her off before she could get going.

"Sorry, hon. I like you, but we already have a wedding planner on retainer."

"So Daniel's planning a wedding?"

"I didn't say that." Miranda wouldn't be caught dead leaking MMP spoilers. "But we always hope our Mister Perfect will find the woman of his dreams and we keep a wedding planner on hand just in case."

"What about the rejected Suitors and Suitorettes from past seasons?" Sidney asked, not above revealing her desperation. "Are any of them altar-bound? Have Marcy and Craig set a date?"

A heavy pause. "Did your business suffer in your absence?"

"We could use the exposure," Sidney admitted.

"Well, it's not a wedding, but we are looking for a few Suitorettes to do publicity appearances in the LA area to promote the show over the next few weeks. You could mention your business. I would have called you, but usually the girls who leave on their own want to wash their hands of the entire franchise."

"*Marrying Mister Perfect* might not have been my path to love, but I still believe in the show. Daniel just wasn't right for me."

"We're talking mostly photo ops with fans of the show and the occasional local day time television appearance—and the pay is terrible—but it's free exposure, if you're interested."

"I'll do it."

"Which one is this?" Josh asked the publicist riding opposite him in the limo as they pulled up in front of Planet Hollywood. He'd done so much promo in the last few days he'd completely lost track of where he was or who he was talking to. But he did the job. Smile, shake hands, answer the same questions and pretend he wasn't jaded.

"MMP Superfans—private Q&A for the online contest winners and then the autograph signing will be open to the public. Daniel has to shoot the Late, Late Show bit, so we brought in some of this season's Suitorettes instead." Cole checked his tablet. "Looks like Monica, Alicia, and Sidney."

Josh froze with his hand on the door pull. "Sidney?"

"The wedding planner, remember? The blonde with legs up to her ears who walked before he could dump her."

"No, I remember her. I just didn't peg her for the publicity event type."

"Last minute replacement. Ready?"

Cole opened the door to the limo and jumped out before Josh could think of a coherent response.

Josh climbed out after him, slapping on his public smile and waving to the small crowd of tourists who had pressed against the red velvet ropes in an attempt to see who was getting out of the limo. They cheered and waved back—even though Josh would bet his next paycheck half of them didn't have a clue who he was except some random semi-famous Hollywood personality. It was all about image. Project an image of fame and the celebrity gawkers didn't need to know who you were to be impressed by you. Which was why the show had arranged the limo and the red velvet ropes.

So much of his life was staged for effect it could be disorienting. He'd seen Suitors and Suitorettes over the years get swept away by the glamour and always tried to remind himself what was real, tried to keep his feet firmly on the ground. Marissa had been good for that— until he realized his life with her was no more real than the red carpet set ups.

Inside, he climbed the stairs to the restaurant's event area where a few dozen MMP Superfans were perched on the edges of their chairs. At the front of the room, an elevated platform had been set up and three Suitorettes waited to one side, speaking amongst themselves as they waited for him.

Josh made a concentrated effort not to look directly at Sidney as he trailed Cole toward the makeshift stage. The publicist would be acting as emcee, as he had at all of Josh's other publicity stops today. It always felt foreign to him—handing over the hosting duties to someone else—but now Josh was grateful he wouldn't have to interact with Sidney any more than absolutely necessary.

She looked gorgeous.

Not that he was looking.

Her long legs were bare. Only in LA would her short ice blue sundress be appropriate attire in January. Her blonde hair was long and loose like a classic California girl. He fought the urge to study her face, to try to detect any of the awkwardness he was feeling.

Did she still have a crush on him? Was that why she was here?

He needed to apologize to her. He owed her that. But he couldn't do it here, with several dozen avid fans looking on.

Some of the Superfans caught sight of him and let out a squealing cheer. Josh waved, beaming at them as Cole trotted up the risers to the stage and grabbed a microphone, launching into his welcome spiel. Josh listened with half an ear, nodding to the Suitorettes in casual greeting.

Even with his eyes locked on the crowd and his public smile firmly in place, he was excruciatingly aware of Sidney shuffling closer to edge up to his side.

Monica was introduced first and Sidney leaned close as the aspiring singer mounted the stairs.

"I'm not stalking you," she whispered.

Josh kept his face carefully blank and tried to speak without moving his lips. "I didn't think you were."

Alicia climbed to the stage next.

Sidney shifted at his side. "I didn't know you'd be here."

"Likewise."

"Miranda offered to let me do some promo stuff for exposure for my business."

"You're up." He nodded her toward the stage,

looking directly at her for the first time—and nearly getting rolled by the look in her teal eyes.

Then she was turning, climbing the stairs, and he fought to keep his eyes off her legs.

His turn was next and the applause that had been perfunctory turned deafening—not surprising. He was a known quantity. America hadn't gotten to know the girls yet. By the reunion special, they would be getting as much of an ovation as he did—sometimes more—but right now they were just pretty girls in a neat little row and he was the star.

Time for him to act like it.

CHAPTER TWELVE

Sidney was an idiot.

She hadn't thought for a second that Josh would be there too. That she would be sitting next to him on the makeshift stage, close enough for his sleeve to brush her arm whenever he leaned forward to engage one of the fans.

What must he think of her? The last time they'd spoken there had been cameras in both of their faces and he'd been oh-so-subtly telling her that she should date Daniel because he would never in a million years be interested in her. Now cell phones snapped pics of them and she was supposed to smile mysteriously whenever someone asked her how she felt about Daniel—when all she really wanted to do was hide under the narrow table. The awkwardness was excruciating.

And her stupid girl parts were still fluttering at his proximity. He must have some super powered pheromones because there was no other explanation for how she could be mortified and turned on at the same time.

At least the publicity appearance was easy.

At first it was all questions about Daniel and the show, with a couple questions thrown at her and the other Suitorettes—which at least gave her the chance to mention Once Upon a Bride in every response—but then the tone of the event turned.

One of the fans stood to ask her question, her face flushed with excitement as the publicist, Cole, handed her a microphone. "Josh, is it true you're single now?"

Sidney felt the subtle tensing of his muscles at her side. "Yes, I am newly single."

"What happened?" Another fan shouted out before Cole could call on her. "Why did you get divorced?"

Sidney looked at him out of the corner of her eye. His smile didn't falter, but she could feel him hesitate. "It just didn't work out."

"Are *you* going to be the next Mister Perfect?" The brunette in the front row batted her eyelashes.

His body was rigid now, though his smile never wavered—his host persona locked into place like a mask. "I think I'm better suited to hosting for now."

A woman in the back row catapulted to her feet. "Will you marry me?"

At that outburst, Cole must have realized how far out of hand they were getting. He held up his hands, regaining control of the enthusiastic crowd and announced the end of the Q&A and beginning of the autographing. The fans lined up eagerly.

The only autographs Sidney had ever signed were on credit card receipts and rent checks, but now these complete strangers wanted her to sign *Marrying Mister Perfect* promo cards.

The line stacked up in front of her, with all of the fans wanting more one-on-one interaction with Josh as he signed their cards. Some of them avoided eye-contact with her, eagerly looking toward Josh, while others asked her questions about herself and she was able to get in several dozen more plugs for Once Upon a Bride. But even as she pimped her business, constantly smiling, she couldn't help overhearing Josh's conversations with his fans—and feel how he grew more and more stiff as they pumped him for information about his divorce and some overtly propositioned him.

He fielded every question with unruffled charm, but by the time they reached the end of the line he might as well have been carved from stone he was so rigid.

Cole thanked everyone for coming and ushered the "talent" out, but instead of leading them out to the street, Sidney found herself with Josh and two other Suitorettes in a small office.

"The limos are stuck in traffic around the corner," Cole explained, "but we always want to leave before the enthusiasm for the event tapers off. Sit tight here and I'll come get you when our wheels arrive."

But Josh didn't sit tight. He was out the door almost as soon as Cole was. Monica and Alicia sat down, trading stories about how great it was to feel famous, but Sidney couldn't join in. She'd never wanted to be famous—it was hard to be invisible and notorious. And now seeing how it made people behave around Josh, she'd just as soon keep fame at bay with a ten foot pole.

Slipping out of the office into the back hall, she glanced around, trying to figure out where Josh would have gone. A back door was cracked open at the end of the hall, letting in a bright shaft of sunlight, and Sidney moved toward it.

The wide back alley was littered with cigarette butts and the stoop was covered with ash, but Josh wasn't smoking. He leaned against the exterior wall with his eyes closed and his face tipped up to the sun. Sidney carefully propped open the door marked Deliveries to keep it from locking them both out, and took a position beside him, holding up the wall.

"You okay?"

He didn't jump, proving he'd known she was there, even if he hadn't opened his eyes at her approach. "Of course."

"They shouldn't have asked you those questions."

That opened his eyes—and the cynicism was bright in their brown depths when he looked down at her. "When you're a celebrity—even a minor one like me—people feel like they have the right to all your secrets. I shouldn't have been rattled."

"It's your business. Your private life—"

"I'm a public figure. I should have been prepared for it." She thought he would leave it at that, but then he grimaced, tilting his face back up to the sun. "I couldn't think of the right thing to say. It's not like I can tell them I'm a failure at marriage. A poor heartbroken schmuck whose wife cheated on him. I'm the host of *Marrying Mister Perfect*. I'm the brand."

"You're allowed to be human."

He didn't seem to hear her. "I'll handle it better next time."

She wanted to argue that there shouldn't *be* a next time, that people should respect his privacy, but then he turned toward her, facing her with one shoulder propped on the wall and she lost her train of thought.

"I was hoping I could talk to you."

"You were?" Was that her voice? So breathless and light?

"I've been wanting to apologize to you for the way things went between us on the show. I never wanted you to get hurt."

"No, I'm sorry. I never meant to put you in an awkward position."

"You didn't."

She'd thought her hope where he was concerned was dead, but it resurrected itself. What exactly was he trying to say? He was sorry he'd hurt her. Did that mean he wanted something more with her now that she was no longer a Suitorette?

"So how's business?" he asked. When she looked blank, he prompted, "You said that's why you're here?"

"Oh, right. Slow, unfortunately. I'm hoping we'll get some exposure from the show, but with me leaving early..."

Josh nodded. "You could always give it another go. They haven't picked the Miss Right for next season yet. I could put in a good word for you."

He thought of her as the next Miss Right—which meant he pictured her dating thirty handsome Suitors. As if she needed more of a hint than that about how he saw her.

Her stupid hopes withered. Dang it. She couldn't seem to stop coming back for more punishment where he was concerned.

"No, thanks. I think I've had about all the reality dating I can handle."

"What happened to the eternal optimist?"

She figured out you were never going to want her. "I'm still an optimist. But I doubt the producers want a Miss Right who walked away from Mister Perfect."

He shrugged. "You might be surprised."

The Deliveries door swung open and Cole's head popped out. "There you are. Josh, your car is here. Sidney, yours will be along in five."

The host shoved himself away from the wall. "I guess that's my cue."

"See ya, Josh."

He nodded to her, distant and formal. "Sidney."

He followed Cole inside, but Sidney stayed behind, refusing to trail after him like a hopeful puppy.

What was it about him? Why did she still like him, even after he repeatedly told her how uninterested he was in her? Was that it? Was her stupid heart fixed on him because he was safe? If he was totally out of her league there was no real risk of heartbreak in crushing on him. Or was she a glutton for punishment? Fixating on a guy who would never think she was good enough because she was in the habit of looking for affection from those who saw her as unworthy.

She could psycho-analyze herself to death, but the truth remained. She still wanted him.

He was tall and handsome, but also wry and funny beneath his smooth host veneer. He was bitter and jaded, but also instinctively chivalrous and surprisingly gentle with the cast of Suitorettes. Except for her. His notorious kindness had taken a holiday when she left. There must be something wrong with her but she kind of liked that he hadn't been sweet with her, because he'd been real instead and reality had been in short supply on the show.

But now all she had was reality. And a crush she really hoped she could make go away.

CHAPTER THIRTEEN

"Once again thanks to Josh Pendleton for being here tonight, and a new season of *Marrying Mister Perfect* begins this Tuesday at eight, seven central."

Josh kept his best smile firmly in place as the late night host wrapped up his segment—a smile which was a little more genuine due to the fact that he was finally done with his promo duties for the day. Not that he was looking forward to returning to his crappy apartment, but at least he wouldn't have to worry about anyone else asking him about his divorce.

It had almost been a relief to throw himself into the show as soon as the divorce was final. For a few months, he'd been able to avoid facing all the ways his life had changed, but now it was all coming back to bite him on the ass.

He'd known he was losing Marissa and the house, but he hadn't anticipated all the little ways his life would suck more now. All of their friends were "couple" friends and she seemed to have gotten them all in the divorce.

His family lived in Washington and he didn't want to worry them, so he didn't tell them how much everything sucked right now. How isolating every single part of his life was. How he was having to figure out how to be him again and he completely sucked at it.

It didn't help that he was asked about it constantly. Five days into promotion for the new season, all anyone wanted to talk about was his failed marriage.

He couldn't escape it. At least this last interview had stayed focused on *Marrying Mister Perfect*.

Josh shook hands with the host, going through the usual we're-such-good-friends-even-though-we-barely-know-each-other bullshit, counting the seconds until he could sneak back to the dressing room, grab his things and escape.

But when he arrived at the dressing room, the sight of the woman waiting there made it clear he wasn't going to be escaping any time soon.

"Miranda. To what do I owe this honor?"

"Josh," the executive producer greeted him as she stood, tucking her ubiquitous tablet under one arm. "How's promo going so far?"

"You know how it's going. That's why you're here."

She cocked her head to one side. "Were you always this blunt? I don't remember you being this blunt."

"I'm turning over a new leaf. How's the focus grouping going?"

"Work in progress." She shrugged. "But this probably won't help your cause."

She pulled the tablet out from under her arm, tapping something on it and flipping the screen to face him. The article on display was for a crappy online gossip magazine—but it had a picture, and pics generated clicks. No one knew that better than the MMP marketing department.

"How did they get this?"

In the photo, he stood close to Sidney. Her back was to the wall and he was facing her, the lighting doctored to give the illusion of night. It looked intimate. Like two lovers caught in a private moment at the backdoor of a club, rather than the smoke-break area behind a Planet Hollywood—which was the only place the photo could have been taken.

He hadn't even seen the photographer.

"Does it matter?" Miranda countered.

"It isn't what it looks like."

"I don't care what it is. I only care about what it looks like," she said flatly. "This isn't what I meant when I told you to date, Josh. You need to stay away from the Suitorettes."

"I am away. That wasn't anything. We were talking after a promo event."

"But it looks like something and image matters. You know that."

"What do you want me to do, Miranda? Maintain a ten foot buffer between myself and any single females?"

"Actually, I'd like just the opposite." She scrolled through screens on her tablet, searching for something as she spoke. "You need to be seen with someone appropriate. I need you to be dating someone—not a Suitorette—so people stop asking if you're the next Mister Perfect. I've clearly been off my game or I would have anticipated the reaction to your newly single state. As it is, we'll spin it. We made sure Jimmy didn't ask you about your divorce tonight, but we've scheduled an afternoon talk show segment for you to tell all next Wednesday. We're negotiating the talking points, making sure it'll be handled in the right way, but in the mean time…Olga."

She turned the screen to him, displaying a picture of a vaguely familiar, skimpily-clad red-head with Bambi eyes and full lips.

"Olga?" he repeated, starting to feel numb.

"She's one of the pros on *American Dance Star*. For reasons of her own, she could use some good publicity right now and dating you will be good publicity."

He frowned, instantly suspicious. "What exactly are those reasons of her own?"

"Nothing sinister. She just wants to transition to acting and she's being turned away for the leading roles because her image is too highly sexualized to appeal to middle America."

"So my job is to desexualize her? Gee, thanks."

"Don't get your panties in a twist. She just needs to date a nice guy with relationship potential rather than the fast-cars-and-faster-women sleazebags she's been seen with lately. And she should be good for ratings—she has a following in her own right. Maybe we can poach some of her fans."

"Are you pimping me out for ratings?"

"I'm pimping you out so you can keep your job. Any ratings boost is just a perk."

He rubbed a hand across his face, feeling the itch of makeup on his skin. "Do I have a choice?"

"Of course you do. You always have choices. But dating Sidney Dewitt isn't one of them."

"I have no intention of dating Sidney Dewitt."

"Good. And just to be safe, I'll make sure you two aren't on any of the same promo events from here on out." Miranda smiled. "You'll like Olga. She's a sweet girl."

"And if I don't?"

"Fake it for a few weeks. At least until viewers get engaged in the new season and forget about your divorce. Be glad America has the attention span of a two year old. You'll be old news before you know it."

"Gee thanks."

Miranda smiled. "I try."

"Aunt Sidney, come *on*! It's starting!"

Lorelei bounded into the kitchen, all knees and elbows and wild black curls as she tried to drag Sidney bodily toward the living room where Parvati and Victoria were popping the champagne for night one of *Marrying Mister Perfect*. Sidney had retreated to the kitchen to grab paper towels to mop up some of the free-flowing champagne—and had been eyeing the fire escape, wondering if she could make a run for it while no one was watching—when Lorelei came to drag her back to the inevitable.

She was about to be on national television.

Why had she thought that was a good idea?

Lorelei latched onto her arm and began towing her toward the living room as the distinctive opening theme played. The girl was a miniature version of Victoria, except for the eyes. While Tori's eyes were ivy green, Lorelei's were whiskey brown—a souvenir from the father Victoria never spoke of.

They walked into the room right as Josh's face appeared on the big screen TV, smiling his smooth host smile—the one that had none of the wry cynicism she saw when his guard was down.

"Dear Lord, that man is gorgeous," Parvati sighed. "Did you hear he was on the market? For like five seconds. Figures a man that hot would only be divorced for about five seconds before some hot Russian model snatched him up."

Sidney's toe caught on a rug and she stumbled. "What?"

"Josh Pendleton," Parvati said without tearing her

eyes from the screen where now Daniel was waxing poetic on the qualities he was looking for in a wife. "He's dating that Olga what's-her-face. The super hot one from that dance show who's the new face of Revlon. Or was it Maybelline? I always get those two mixed up."

No wonder he'd turned her down at every opportunity. He was dating a makeup model. "Of course he is," Sidney murmured softly as Tori shoved a full glass of champagne into her hand and Lorelei dragged her onto the couch.

"Aunt Sidney, when do you come on?" Lore asked, bouncing on her chair.

"I don't know. They shoot so much footage and we never know what they're going to use. I could be on screen for half an hour or twenty seconds."

She'd seen the show enough to know that some of the girls would be virtually invisible the first night—and while the exposure for the business would be better if they featured her often, she found herself secretly hoping to go unnoticed, dreading the moment when she would appear on screen.

After the first commercial break, Josh led the viewers into a collection of intro packages—and excited squeals rang through Victoria's apartment as Sidney appeared on screen.

Her stomach pitched.

"Oh honey, you look gorgeous!" Parvati gushed.

"Shh! She's talking about Once Upon a Bride!" Victoria bounced, as giddy as Lorelei at the free publicity.

Sidney cringed, trying to fade into the couch cushions, but gradually her friends' excitement began to penetrate her self-consciousness. Seeing the show through their eyes, it wasn't so terrible after all.

They drank champagne—except for Lorelei, who had sparkling cider. Laughing and groaning at all the cheesy over-romanticized set-ups, Sidney found herself actually enjoying herself—pointing out Caitlyn as her best friend in the house and pleading no comment when Parvati declared Elena the Suitorette most likely to get naked in front of Daniel by week four.

By the time the Elimination Ceremony rolled around, they were all pleasantly buzzed and giggling. When Daniel called Sidney's name to give her the ceremonial ring, a cheer went up and Lorelei leapt up to take a victory lap around the living room.

"Do they let you keep the rings?" Parvati asked of the simple gold bands embossed with the MMP logo.

"Yep. I have them upstairs. No idea what I'll do with them."

"We can display them downstairs," Victoria said instantly. "On one of the ring-bearer pillows. Every week after the Elimination Ceremony, we'll add another ring, for as long as you're on the show." She tapped a manicured fingernail to her lips. "Do you think we should get a banner made? Once Upon a Bride – Home of *Marrying Mister Perfect*'s Sidney?"

"We'll have to get the show's permission to use their name, but I can ask."

"This is going to be good for us," Victoria said as onscreen Daniel made his final selections. "I can feel it."

Sidney nodded, distracted by the Coming Soon package running to close the show. She heard snippets of her own voice and saw shots of the back of her own head in addition to the voices and hairstyles of the girls in the house. It looked like Caitlyn went far, if her distinctive red hair on a tropical island was anything to go by—no surprise there. And that Elena did as well—

even less surprise.

When the show was over, Tori ordered Lorelei off to bed and trailed after her to tuck her in, leaving Parvati and Sidney in the living room with the last of the champagne.

"Are you okay?"

Sidney tore her eyes off the muted television, where the local news was now playing. "What?"

"We've been best friends since we were six, Sid. I know you a little bit. And I could tell you were super uncomfortable being filmed. You weren't really *you*."

"It was harder than I thought it would be," she admitted. "The interview set ups never bothered me, but the hidden cameras and the roving cameramen... never knowing if you were being filmed... it brought back that feeling, wanting to disappear so no one would judge how I look."

"You looked amazing," Parv said.

"Thank you. Seeing myself, it was better than I thought it would be, but it reminded me of how uncomfortable I was on the show. Like I'm still a chubby girl, just in a skinny body now."

"We don't have to watch it if you'd rather we stop."

"No. No, I liked watching with you. I don't think I could have done it by myself."

"Was the rest of it hard?" her friend pressed gently. "Seeing him again? Seeing yourself see him for the first time? You seemed so excited to meet him—all blushy and starry-eyed."

"Not hard." At least not because of Daniel. It was tempting to tell Parv that it had been Josh who made her star-struck, but then she would have to admit that she threw away her time on *Marrying Mister Perfect* because of a celebrity crush.

Seeing it again, she'd been reminded of the way Josh had stepped out of the night just minutes in front of Daniel. Reminded of his wry, not-for-camera smile and the way he kissed.

"It was a good moment—all promise and potential," she acknowledged. "Then reality set in."

And the reality was that she and Josh Pendleton lived in different worlds. He was kissing a supermodel now.

She felt a flicker of irritation. Not jealousy, but anger that she wasn't even allowed to date yet because it would be a spoiler for the show if she was seen with anyone, but Josh had already moved on. She had wanted to beat him to the punch. To prove to him that she wasn't still pining for him. And maybe prove to herself in the process that Josh Pendleton wasn't her personal romantic kryptonite.

CHAPTER FOURTEEN

"Smile, darling. We are madly in love, remember?"

Josh forced his lips to curve as Olga plastered herself to his side, beaming for the cameras. It was their third red carpet this week and it was getting harder to pretend walking very slowly past a thousand cameras was his favorite pastime. But this was the deal.

He and Olga needed to be seen together and this was how Hollywood couples were seen. Even if the relationships were completely fake.

From the second they'd met, it had been obvious that their "relationship" would be a business arrangement.

She was exquisite—that certainly wasn't a problem. Often called "petite and powerful" by the producers of *American Dance Star*, the top of her artificially red curls barely reached his sternum and if she weighed even a hundred pounds it was only because her body was composed almost entirely of muscle. Though it was very shapely muscle.

When Miranda had introduced them, she'd smiled her cat-like smile and purred, "So you are my leading man." Her English was flawless. He'd learned she only amped up her accent when she was trying to play up her Russianness for the fans.

She didn't want a relationship, she'd told him bluntly. She just wanted the job offers being in a relationship would bring her. He'd agreed that he didn't want a relationship either—but he needed to be safely off-limits to avoid hassles in his job. And an alliance had been formed.

Olga did her part—cooing over him in public, gushing to the tabloids about how sweet he was and how much she enjoyed their quiet, domestic life together. And Josh did his part—providing escort for every red carpet event and photo op in Hollywood with his smile firmly in place.

"Josh! Olga!" One reporter from a popular industry show waved them over. She gushed for a moment about the importance of the charity they were ostensibly honoring that night in the See-And-Be-Seen Sweepstakes of Hollywood, then segued smoothly into her real question, "So, you two, do I hear wedding bells?"

Only years of experience kept him from physically recoiling from the thought. He laughed his charming host laugh and shook his head wryly. "Give us time. We're still enjoying getting to know one another."

Olga cuddled close, playing her part to perfection. "We don't want to rush into anything and become another Hollywood statistic. For now, I have him exactly where I want him."

She winked and Josh almost snorted at the truth of that statement. She had him on the red carpet and nowhere else. Talk about a Hollywood statistic.

But if it kept him employed, he wasn't going to complain. Even if he sometimes wondered about long, lean blondes with improbably teal eyes.

Sidney took off her shoes at the base of the stairs, creeping up toward her apartment on stocking-covered feet as stealthily as possible.

It had aired last night. The show where she walked out. Now everyone knew she was the Suitorette Who Walked Out.

Business had started picking up immediately after the first show aired. The phone had started ringing the very next day and they'd been getting more and more drop-ins. Most of their new visitors were curiosity seekers, but they had more and more appointments for bridal consultations and several of those had already turned into clients.

Would they demand their money back now that they knew she'd given up on finding love?

She hoped not. She'd told herself she was overreacting. That it was ridiculous to think everyone would disapprove of what she'd done, but all she could hear was her mother's voice telling her that Dewitts didn't quit.

She still hadn't seen the full show, but she'd seen clips of her departure, over and over again during the last two days as she ran the publicity gauntlet, being interviewed on morning talk shows and daytime talk shows and late night talk shows. *Marrying Mister Perfect* had all the time slots covered.

Last Season's winner Craig had interviewed her via satellite for one of the New York wake-up shows, then she'd had a series of interviews with bloggers and vloggers before she was interrogated by the ladies of *The View*, or *The Chew*, or *The Talk* or whatever new midday gossip show had sprung up overnight.

The show's producers had prepped her. She'd known what to expect—the same questions over and over again.

Why did you leave? Do you still believe in love? Are

you seeing anyone? Do you believe the show can work? Would you consider being the next Miss Right?

She had made her love life public property and now she was reaping what she'd sown.

Only the last question had surprised her. She hadn't expected America to rally behind the Girl Who Left, but apparently the producers had framed her departure so she came across looking noble rather than picky.

The support had startled her—a surprising number of her interviewers echoing her own thoughts about Daniel seeming more interested in being Mister Perfect than finding love, several openly admiring the brave move of following her heart when it was guiding her away from him, and one even commenting on how much pressure the Suitorettes were under to *feel* something all the time.

Do you believe it's even possible to fall in love so quickly? Let alone on a national stage? her last interviewer of the day had asked.

The problem was she *did* believe. She'd just fallen for the wrong guy.

Carrying her heels, Sidney tip-toed up to her landing and began fishing in her bag for her keys.

The exposure was good for business. She'd mentioned Once Upon a Bride at least twice in every interview and reaffirmed that she believed in love more than ever now—but the words were starting to sound hollow to her.

She unlocked the door, easing it open carefully in an attempt to avoid the usual squeak.

She might as well have spared the effort.

The lights were on. Parvati and Victoria sat on her couch, two pairs of concerned eyes turned toward her as she hesitated on the threshold.

"This isn't why I gave you guys a spare key," she told them as they rose.

"We've been waiting for you," Parv stated the obvious. "We've been talking about it and we both thought we would understand why you left when we saw the show, but we're more confused than ever."

Sidney set her purse on the table by the door and shrugged out of her jacket to hang it on a hook. "I'm sorry. I know it could have meant a lot for Once Upon a Bride if I'd stayed—"

"Stop," Tori interrupted. "This isn't about the business."

"This is about you," Parvati added.

"It's a little about the business," Sidney insisted and Tori made a face.

"Fine, I'm selfish. I wanted the sales bump being on national television would get us, but things have been looking up and I believe in your three-pronged plan. What we want to know is what happened? *Something* made you want to leave. Something they didn't show on television."

"Oh my God." Parvati's jaw dropped, her eyes widening as realization hit. "You fell for someone else, didn't you? Not—holy crap, it was Josh Pendleton, wasn't it?"

Parvati knew her too well. She should have known she wouldn't be able to hide it. Sidney sank down onto the chair facing the couch, admitting defeat. "I may have had a stupid crush on him."

"The *host* Josh Pendleton?" Victoria frowned. "I thought he was dating some Russian girl."

"He wasn't at the time." At least she hoped not.

"Oh. My. God," Parv gasped, her eyes gleaming with greedy excitement. "I saw that tabloid article, but I didn't think those things ever had a shred of truth to them. You and Josh Pendleton! Josh. Pendleton. Did you and he...?"

"No. Nothing happened." Honesty forced her to add, "Well, we kissed once, but he wasn't actually interested in me. I was just a Suitorette to him."

"He kisses the Suitorettes?" Tori asked skeptically.

"No, but he was drunk and we were in his hotel room and it just sort of happened. Or I made it happen. I don't know. I know he regretted it."

"Did you?"

Sidney looked at Parv. "Did I regret kissing him?" She released a huff of breath, a distant cousin to a laugh. "Not for a second. Even if it was stupid."

"Do you regret leaving the show?" Tori asked, without a trace of judgment in her tone—bless her.

"Honestly? No—except when I think about what it could have done for the business. With Daniel... it just wasn't there. And the more I watch the show, the more I see him with the other girls, the gladder I am that I left when I did."

"But?"

Sidney hesitated. It had become habit to keep it all to herself, but these were her best friends and she realized she wanted to tell them all the things she hadn't been able to say. "I really thought there was something there with Josh. That night..." She grappled for words. "You know that zing? That feeling I get when I know a wedding is perfect and the couple is going to be happy? Like everything has fallen into place and I'm exactly where I'm supposed to be? I felt that with him. When he smiled at me, I lost all my good sense."

Parvati sighed, pressing a hand to her heart.

"My instincts were screaming that he was it. He was

The One. But he flat out said he felt nothing for me. Nothing. I always thought I would know when it happened, that I would know when my guy came along, but was that all wishful thinking? Are my instincts wrong?"

"Don't ask me," Tori said. "I'm the single mom who hasn't been on a date in years."

"You know I'll stay with Lore anytime you want to—"

"I don't want to."

"Not to dismiss Tori's dating woes," Parvati chimed in, "but can we get back to the part where Sidney kissed Josh Pendleton?"

"Can we not?" Sidney asked. "I'm lucky he didn't bring me up on sexual harassment charges."

"How did you get in his hotel room anyway?"

Sidney flushed. "It was the night before the show. I ran into him in the hallway. Literally."

"And he invited you into his hotel room?" Tori's sculpted eyebrows arched high.

"It wasn't like that. We were trying to avoid the producers—it doesn't matter. What matters is there's no future there. Josh Pendleton is a fantasy. End of story. Even if he had wanted me, he isn't allowed to date a Suitorette."

"Not even a former one?" Parv asked.

"Does it matter? He's dating a supermodel."

"She's more of a dancer who happens to do some modeling."

"That isn't helpful, Parv."

"It's celebrity gossip." Parvati flapped a dismissive hand. "You know how reliable that stuff is. Speaking of which—have you talked to Caitlyn? There's an article on TMZ about her having hot revenge sex with a fireman after Elena got topless with Daniel in the hot tub."

"Parv, focus," Tori said sharply.

"No. Don't focus. There's nothing to focus on. Except landing a celebrity wedding and making the *Veil* list. Josh Pendleton is nothing more than a distraction and I refuse to be distracted."

CHAPTER FIFTEEN

"Samantha's out."

"Excuse me?" Josh froze halfway into his chair. Miranda hadn't even waited until Josh sat down across from her at the trendy Beverly Hills bistro before dropping her bomb.

"Remember how her family kept saying she was still in love with her ex when we filmed her Meet-the-In-Laws segment? Turns out they were right. She's engaged. So no Miss Right for Sam."

The network always preferred to be able to announce the next season at the reunion special, but if Samantha was out, it looked like that wouldn't be happening.

"So who? Elena?" He settled himself in his chair and picked up his menu.

"Too controversial for the network. The backlash against her for the Jacuzzi incident was much more intense than I'd anticipated."

Josh grimaced. Elena would have been a great Miss Right—sexy, impulsive and living for the fame—but after going topless with Daniel in a Jacuzzi she'd been hashtagged as "the Slutty Suitorette" on Twitter and there was no going back from there. "Caitlyn?"

Miranda shook her head. "I know she and Daniel are on the outs, but he wants the chance to win her back on the reunion special next week. If he wants to re-propose on national television, I don't want to bias her against saying yes by dangling Miss Right in front of her. If she turns him down, feel free to ask her on the spot to be our next Miss Right, but I already have someone in mind if she isn't interested."

"Who's that? And why did you need to see me? I'm not normally a part of these decisions." He'd been sure she was going to tell him he was fired because the focus groups had gone badly, but instead she just wanted to talk about the next season.

"I'm thinking Sidney," Miranda said, watching him closely. "I just wanted to make sure that wasn't going to be a problem for you."

Josh kept his expression impassive. "Why would it be a problem?"

"We have cameras in the Old Grotto."

Panic spiked through him until he remembered they hadn't done anything in the grotto.

"We don't have audio, so I have no idea what you two were talking about, but you seem awfully close and I wanted to be sure it wasn't going to be a problem having her as our next Miss Right."

"Of course not. In fact, I told her she'd make a great Miss Right."

"So you two are just friends."

"I barely know her."

Miranda eyed him skeptically. "If you say so. I just wanted to give you a heads up that we'll be asking her after the reunion special."

"Excellent. Can't wait."

"Uh-huh."

"Who do you think it will be? Elena or Caitlyn? My

money is on Elena. Men make decisions with their dicks. I bet she turned him down flat—more publicity that way and we all know she wasn't there for the Right Reasons. Caitlyn's a sweetie, but I don't think she even slept with him during the two-day dates and you can't win with your knees glued shut. You guys were friends, weren't you? Do you think she's gonna be the next Miss Right?"

Sidney made a noncommittal noise, listening with half an ear as her makeup artist chattered merrily away.

Tabloid rumors had been swirling around the show. She supposed they always did, but this year it seemed even more extreme than ever. Every day it seemed like there was a new story about Elena's scandalous ways, Daniel partying with bimbos in LA or Caitlyn's secret relationship with a fire-fighter in her hometown.

Sidney had tried calling Caitlyn to make sure she was all right, even though she knew her friend couldn't tell her what the result of the show had been, but Caitlyn had been distant and evasive on the phone.

In the mirror's reflection, Sidney could see the open doorway behind her, her attention repeatedly veering back there. The soundstage where they would be filming the reunion special was a hive of activity and every five seconds another crew member rushed past the open door—but never Josh. He probably had his own luxurious dressing room—not like the main green room where she sat with five other Suitorettes as the show's battalion of stylists made them presentable.

Daniel, Caitlyn and Elena waited somewhere in the building for the big reveal. In a few hours, the finale show would air on the east coast and Daniel's choice would be revealed. Throughout the show, Josh would be breaking in from the live reunion special, talking with the rejected Suitorettes as Daniel recapped his journey and discussing the major dramas of the season.

Sidney didn't know who all he would be talking to, but the producers had explained that her choice to leave on her own would be part of the fourth segment. She'd be brought up center stage and Josh would walk her through her own departure before asking her to elaborate on it. Easy.

Which did nothing to explain the little sizzle of nerves that kept whispering across her senses every time another person walked past the doorway.

He was taken. He'd been *extremely* clear that he was uninterested. What was wrong with her that she couldn't accept that and move on? What was so freaking perfect about Josh Pendleton anyway? Obviously he was hot, but she firmly believed that what was under the skin was a thousand times more important than the pretty trappings, so why this stupid obsession? Why couldn't she kick it?

Sure, he'd been the only thing that felt real on the show, but that had probably been a function of the fact that her time with him had been the only time she wasn't being filmed. Her relief at not feeling that crushing self-consciousness must have distorted her reality.

"There. You're all set, sweetie," the makeup artist declared, and Sidney thanked her, rising from the makeup chair.

She retreated to the opposite side of the large green room where craft services tables had been set up. She couldn't see the door from here. So maybe she would stop looking for Josh every five seconds. At least that was the theory.

She grabbed a sparkling water—more to have something to do with her hands than due to thirst—and perched on a chair next to Samantha.

The other Suitorette was the last one to make an exit from the show and third place looked good on her. She'd always been composed and elegant, above the fray on the show, but now there was a difference in her eyes. She looked... happy.

Her rejection had been months ago, but this was a far cry from the girl who'd been dejected and demoralized on last week's episode.

"You look happy." A suspicion rose up in her mind. "Are you the next Miss Right?" Sidney asked, keeping her voice low to avoid being overheard by the other Suitorettes and stylists crowding the room.

"Just happy it's almost over." Samantha avoided her gaze.

Sidney resisted the urge to tell her that it wasn't going to be over for a long time yet—they weren't going to suddenly stop being tabloid fodder or stopped on the street for their autographs just because the show was no longer actively airing, though it would probably get better when the next season began and focus shifted to the next batch of hopefuls. Unless you were Miss Right.

"You'd be great. I'm surprised they haven't asked you."

"They have," Samantha admitted, her gaze still evasive. "But it's hard to imagine going through all this again. I'm not Elena."

Elena had seemed to thrive in the bizarre atmosphere of the show, but Sidney had to wonder how she was doing now that she'd earned the charming appellate of The Slutty Suitorette. Although knowing Elena, she probably loved the attention.

A PA swept into the room before she could reply. "Ladies, time to find your places, we're live in ten!"

"Daniel certainly has a difficult decision in front of him. And after the break, we'll sit down with the Suitorette America fell in love with, who followed her heart away from Mister Perfect. That's right, Sidney is here and ready to talk about what has happened since she walked away from Daniel. All that and more, when the *Marrying Mister Perfect* finale and reunion special returns."

Josh kept his host smile in place until the director called that they were clear and a makeup artist rushed forward to blot his face. The lights burned even more brutally hot than usual, but TV's Josh Pendleton could not be allowed to sweat on camera. He held still for the blotting, staring straight ahead as the producers guided Sidney away from the Suitorette couches and up to the loveseat opposite his chair center stage.

They swarmed around her, making sure her microphone was hidden and touching up her own makeup before retreating again, leaving him alone with Sidney in front of a live studio audience with sixty seconds still on the clock before they came back from commercial.

He nodded to her. "Sidney."

"Josh. How've you been?"

"Good. And you?"

"Good. Thanks."

Awkward silence fell, the seconds ticking by with excruciating slowness until the director finally called him to attention and the red light on camera one lit.

Josh smiled, instantly comfortable as he read off the teleprompter. "Welcome back." He went through his usual spiel, reinforcing the drama of the decision Daniel was about to make, before pivoting to talk about Sidney's decision to leave the show. The screens in the studio lit as they all watched Sidney's departure over again and another camera zoomed in on her face to get every microscopic detail of her reaction on film. When they returned to a wide shot, Josh was ready, facing Sidney with a practiced smile in place.

"Sidney, welcome." She murmured the usual pleasantries about how happy she was to be there and Josh continued, keeping to the script. "You were among the early front runners and America certainly loved you—as Daniel seemed to—but then you shocked us all by walking away from this journey to love. Any regrets?"

"None," she said, looking straight into his eyes. "Daniel may not have been my Prince Charming, but I have to believe he's out there and that somehow *Marrying Mister Perfect* is part of my path to a happily-ever-after."

Shit. Josh forced his expression to remain pleasantly encouraging when dread shivered through him at her words. Was she still hung up on him? Was that what she meant? Or had Miranda already talked to her? Was she trying to imply she was planning to come back as Miss Right?

He was worse than the Suitorettes, parsing every syllable for clues as to what she really felt.

A voice buzzed in his ear, prompting him, and he returned to the script. "You famously said your heart was leading you in another direction. I think all of America is wondering, did you find what you were looking for there?"

"If you're asking if I'm seeing anyone, the answer is no. I'm still looking for my own Mister Perfect."

"Speaking of which, are you aware of the Twitter campaign that is currently going strong, asking for you to be the next Miss Right?"

A flush lit her cheeks. "I didn't know. Though of course I'm flattered."

"You've often been quoted as saying you believe in the show. Would you consider it, from the other side? Are you still that romantic optimist who met Mister Perfect at the altar on night one?"

"I don't think you can be a wedding planner if you aren't a romantic optimist, and I will always fall into that category. And I definitely still believe the show can lead to true love—no one who has ever seen Marcy and Craig together can deny it—but I don't think I—"

Miranda's voice crackled through his earpiece. *"Cut her off. Leave it open."*

"Let me stop you there," Josh broke in smoothly. "And we'll just see what the future holds."

A small frown puckered her brow.

"Wrap it up."

"I just have one final question for you, Sidney. Who do you think Daniel will choose? Caitlyn or Elena?"

"Whoever he chooses, he will be a very lucky man. They are both extraordinary women."

Josh pivoted to the cameras and took them into the next pre-recorded segment, feeling Sidney's eyes on him the entire time.

As soon as the director called that they were out, she reached up to yank off her mic. "What was all that? You wanted to ambush me with that Miss Right stuff?"

"The producers wanted to test the waters for you as a potential Miss Right and they figured you would react more naturally if you didn't know it was coming."

"And if I'm not interested?"

"You should really consider it," he encouraged, pretending he didn't understand why she wouldn't want to subject herself to the cameras again. "That whole *both extraordinary women* bullshit only proves you're already good at playing the game. You'd be great and just think what it would do for your business."

Irritation flickered in her eyes, but then her gaze shifted over his shoulder and she asked, "Does your new girlfriend know what a cynic you are?"

He glanced over his shoulder to where Olga sat, front and center. Miranda had given her a seat that would guarantee she was "accidentally" on camera at least five times throughout the broadcast, reinforcing their romantic attachment.

"Oh, she knows," he assured Sidney.

Though it might be the only thing Olga knew about him.

Sidney swallowed her irritation. Part of her had hoped that Josh's relationship was just a publicity stunt, but if she really knew him…

"I'm glad you've moved on and gotten over your ex. Everyone deserves to be with someone who makes them happy. Especially someone who is guiding others to romantic happiness," Sidney said—trying to force herself to mean it.

"Thank you."

One of the producers approached, guiding her back to the Suitorette couches. She watched as he chatted with Samantha about her heartbreak—though she seemed the least heartbroken person in the room. Then they all watched Daniel reject Elena—tears glistening artistically on her lashes—before getting on one knee in front of Caitlyn.

On the giant screens, Caitlyn said yes—and the entire studio audience sighed happily—but when Daniel and Caitlyn appeared together in public for the first time, they were sitting as far as possible from one another on the loveseat and Caitlyn wasn't wearing the ring anymore. Josh walked the audience through their break-up, highlighting the difficulties of a long-distance relationship in the public eye—and Caitlyn's understandable difficulty watching Daniel rubbing up against Elena every week.

Sidney wanted to talk to Caitlyn, but as soon as Josh wrapped up the show, tempting the audience with the promise of the next season, a swarm of MMP staffers descended on the former Suitorette and she was whisked away. Several of the other girls were making plans to go out dancing, but Sidney plead exhaustion and a desire to get home. Most of the girls were in from out of town and staying in hotels, but she'd just come down for the day and was eager to get back to her real life.

But before she could make her escape, Miranda Pierce caught her in the green room.

"Sidney. Just the woman I was hoping to see."

"You need a wedding planner?" she said optimistically.

"I need a wedding planner beloved by America who wants to be romanced by thirty hot men on the next season of *Romancing Miss Right*."

"No." Sidney edged around the producer, heading for the door.

She should have thought about it more. The exposure for Once Upon a Bride would be brilliant—but she wouldn't be able to hide in the shadows if she was Miss

Right. She'd be front and center twenty-four-seven.

And Josh would be watching the whole thing.

As much as she might want to believe he wouldn't be a distraction, she was realistic enough to face the truth. There was no way she would be able to concentrate on falling in love with someone else when he was standing beside her at every Elimination Ceremony, watching the proceedings.

"At least consider it," Miranda urged, pacing her as she walked down the hall toward the private exit.

"If you need a wedding planner, I'm your girl," Sidney promised. "But I'm not cut out for being Miss Right. Sorry, Miranda."

CHAPTER SIXTEEN

"She said no."

Josh finished washing off the last of the makeup and looked up to find Miranda standing in the doorway of his dressing room. "Sorry?"

"Sidney. She turned down Miss Right. Thought you might want to know."

"Why would I want to know? It has nothing to do with me."

Miranda snorted. "You're slipping, Josh. You want the world to think Sidney is just another Suitorette, but if you want me to buy that, you have to react naturally. You should be worried that we're out a Miss Right. Caitlyn said no. Samantha said no. Elena is universally hated. And now Sidney has said no. It's your job to care that we might not have another season."

"There will always be another season. *Marrying Mister Perfect* will never die."

Miranda's eyebrows flew up. "Do you want it to?"

"Of course not." he insisted, even if he sometimes had the feeling that his life had become a machine and he couldn't stop it or change course without getting crushed in the gears.

There hadn't been a happy ending this season. Mister Perfect hadn't gotten the girl—and Josh couldn't help but wonder if he might have dropped the ball somehow.

It wasn't their first unsuccessful season—the romantic triumphs were much rarer than the defeats—but it was the first time he wondered if he could have done something differently, offered different counsel, and done a better job of guiding Mister Perfect to his future happiness.

Maybe he wasn't cut out for this job anymore. Too jaded. Too cynical. But if he wasn't Josh Pendleton, Host of *Marrying Mister Perfect*, who was he?

"You don't have to sell me," Miranda said. "I might be getting off the merry-go-round myself."

"What?"

"Bennett wants me to defect over to *American Dance Star*. I'm still making up my mind."

Jesus. Even Miranda might leave the show. "I hope you'll stay. It won't be the same without you."

"Maybe it shouldn't be. Maybe it's time for a change. You said it yourself. This season felt different." She shrugged. "Don't worry about it now. Your girlfriend is waiting for you."

His girlfriend. His relationship was a fraud designed to keep a job he was no longer sure he could do, and beyond that...

He didn't know what there was beyond that.

"Are you sure you don't want to be Miss Right?"

Sidney looked up as Victoria walked into the back office of Once Upon a Bride. "Positive. What's wrong?"

"Another cancellation." Tori tossed herself onto one of the chairs facing the desk. "Parvati has started calling it the Curse of Mister Perfect."

Sidney cringed and Tori's expression softened.

"She's kidding. Every business goes through ups and

downs. There's no way you going on that show is causing all our brides to suddenly decide they don't believe in marriage."

"I don't know," Sidney said. "I scoffed in the face of love. Maybe the universe is taking revenge."

"You didn't scoff in the face of love. And the universe taking revenge is about as likely as all our financial woes being solved by hopping backwards around the block until our luck changes, like Lorelei suggested."

"Are our finances really woeful?"

Victoria made a face. Considering she was the one who balanced the books each month, it was not a comforting face.

"If you think me being Miss Right would help..."

Thankfully, Victoria was already shaking her head. "God no. If things get dire we'll try hopping backwards around the block, but for now—"

The phone at Sidney's elbow rang. "Maybe that's someone wildly famous who wants nothing more than to book us for a ridiculously lavish wedding." She picked up the phone, but the caller-ID told a different story. "It's Caitlyn."

Victoria frowned. "The Suitorette?"

Sidney nodded, connecting the call. "Caitlyn! It's so good to hear from you! I wanted to talk to you after the reunion special, but you just vanished."

"I had plans to make. Had to win back the love of my life."

"Daniel?" Sidney asked, incredulous. He had seemed far from the love of Caitlyn's life at the reunion special.

"No. My neighbor, actually. Here in Tuller Springs, if you believe it. And I have some big news. We're getting married. And I was hoping you might plan it."

Sidney was glad Caitlyn couldn't see her jaw fall. "Don't tell me you're marrying the firefighter all the tabloids were talking about."

"Yeah, that's Will. I'm sorry I couldn't talk to you about it—you know how the show is with the confidentiality crap. But I was really hoping you'd forgive me."

"Caitlyn, there's nothing to forgive."

"So will you plan my wedding? You'll have to deal with my mother—which is a trial in itself. And all of Will's sisters will want to help."

"Don't worry. I'm great at dealing with bossy in-laws."

"So you'll do it?"

"Of course." It was practically the celebrity wedding they'd been praying for. And even if it hadn't been, it was Caitlyn.

"Oh, thank goodness. I didn't even know where to start. Will and I thought we'd just do a quiet thing here in Tuller Springs, but my mother was pushing for a splashy New York society wedding and somehow we found ourselves compromising with something tasteful but private on the beach, and I know you said you do beach weddings sometimes—"

"There's a gorgeous resort here in Eden. It might be just what you're looking for, if you'd like to fly out and take a look."

"Will and I were thinking of flying out in a couple weeks—and I think my mother will probably invite herself along. But there's one other catch you should know about. The show will have to approve the venue."

"*Marrying Mister Perfect*? What do they have to do with it?"

"Crud, did I forget to tell you that part? I don't know

what has happened to my brain lately. *Marrying Mister Perfect* offered to pay for the wedding—with a bonus for Will and me. I thought Will would balk at the idea and at first he did, but then he said if they want to pay me to marry him, we should take the money and have an amazing honeymoon with it. We negotiated so they won't be able to televise the ceremony or anything on the actual day and the photos will be limited, but in order to get them to agree to that, we had to promise them a special."

"What kind of special?"

"A Making-a-Mister-Perfect-Wedding special. They want to record us doing all the prep—picking the perfect dress, finding the perfect venue, perfect caterer, cake tastings, the whole nine."

Greed and terror mixed in equal parts in her gut, her heart beginning to race. That kind of exposure could take Once Upon a Bride to a whole new level. She'd joked about a big celebrity wedding landing in her lap, but that was exactly what this was. She would plan Caitlyn's wedding if it was a private ceremony of five people on top of a mountain in Colorado, but if MMP was footing the bill it was going to be an event.

The kind of event *The Veil* magazine paid attention to.

It would completely wipe the slate clean from her early departure. But if she had to be on camera again…

"Us?"

"You, me, and the MMP wedding rep. They want to have their person there to make sure everything is being done the MMP way, but I figure if anyone knows how to keep the MMP people from shoving them around, you do."

She'd been so relieved when she thought her time on camera was over, but this was too good to pass up. The entire country would get to watch her being the fairy godmother. She may not know shit about being Cinderella, but *this* she could do. And if she had to suffer through a few awkward on-camera moments, she would.

"It's going to be perfect, Caitlyn."

Her friend laughed. "I'm not looking for perfect. I'm just excited to be marrying Will."

"Josh! How's my favorite client?"

Josh grimaced at his agent's familiar greeting. The cheer in his voice sounded like just another layer of Hollywood bullshit shellacked over the suckage of his real life. "I'm hoping you're calling with good news."

"Good news? Try great," Harry bragged. "The network wants to re-up your contract. Lock you in for four more years."

Relief shuddered through him—heavily laced with dread. "I'm guessing the focus group data came back in my favor."

Harry laughed, smug arrogance resonating in the booming sound. "Turns out no one gives a shit if you're married or not. You're the face of *Marrying Mister Perfect* and they adore you. I'm probably going to be able to get you more money, thanks to those fucking focus groups."

Josh heard a horn blare in the background and realized his agent was probably screaming down the highway as they talked.

"Awesome." He'd wanted this, but the words felt thin.

"I'm still negotiating the details," his agent charged on, blissfully oblivious to his misgivings. "Fair warning, it looks like the morality clause is gonna be tighter than a nun's ass—but we're talking eight more seasons. That kind of job security is unheard of in this town. I couldn't get Tom Cruise this deal. They just want you to do one little thing while we're working out the fine print."

"Of course they do."

CHAPTER SEVENTEEN

The Los Angeles Bridal Expo tried to be elegant and refined—with champagne and canapés for the girls who paid up for the VIP experience—but the result was more tulle-covered feeding frenzy than tea time at the Plaza. Sidney had been to the smaller bridal shows in Santa Barbara and Malibu, but this was the first time she and Victoria had ponied up the big bucks for a vendor's slot at The Big One. It was exciting—and mildly terrifying.

Victoria had brought along their *as seen on Marrying Mister Perfect* banner to decorate their booth, along with their sample binders and buckets of promotional items.

Thanks to Sidney's recent brush with celebrity, the booth was jumping—though most brides wanted to talk about the show more than they wanted to hire her as a wedding planner. Even so, Once Upon a Bride was making contact, being remembered, and building their brand. The brides ran them out of logo pens and fridge magnets in record time—and they kept coming.

By noon, Sidney's eyes were glazing over with exhaustion, but she was still smiling—the plan was working. Between Caitlyn's wedding special and the exposure she'd already gotten from her experience on the show, their luck was turning around.

Her phone buzzed on her hip when she was talking to a bride who had driven up from San Diego just for the

Expo. She checked the caller-ID on auto-pilot and, seeing Caitlyn's name, excused herself. "I'm sorry, it's one of my brides. I should take this, but my partner would be happy to answer any other questions you have about weddings in Eden."

She directed the San Diego girl toward Victoria and stepped to the back of the booth to connect the call, smothering her panic. There could be dozens of reasons why Caitlyn was calling—she'd called at least once a day ever since hiring Sidney to talk about her vision for the wedding, the definition of an eager bride—but Sidney couldn't help her nerves that the other shoe was about to drop.

"Caitlyn, how are you? Did you and Will have any more thoughts on possible dates?" she asked, as if leading with talk about dates could forestall any bad news. *Please don't be calling to cancel.* She'd been the recipient of too many of those calls lately.

"Sorry to bother you! I know you said you were doing a bridal expo today, but the dates are actually what I wanted to talk to you about," she said, with a short laugh. "Turns out we might need to rush things a bit. I'm pregnant."

Four thoughts flashed through Sidney's head in rapid succession—*Is it Will's or Daniel's? Are you still getting married? When are you due? Will you still want a big public wedding if you're showing?*—but thankfully the right thing somehow came out of her mouth. "Oh wow, congratulations."

"Thank you! But please keep it quiet. We're trying to keep it out of the tabloids as long as possible."

"Of course."

"I had to tell the show people—of course they were thrilled until I told them there was no way in hell I was doing an on-air ultrasound. I thought they were going to drop the wedding bills on us, but turns out they like the idea of moving the wedding up to May—as far as they're concerned, the faster I get married the better because I'm trendy now and they want to capitalize on that as much as possible."

"May?" Sidney's heart thudded hard. That was only two months away.

"We were thinking Memorial Day weekend. And I know that's asking for miracles, but if anyone can do it, you can. Will and I are moving our trip out to plan things up to next weekend, if that works for you."

"That'll be perfect. Everything will need to happen fast," Sidney agreed, already mentally mapping out a whirlwind weekend of tastings and viewings and dress shopping. The major resorts would already be booked solid for Memorial Day, but if she thought outside the box for the venue she might be able to come up with something even better.

"My thoughts exactly," Caitlyn said. "Which is why the MMP wedding rep is going to meet you at your booth at the bridal expo at two."

"That sounds perfect. I'll keep an eye out for one of Miranda's many minions."

Caitlyn laughed. "Do that."

Sidney hadn't heard anything from Miranda, but the MMP wedding rep was almost definitely the wedding planner they had on retainer. She wasn't overly excited about having to co-plan the wedding with someone else, but giving Caitlyn the wedding of her dreams would be worth any battles she had to fight to keep Will and Caitlyn's vision intact when the show consultant tried to hijack the wedding and make it more commercial.

She ended the call with Caitlyn moments later and

moved back to the front of the booth where Victoria was enjoying a rare lull. She grinned when Sidney approached. "We have a new client from San Diego."

Sidney's eyes widened in surprise. "You landed that bride? I didn't think she was seriously looking for a wedding planner."

"She wasn't, but she was so impressed that you refused to ignore a call from one of your brides, even in the middle of the expo, that she said she wanted someone who took care of her like that. So, technically, *you* landed her."

Sidney returned Victoria's grin. She didn't want to jinx it, but it certainly felt like the tide was turning.

For the next two hours the traffic in the booth was slower, but the brides who did stop by almost all signed up for their newsletter—and at least half a dozen took advantage of the Expo Special Rates to hire them on the spot. Several even said they trusted her as their wedding planner because they felt like they knew her from the show—and all of them respected her decision to hold out for true love rather than trying to force things with Daniel.

Leaving the show was turning out to be the best business decision she'd ever made.

Her life was finally getting back on track. She was starting to feel downright cocky.

So of course Josh Pendleton chose that moment to walk into her booth.

Of all the booths in all the bridal expos in all the world...

His host persona was firmly locked in place. Nothing wry or cynical touched the cheesy smoothness of his smile. A cluster of women just beyond the booth snapped pictures of him on their cell phones, whispering among themselves. "Sidney, it's good to see you."

"Josh," she returned his fake smile. "This is unexpected. I didn't figure bridal expos were really your thing."

"Believe it or not, I'm a regular at these events. This is the heart of our demo, so MMP likes to have a presence here. And I am ordained, after all. You'd be surprised how many people want me to perform their ceremonies."

"I forgot the show had you ordained so you could perform ceremonies on the spot at the reunion specials."

"Always be prepared, that's the MMP motto. Or the Boy Scouts. They're so similar."

And there it was. The wry little glint in his eyes, self-deprecating and devastatingly hot. Why did she have to find him so attractive? "It's nice of you to drop by for a visit while you're here…" The rest—*but what the hell are you doing here?*—remained unspoken, but Josh seemed to hear it, eyebrows arching.

"I thought you were expecting me."

"Expecting…?"

"MMP sent me. I understand we're planning a wedding together."

Sidney's jaw fell open in gauche shock—right as one of the onlookers grew bold and rushed forward to snap a picture of the two of them. Within seconds, that single shot had triggered a hurricane of selfies and cell phone snapshots. Everyone wanted their picture with Josh and her. Sidney smiled, her face feeling rubbery and strangely cold as picture after picture was snapped and those words echoed in her head. The death knell of her hopes that she might be able to get over him soon.

I understand we're planning a wedding together.

CHAPTER EIGHTEEN

By the time the photo frenzy died down, Sidney had most of her composure back. She was a professional and he was only a man—even if he was an extremely distracting one. She was perfectly capable of planning an amazing wedding with him. It would probably even be easier than if she'd had to work with another professional wedding planner. Josh was unlikely to try to overrule her.

When the last of the cell phone wielding fans finally gave them a few feet of breathing room, Sidney was feeling remarkably optimistic about the entire situation. And then he spoke.

"Why don't we have dinner tonight?"

"Dinner?"

Dear God. Was Josh Pendleton asking her out? She felt her face flush as her heart rate accelerated.

He was half-turned away from her, aiming a smile at a group of giggling fans. "It's obvious we aren't going to have any privacy as long as we're here and I expect you'll be famished when you're done. I know a great Italian bistro not far from here where we can discuss what needs to be done to get this wedding rolling."

"Right." Business. "Of course."

Not a romantic candlelit dinner for two, but a business meeting during which he was being considerate and efficient by grabbing food at the same time. She needed to stop seeing romance at the drop of a hat with him. She couldn't keep being flustered by every innocent sentence he uttered because her hormones were out of whack where he was concerned. Who cared if he smelled amazing and made her stupid heart race when that rare wicked glimmer appeared in his eyes? This was business. End of story.

"That sounds logical." She flipped open her card case and plucked out a business card. "Why don't you text me the directions and I'll meet you there at five-thirty?"

"Excellent." He pocketed her card and extended one of his own.

The exchange was very businesslike and put her feet back on the ground. He was just a guy.

She barely even remembered how he kissed.

Josh flicked idly through the emails on his phone, killing time as he waited for Sidney at Mama's. She was already ten minutes late, but he wasn't worried about being stood up. She'd probably been held up at the expo. Though from the look on her face when he'd told her they would be planning the wedding together, she might be on her way to the airport to catch the next flight to Brazil.

Obviously she still wasn't completely comfortable with him—and he couldn't blame her. He needed to find some way to erase their past and start over. He could try ignoring their odd history, but maybe he needed to come at it head on. The last thing he needed was for things to be awkward between them for the next two months. They were going to be working together, since Miranda had officially left the show and the higher-ups wanted him to produce the wedding special as the face of the brand.

The front door of the tiny Italian bistro flew open and Sidney rushed in, looking harried, flushed, and sexy as hell.

Josh slammed the brakes on that line of thinking, rising from his chair to catch her attention as she scanned the small restaurant. The tightness in her expression eased when she saw him and she began to wend through the small tables with their checkered plastic table cloths.

"Sorry I'm late," she said as she shrugged out of her light jacket and hung it over the back of her chair. "I drove past here three times. I wasn't expecting the great Josh Pendleton to frequent a restaurant in a strip mall."

"Don't judge until you've tried the cannoli. You'll think you've died and gone to culinary heaven."

She smiled, a harried little grin and he thought for a second he'd been wrong, that he'd been imagining the tension between them, hyper focused on interpreting imaginary signals from her because of the show.

Their waitress, the owner's granddaughter Carolina, came over to take their drink order. Josh ordered the house red and Sidney followed his lead, but as soon as Carolina stepped away, she began to babble, discomfort flowing off of her in waves.

"I'm sorry about earlier. You caught me off guard. I was expecting the show to send the wedding planner they have on retainer or maybe one of the producers. I should have considered that it might be you, at least for the on camera portions—"

"Actually, I'm going to be your shadow for all of it," Josh interjected. "I've been around the block enough times with the show to know what their requirements are and with Miranda leaving the big bosses asked me to produce."

"Miranda's leaving?"

"Poached by *American Dance Star*. She's still going to oversee the Wedding Special, but only until they can name another EP. After that, she's out."

"But she *is* MMP. Almost as much as you are."

"That's why I'm here. Because I *am* MMP." *Whether he wanted to be or not.*

The other part of what he'd said finally made its way through her nerves. "*You* are going to be producing?"

"Disappointed?"

"No, I just…" She trailed off, but Sidney was nothing if not resilient and she rallied quickly. "Should we get started?" she asked, pulling a tablet from her purse. "We'll need to move fast."

"Can't we at least wait until the wine arrives? We have two months."

"Two months is a millisecond in wedding time. Caitlyn and Will should already be sending out invitations and we can't do that until we have the venue and dates confirmed. I want to have at least three viable venue options to show Caitlyn next week and all the best places are already going to be booked for Memorial Day weekend, so I'll be thinking outside the box this week and looking at some places that others might have overlooked. We can hope for a cancellation, but we can't rely on that—"

"It's *Marrying Mister Perfect*. When the resorts hear that won't they magically have some cancellations to make room for us?"

"Booting another wedding off their special day to make room for us isn't how I do things—and it isn't how these resorts operate either. The bridal community is tight. These venues don't want to get a reputation as being unfriendly. Besides, it's bad wedding karma."

"And the bridal superstitions commence." The wine arrived and he clinked his glass against hers before sipping the delicious red. "There's always the MMP mansions."

Sidney choked on her wine, sputtering and glaring. "Don't even joke about that."

"Is it such a terrible idea? The gardens are gorgeous. I could officiate."

"You think Will would like to get married on the spot where another man courted his fiancé?"

"Kidding." He held up his hands in surrender. "So when do we look at these alternative venues?"

Her face flushed so red it was visible even in the low light of Mama's. "I just assumed you'd be busy. I know your schedule must be insane."

"During the show it is, but we're between seasons, so I'm all yours. I'll go with you and earmark a few places—good and bad—where we can return with a camera crew. Just think of me as your friendly stalker." Carolina reappeared and he smiled. "Shall we order?"

If someone had told her a year ago that she'd be sitting in a hole-in-the-wall Italian restaurant with Josh Pendleton while he explained his intention to dog her steps while she planned a celebrity wedding, she would have promptly checked them into rehab because they had to be on something.

But here she was. And here *he* was.

He offered to order for them both and she took him up on it, her brain no longer reserving any space for thoughts of food. Any equanimity she'd managed to gain since his bombshell at the bridal show was rapidly evaporating with his revelation that he planned to be involved day to day in a hands-on way.

Not that she would object if Josh wanted to put his hands anywhere, a sly little voice whispered in her mind.

She chalked the voice up to exhaustion and starvation, taking another sip of the wine to balance her nerves. The red was surprisingly complex—surprising mostly since the plastic tablecloths and paper placemats had not inspired confidence, but she should have known Josh wouldn't suffer anything but the best.

The waitress retreated to put in their order and Sidney eyed her new partner over the rim of her wine glass. "Do you come here often?" she asked—and then cringed at how it sounded.

The glimmer in Josh's eyes acknowledged the cheesy line, but he answered without teasing her about it. "More often than I should probably admit. I always liked it, but since the divorce I've taken to eating here a couple times a week. It's quiet. I know no one will bother me. And the food—trust me, once you've tried it, you'll understand."

"I take it your wife was the cook."

"Marissa could burn water. I can make ramen with the best of them, but that's the extent of my culinary expertise," he said, that knee-buckling grin flashing out—luckily she was sitting down. "Thank God for carry-out or we'd have starved in the first year of our marriage."

"And Olga? She doesn't like to cook?" she asked to remind herself that he was off the market.

He blinked, seeming startled by the question, but he rallied so quickly she found herself wondering if she'd imagined the momentary lapse. "We tend to go out more than we dine in."

"Of course." This was Josh Pendleton she was talking to, after all. She couldn't expect him to spend his nights at home, cooking and watching cheesy romantic comedies—or the latest episode of *Marrying Mister Perfect*.

Even if he hadn't been with Olga, their lives were miles apart. Why couldn't she remember that when she was with him?

Tension settled again in her shoulders and thinking of something clever and neutral to say became a herculean task. "Ah... so this week... um, Caitlyn wants a beach wedding and the, uh, the resort will need to be big enough to accommodate a sizeable wedding— they're still working on the guest list but at first count I think we're looking at a couple hundred, and the venue will need to be someplace we can manage security. My brother does private security, so I might hire him to at least help us vet the places we're considering, and we can hire his firm on the actual day if the show approves—"

"We have our own security, but extra is always welcome at events like this."

"Right. Good." She traced the checks on the tablecloth, incapable of meeting his eyes, but at least she knew what she was doing when it came to the wedding. "Caitlyn mentioned an outdoor ceremony with the reception close enough that people can walk between the two, but she also said something about a chapel, so if there was a resort with a chapel on site, that might be a good option to show her when she arrives on the weekend." Sidney took another sip of her wine and forced herself to look at Josh. "So you can see this week

I'll mostly be running around narrowing the venue list down. There's no need for you to join me…"

He braced his forearms on the table and she fought the impulse to look down at the taut biceps revealed by his rolled up sleeves. "Sidney, I know you know more about weddings than I ever could, but I've worked with MMP for a lot of years now. I know what they can make happen, what sort of things they're likely to approve, and what will be deal-breakers for them. Use me. I'm at your disposal. I'm not going to try to do your job for you, but I am going to see different things at these venues than you see. And if the only reason you don't want me coming with you is because you think it will be awkward because of our history, that's something we probably need to discuss."

CHAPTER NINETEEN

He wanted to discuss their history. Dear God.

The waitress arrived at that moment with her arms loaded with plates which she set in the center of the table, family style.

"Oh look! The food!" Sidney was prepared to babble about the pasta for as long as possible to avoid talking to Josh, but his voice was low and implacable when the waitress moved away and they were once again alone.

"Sidney. I don't want things to be awkward between us for the next two months."

"No, of course, I don't want that either," she said, keeping her eyes on the array of food in front of her—which did indeed smell like heaven on a plate.

"Sidney." She made herself meet his gaze. There was nothing cynical and wry there now. It was just probing and understanding. "Do we need to talk about what happened before?" he pressed. "When you turned down Miss Right, I wondered if it had something to do with me."

"No! Of course not!" she lied. "I just hated the cameras."

"And now you're back in front of them again. I know that isn't easy for you. When they told me you were going to be the wedding planner on the televised special, I almost didn't believe them."

"This is different. It's what I'm good at." She waved her fork like a wand. "Fairy godmother."

"And you didn't know I was going to be part of it."

"I admit I was surprised they picked you as the representative, but not because I'm trying to avoid you."

"Look, the night we met I made a mistake—I'm not trying to pretend otherwise. Things shouldn't have gone the way they did. But I like you. And I'd like us to be able to be friends."

"Of course we're friends." He was off-limits on a romantic level, but she wasn't a slave to her hormones. Just because she was attracted to him in a way that scrambled her senses didn't mean they couldn't be buddies. Even if he did think their one kiss had been a mistake. "You're TV's Josh Pendleton. Your job is to be everyone's friend, isn't it?" she tried to joke, but it came out awkwardly.

"Yeah. I'm everyone's friend," he said, but the words were sad and seemed to say something else.

She found herself remembering how he'd spoken about his celebrity. How everyone wanted to use him and no one knew him. Was Josh Pendleton lonely?

"So we're good?" he asked.

"Yeah. Of course. I can't wait to work with you." She held up a fork dripping with cheese and sauce. "Now can I eat this and find out if it tastes as good as it smells?"

"Better," he promised, reaching for the utensils to serve himself from the steaming hot plates.

And, in typical Josh Pendleton fashion, he was right.

"This place is perfect," Josh declared, taking a slow turn with his hands in his pockets. "As long as Caitlyn thinks the smell of fish is romantic."

Sidney shot Josh a glare before turning to the inn's events manager with a soothing smile. "Ignore him. He's a cynic who lacks vision. You said the fishery takes in a fresh catch twice a day?"

The events manager answered her questions before departing to fetch a pricing brochure, leaving Sidney and Josh alone on the rustic dock. It was a gorgeous spot, the old inn fully refurbished and tucked into a picturesque natural cove. Unfortunately, the scent that drifted over from the fishery upwind was distinctly... pungent. And the ballroom was far too small.

"You really don't see a problem with the aroma?" Josh asked, his eyes watering from the waft of fish on the breeze.

"It is less than ideal," she acknowledged, but wasn't ready to completely concede. "But if we time it so the fishery is inactive... with a carpet of flower petals running down to the water to counteract the smell..."

He burst out laughing and her own lips twitched. "Always the optimist. Come on." He took her arm and steered her toward the path from the dock up to the main building.

Planning a wedding with Josh Pendleton was turning out to be almost *fun*. In spite of their luck.

It was their second day of looking and the fifth place they'd seen today. Sadly, this was also the most likely contender so far. They were working their way up the coast, hitting all the resorts and hotels that had bookings available for Memorial Day weekend, but the pickings were extremely slim.

At least the company was good.

The rest of their dinner at Mama's had been remarkably comfortable. *Friendly*. And ever since Josh had picked Sidney up at Once Upon a Bride the previous morning to begin vetting venues—shocking Tori into a rare moment of speechlessness—there had been an easy rapport between them.

She'd even managed not to be rattled when three of the event managers they met with assumed they were the bride and groom of the upcoming wedding. Josh had played into the misconception with a wink—which would have gotten her stupid hopes up if she hadn't reined them in sharply with a single word: buddies.

They were buddies. And colleagues. End of story.

"Would you really plan a wedding here?" Josh asked when they reached the porch at the back of the inn, eyeing their picturesque—and aromatic—surrounds dubiously.

"If the bride wants it, you make it work. Obviously I recognize this place isn't ideal. In a perfect world Caitlyn and Will would be married at the Paradise Resort in Eden because it's heaven, but they're booked solid until *next* Memorial Day, so I'm adapting to the circumstances. It's what wedding planners do. We adapt."

"Admirable. Did you always want to be a wedding planner?"

The events manager returned then with the brochures and Sidney was distracted thanking him and taking their leave. She'd figured Josh was just making conversation, so she was surprised when he said as they made their way to the parking lot where his silver convertible waited, "You never answered my question."

"About when I knew I wanted to be a wedding planner?"

"That's the one." He beeped open the car locks, but still walked straight to the passenger side, opening her door for her. Always chivalrous, even when no cameras were looking, that was Josh.

"I was eight," she admitted as she settled onto the passenger seat, setting her attaché case with all the wedding notes at her feet.

Josh rounded the hood of the sleek little car and climbed into the driver's seat. "I'm guessing there's a story there." He punched a destination into the car's GPS. The Paradise Resort.

Sidney frowned. "We can't get the Paradise. It's booked forever."

"And we'll say that during the film package, but I want our viewers to understand the constraints of planning a wedding last minute, even when you can throw around the weight of the *Marrying Mister Perfect* franchise. And I want to know what heaven looks like. Especially since I'm unlikely to get there the traditional way." He winked at her and threw the car into gear, whipping out of the parking lot and zipping toward the Pacific Coast Highway and back toward Eden.

"Besides," he added, "this way I'll know exactly what you're looking for in case I trip across something ideal when I'm not with you."

She wasn't sure she trusted the calculating glint in his eyes, but he had a point—and he knew what they needed. "To the Paradise, then."

"Women are always telling me they want me to take them to Paradise. You're the first one who's been so resistant."

She rolled her eyes. "Very funny."

"I try." He grinned. "Now you have—" He glanced down at the GPS. "—seventeen minutes to tell me the story of how eight-year-old Sidney Dewitt discovered she was destined to be a wedding planner."

"I went to a wedding and the wedding planner seemed magical. That's all."

Josh instantly spotted the lie. "Oh, I'm sure there's more to it than that. Whose wedding was it?"

"You know, I don't think I ever knew. My father was trying to clinch a deal with the father of the bride, so we were there to make a good impression. I didn't see the romance of it. I was just bored and jealous of my brother who got out of coming too because he was away at football camp. My mother shushed me and told me to stop squirming, but when has that ever worked on a child?"

Josh didn't answer, just gave her a listening look and she continued her story.

"I tried to bolt for the buffet table as soon as we got into the reception, but my mother sat me down and began to scold me about something—I don't remember what—and then a miracle occurred."

"Cake?"

"Better. My mother spotted a business associate she just had to speak to for a moment and I was supposed to be good, be quiet, and stay out of trouble at our table for just a moment while my mother rushed over to grab whatever board member was in her sights."

"And were you good and quiet and far away from trouble?"

"Of course I was." She grinned impishly. "For about thirty seconds. Then I saw another kid walking past with the biggest glass of grape juice I'd ever seen and the siren call of that purple deliciousness was too much to resist."

Josh's smile flashed out along with his real laugh—not his camera-ready chuckle.

"The bartender was a sucker for kids. He handed me

a cup of grape juice full to the brim. But it was just a little too full."

"Uh-oh."

"Yep. As soon as he turned away to help someone else, before I'd even taken a single step back to my table—*fwoosh*. I'm sure it wasn't a very big spill, but I remember watching in horrified slow motion as this tsunami of grape horror rose up over the lip of the cup and descended toward the pristine whiteness of my skirt. I knew my mother was going to kill me. I was just working out the details of *how* I was going to die when another miracle occurred. A fairy godmother appeared."

"The wedding planner."

"The very one. Even now when I think about her she seems more like a magical being than a human. She was so tall, with a tight brown bun, and this little knowing smile—like nothing could ever rattle her. She took the grape juice out of my hands before I could spill more and said, 'Don't worry. I have just the thing for that.' I'm sure it was club soda or stain guard or something, but at the time it seemed like magic. She reached into her purse like Mary Poppins and pulled out a spray bottle. A few squirts and the Grape Disaster began to fade before my very eyes. So of course I asked her if she was a fairy godmother."

"What did she say?"

"She said, 'Close. I'm the wedding planner.'"

"And you knew it was your destiny to lift grape juice stains at wedding receptions?"

"Actually, I was disappointed at first. My parents' marriage was more a business arrangement than a love affair, and the one wedding I'd been to was boring and slow. I didn't see anything magical about the marriage business and I told her so."

"I bet she loved that."

"She gasped, making this big show of pretending I'd shocked her, and informed me that wedding planning was the single most magical profession in the world because she could make invisible things appear for just one day."

"How does that work?" Josh asked, as skeptical as she had been at eight.

"She boosted me up onto a barstool, so I could see over the crowd to the dance floor and then she pointed to where the bride and groom were just stepping out to take their first dance. And then she said, 'Do you see the love? Some days we feel the love. Sometimes we forget to even do that. But at a wedding, for one day, we can all see it if we look closely. Do you see it? The little glow around them? It's hard to see, so you really have to want to, but if you do, the love will let you see it on a day like today. Weddings are magical like that. But love is shy. If people are cross about silly things, it doesn't want to come out. So the wedding planner takes care of seating charts and floral arrangements and grape juice stains, so the bride and groom can focus on each other and letting us all see the love. And that's the magic. Do you see it?' And I did. I saw love. The bride and groom radiated it. Their families glowed with it. And I fell in love with it."

"No wonder they picked you for *Marrying Mister Perfect* if you told them that story. Did you become the wedding planner's protégé?"

"Actually, I never saw her again. I never even knew her name. My mother found me then and dragged me back to our table, but from that day on I was hooked. My mother never understood where my sudden romanticism came from. Both of my parents were baffled when I wanted to become a wedding planner, but from my very first wedding I knew I was doing exactly what I needed to be doing with my life."

"That must be nice." A slight frown pulled at Josh's lips, but before she could press him the GPS binged and they turned into the long winding driveway down to the Paradise Beachfront Resort. "Here we are," he announced unnecessarily. "Paradise."

CHAPTER TWENTY

Sidney had called the Paradise Resort heaven and if this was what heaven looked like, he might have to make more of an effort to get in.

The lush grounds of Eden's premiere resort sprawled over a hillside before descending down to a white sand lagoon where the water was tranquil—and the exact shade of Sidney's improbable eyes.

The resort's main building was angled to give the maximum number of rooms the breathtaking ocean and lagoon views. A five star restaurant looked out over the water from the north wing, but Sidney guided him to the south wing, where a private patio had been set for an event later in the day.

The sprawling stone patio was like something out of a magazine—or a set for *Marrying Mister Perfect*—with a raised area for the band and an awning that could roll out to cover the entire expanse in the case of rare southern California rainfall. Two paths led away from the patio—one up a slight incline to the chapel overlooking the surf while the other wended down toward the secluded lagoon beach, perfect for weddings in the sand without the noise of the crashing waves of the Pacific.

Josh hesitated when he saw the spread laid out on the patio. "We should have called for an appointment."

Sidney glanced at him over her shoulder, already skirting the patio and heading toward the lagoon path. "I've done half a dozen weddings here. The events planner knows me. He won't mind. Come on."

Josh trailed after her, his hands thrust deep into the pockets of his khakis as he tried not to notice the way her skirt twisted around her tanned legs in the breeze. At the lagoon she turned back to face him.

"This is exactly what Caitlyn described. But it's also impossible. People plan years in advance for the Paradise."

"We should get the names of the people getting married over Memorial Day weekend and have the show bribe them to move their dates," he said, only half joking.

Sidney rolled her eyes. "Wedding karma, Josh."

"How is it bad karma if we give them a stack of cash to start their new lives together? We wouldn't force them to switch. We'd just make an offer."

"An offer they can't refuse?"

Josh snorted. "We aren't the mafia. We're reality television."

"There's a difference?"

"Does that make me Marlon Brando?"

"Dream on. Miranda is the Don. Or she was."

"Too bad we can't get her to strong arm the events planner into giving us the names."

"No one is strong arming anyone." She pursed her lips—and he realized he was only pushing the point because she was so adorably determined to push back against him.

"Come on. Does it hurt to ask? Maybe the couple are secretly hoping for an excuse to change their wedding date."

"Don't get ahead of yourself. We don't even know if Caitlyn is going to like this place."

Of course Caitlyn loved it.

"This. This is what I want. Are you sure it's booked?"

"Positive." She'd already put their names on the waiting list, but she wasn't holding out much hope.

"We'll just look around for fun then," Caitlyn said, grabbing Will's hand and pulling him down the lagoon path.

Sidney could almost hate Josh for insisting they show her something Sidney couldn't deliver. She would just have to make sure whatever she found was even more perfect.

No pressure.

Caitlyn and Will walked ahead, completely wrapped up in one another as Sidney trailed behind with Josh. This was their last stop of the day and the sun was just dipping beneath the horizon, casting its last pink light over the water.

The rest of the day's appointments had gone miraculously well—which was the only reason they'd had time to swing by the Paradise for a peek. Florists, cakes, place-settings, stationary—Caitlyn and Will had proved to be that rare decisive couple who had no trouble making choices quickly. Though perhaps that had something to do with Josh. He was, Sidney was forced to admit, incredibly good at guiding people toward decisions without pushing them or railroading them into accepting something they didn't want.

No wonder he was so good as host of MMP.

He'd filmed Caitlyn and Will at several of their stops with a little hand-held camera, but thankfully there hadn't been a full camera crew following them around all day. Next week for wedding dress shopping, a full crew would be on hand, but this weekend they wouldn't have gotten anything done if they had to keep waiting for lighting set-ups to be perfect. Instead, Josh and Sidney would return later to each of the locations and add in the necessary exposition, with adorable shots of Caitlyn and Will feeding one another cake samples spliced in around the edges.

He was a good producer too, she realized partway through the day, seeming to have a natural feel for what shots they would eventually need when they put the show together. She hadn't even felt self-conscious when he turned the camera her way. He could put anyone at ease.

And he had an incredible eye for detail and romance—even if he was a bred-to-the-bone cynic.

Josh walked beside her now, hands thrust into pockets, his eyes on the couple ahead of them as Will caught Caitlyn and lifted her off the sand for a kiss.

"You think they're going to go the distance?"

"Caitlyn and Will? Absolutely."

She'd only met Will that morning, but from the first second she'd had that feeling of certainty, that hunch. Caitlyn lit up around him, and he looked at her like she'd hung the moon. He was only interested in the wedding stuff because it was important to Caitlyn, but he never once complained.

Caitlyn's mother had decided not to come on this trip—choosing instead to fly out the following week with just Caitlyn for a full weekend of dress shopping—so it was just the lovebirds Josh and Sidney had been taking on a whirlwind planning expedition.

She tried not to focus on how much the day had felt

like a double date.

She and Josh had spent three days this week looking at alternative venues and though each day had been a failure, she'd had fun with him. He was grumpy and cynical, but beneath it all lurked the soul of a sappy romantic. He may have been burned, but he still smiled at Caitlyn and Will's antics, even if it was in spite of himself.

"Did you mean it when you said you always believe your couples are going to make it?"

"I want to." But honesty forced her to admit, "Though sometimes there are signs. You can sort of read a wedding like tea leaves and see that some couples are going to have a rougher road in front of them."

"I wonder what you would have seen if you'd read my wedding." He looked out over the water, where the sun had now completely disappeared. "It's easy to get paranoid when you're blindsided by your life falling apart, to think that everyone saw it coming but you. You know how you were talking the other day about that wedding planner? About seeing the love? There used to be these moments on the show—when I saw Jack with Lou or when Marcy met Craig—when I felt like I was privileged. I was being allowed to watch something amazing happen. But this season was different and I don't know if it was Daniel, or you, or me. I just don't know if I believe in the show anymore. I've been clinging to it because it's the last thing left of the life I always thought I wanted, but I'm not even sure I like who I am now. But if I'm not the host of *Marrying Mister Perfect*, who am I?" Josh made a face. "Shit. I'm Divorce Guy, aren't I? I've become that guy who can't go for five seconds without whining about his failed marriage and his pathetic life."

"It's understandable." And she didn't mind. This was the Josh Pendleton she'd met the first night. The one who stopped trying to hold the entire world outside the walls of his hostly persona and dropped all his shields, becoming a cynical smart ass. She'd missed him.

"Yeah, but it isn't who I want to be. I don't want to be the guy who's bitter about *picnics* because I proposed to my ex on one. I freaking loved picnics. Now it feels like I'm losing everything I used to love along with losing her."

"So take picnics back."

"Just like that?"

"Does it have to be more complicated than that? You're not Divorce Guy. You're Picnic Guy. So who else are you?"

Sidney's question seemed to trail after him as they made their way back to her car and dropped Caitlyn and Will at their hotel. He'd left his convertible parked behind Once Upon a Bride, so it was just the two of them as she drove down Eden's adorable Main Street.

Other people had told him to get over himself and get his life back, to fucking cheer up already, but somehow Sidney asking him who he was when he wasn't Divorce Guy was different. It snuck through his layers of bitterness, past the stubborn part of him arguing that he didn't deserve what had happened to him. It pierced his asinine insistence that he had the right to be miserable if he goddamn well wanted to be, and asked him what kind of an idiot *wanted* to be miserable when he could be something else. He could be Picnic Guy. Or Surfing Guy. Or Wine Tasting Guy.

He may not be able to get his dream life back, but

that didn't mean he had to be pathetic and wallow in it.

Hell, maybe he'd even be Dating Guy again sometime soon.

She pulled into the lot behind Once Upon a Bride, parking her small SUV in the space beside his Beamer and cutting the engine.

"You were a big help today," she said in the comfortable cocoon of the silent car. "Thank you."

"I didn't do anything. You're the master. I just sat back and let you work."

"You can pretend you didn't do anything, but you're good at this. At directing people through decisions. It's part of what makes you such a great host. You help clarify things."

"Funny, I feel like that's what you do for me." He shouldn't have said it. He knew the second her face softened that it sent the wrong message—the message he seemed to keep sending her whenever he wasn't on his guard. "Forget I said that."

"It's okay to be real with me. You don't always have to be *on* around me."

"I'm not." That was the problem. He needed to keep his distance from her, but when she was looking at him the way she was right now—like she understood him and didn't think he was half as pathetic as he really was—the normal filters didn't apply. Somehow he could tell her all the things he didn't want anyone else to know.

Like how lonely he was, how out of his control his life felt right now—but neither of those things applied when he was with her.

He needed walls between them, STAT. "Look, Sidney, you know I can't date you. It would violate every morality clause in my contract if I'm caught getting too familiar with a Suitorette—even a former one. I'll lose my job and my reputation will be shot."

"No, of course I understand," she said softly, but she didn't withdraw behind a defensive wall as he'd hoped. Her eyes were still open and on him.

"I know I kissed you—"

"Technically, I think I kissed you."

"Potato, potahto." He waved away her clarification. "The point is I'd like it if we could just forget it ever happened."

"Then why do you keep bringing it up?"

Something dangerous seemed to lurk in the silence after she asked the question—something that said they both knew he was lying when he said he wanted to forget.

Shit. "I should get going."

He climbed out of her car, fishing out his keys as he heard her door open.

"Josh." She came around the hood, her attaché case slung over one shoulder. "Do you want to date me?"

He froze, his keys cold in his hand. "What?"

"You said you can't, but if you could?" She stopped close to him, big blue eyes questioning in the low light of the lot. "Would you?"

He'd gotten in the habit of saying no to her. It was the only answer, so he didn't think about what ifs and might have beens. He didn't consider liking her because reciprocating any feelings she might have had for him was out of the question.

But when she was looking at him like that, all vulnerable and hopeful, he couldn't lie.

And he couldn't resist.

CHAPTER TWENTY-ONE

Just like the first time, he didn't form any conscious decision to kiss her. It wasn't intentional so much as inevitable.

Somehow he was just kissing her.

Her lips were sweet and soft, inviting him to angle his head and tease his way between them, a tentative flick of his tongue quickly segueing into a decadent exploration. Every movement was slow and steeped in sensuality, a lingering coaxing caress of his lips over hers, stoking the fire between them. It felt like this moment had been building for months, but he wouldn't rush it. He couldn't. The spell they were under demanded an unhurried discovery.

He wasn't aware of lifting his hands, but one cupped the side of her neck, his fingertips tangling in the fine hairs at her nape, as the other slid around her waist, sneaking beneath her coat to tug her flush against him. When their bodies came into contact, she released a whisper of sound into his mouth—half gasp, half moan—and he groaned.

A crash sounded above their heads seconds before light poured out of the window in the apartment above them.

Sidney jerked back, the spell broken, and Josh stared at her wide teal eyes, trying to redirect some of the blood flow in his body back to his brain. Her eyes were filled with questions—and the only response Josh could think of was a low, muttered curse.

"This can't happen."

She leaned back, but his hands were still on her and she didn't try to break his hold, her own braced loosely on his waist. "Are you still seeing Olga?"

The lie came to his lips faster than thought. "Yes."

She did pull away then, casting her gaze down to the pavement. "I'm sorry. I should go."

He let her get as far as the back door to her shop before her name burst out of him raggedly. "Sidney."

She looked back at him, her hand on the knob, blond hair bright in the light filtering down from above.

"Are we still good?" he asked. "Still...?" He wouldn't say friends.

Her smile held layers of sadness and understanding he couldn't begin to comprehend. "Yeah. We're good. G'night, Josh. Get some sleep. We have caterers tomorrow."

He grinned, relieved. "How tiring can eating be?"

"You'd be surprised." She gave him one last smile before disappearing inside and he leaned against his car, watching her go.

Sidney Dewitt.

Something about her just reeled him in.

He'd kissed Olga—in public, for the cameras—but he'd never *kissed* Olga. Even with Marissa, things had grown perfunctory—never claiming all of his attention. He couldn't remember the last time he'd forgotten himself in a kiss like that, until all he was narrowed down to lips and lust.

Except he could. It was the last time he'd kissed Sidney.

"Shit." Josh scrubbed a hand over his face and climbed into the convertible, firing it up, but not putting it into gear.

It had been instinctive to lie. To throw Olga between them like a human shield.

After he'd learned his contract was being extended and Olga had landed a part in an upcoming made-for-TV movie, the two of them had agreed that while they would still technically be "together" if anyone asked, that they would dial back their public appearances. He hadn't seen her in weeks and had no plans to see her in the future—but what Sidney didn't know could save them both a lot of heartache.

He couldn't get involved with a former Suitorette.

No matter how she kissed.

Josh put the convertible in gear and pulled out of the lot.

Sidney leaned against the inside of the door until she heard Josh pull out, part of her hoping he would change his mind and follow her inside. Which was wrong. He was with Olga the Gorgeous.

"Sidney?"

She pushed herself away from the door, moving to meet Victoria at the base of the stairs. "Hey." She jerked her chin toward the upstairs window that looked over the back lot—Lorelei's window. "Nice timing. Lore?"

"Apparently she was spying on you and fell off her dresser." At Sidney's expression of concern, Victoria assured her, "She's fine, but I thought I'd come down to make sure you were." Tori looked toward the closed back door. "Was that Josh?"

"Yeah."

"Ah." Tori nodded without judgment, waiting for Sidney to say more.

"He's still with Olga."

"Ah." Another nod.

Sidney grimaced. "Apparently that stupid show got me in the habit of making out with guys who are dating other women. Because *that's* a healthy mindset."

"So you made out."

"Didn't Lore see?"

"It was dark. I think she missed most of the good stuff. All she knew is that you were down there with someone."

"He kissed me. Or I kissed him. I never seem to know how it happens. One second he's telling me that he'll lose his job if he dates a Suitorette and the next my brain has evaporated into pure lust."

"Wait, he'll lose his job? You aren't even a Suitorette anymore."

"Apparently there are morality clauses and former Suitorettes count."

"Damn."

"Yeah," she sighed in agreement. Because Josh Pendleton was definitely sigh worthy. Even if he was dating a Russian dancer.

Except part of her didn't believe they were really together.

And how delusional was that? She was so hung up on him she was convincing herself he didn't really love the woman he was with. Just because she'd seen some photos of them together online.

She'd sought out the pictures, expecting them to help her get some distance from her stupid crush back when she first found out he was dating Olga the Gorgeous. She'd thought seeing proof of exactly how out of her league he was would be the straw that would break the back of her enduring infatuation.

But all she'd seen when she looked at the pictures was Host Josh smiling for the cameras. Real Josh was nowhere in sight. There was nothing wryly self-deprecating about his smile. No glint of mischief or cynicism in his eyes. And no connection with the woman at his side. She might as well have been a prop. A gorgeous size zero prop, but inanimate for all the connection between them.

But it didn't matter. Whether he was or wasn't with Olga, he'd made it very clear that he couldn't be with her. Regardless of what either of them wanted.

"We're friends," she told Victoria, who looked on skeptically. "We're working together to plan the wedding that's going to put Once Upon a Bride on the *Veil* list. I'm far too busy to think about anything else right now anyway."

"If you say so."

"I do. Josh Pendleton is just a friend. End of story."

Victoria hesitated, but she'd never been one to hold her tongue. "Sid, you know I love you, and I just want you to be happy, but this thing with Josh Pendleton has already gotten in the way of what you wanted out of *Marrying Mister Perfect*. I just don't want to see him get in the way of what we want for Once Upon a Bride too. If you need me to step in on Caitlyn's wedding, or if we should ask the show for a different liaison—"

"No. I'm good. I've got this."

"You said he was a distraction—"

"He isn't in my head," Sidney insisted. "The kissing thing tonight was an aberration, but we've been working well together. Things went really well with Caitlyn and Will today. They're going to go great tomorrow—and as soon as I find us a fabulous venue that isn't already booked, we'll be home free. Nothing is going to stand in the way of us hitting that list. I promise."

Sidney knew better than to make promises when it came to weddings. The Matrimonial Gods were always listening, and they loved to laugh in the faces of mere mortals.

So she shouldn't have been surprised to come downstairs the next morning to find her car battery deader than dirt. She'd gotten cocky and the Marriage Gods had found it necessary to smite her.

Or she'd left the car door slightly ajar and the stupid dome light had been on all night, which she hadn't even noticed because she was too stupidly wrapped up in Josh Pendleton and his stupid distracting kisses.

Either way, she was due at the first catering tasting in twenty minutes.

Victoria was thirty minutes away having brunch with her mother and Lorelei. Even if the timing hadn't been an issue, she wasn't about to call Tori for an I-told-you-so about how Josh screwed with her focus. Caitlyn and Will's rental car only fit two. Which left one option. The devil himself.

He picked up on the second ring. She heard the whip of wind and road noise in the background and knew he must be using his Bluetooth with the top down. It was a classically gorgeous morning. "Hello."

"Josh? It's Sidney. Would you mind swinging by to pick me up? My car won't start." She refrained from mentioning why.

He agreed without question and ten minutes later the silver convertible pulled into the lot, Josh in the driver's seat looking like a BMW commercial with his mirrored sunglasses and sharp white teeth bared in a smile. He really was too good looking for his own good.

He pulled into the empty space beside where she stood, grinning at her. "Did someone call for a knight in shining armor?"

She tossed her attaché case into the back and opened the door to slide into the passenger seat. "Thank you for coming. I owe you."

"Be careful throwing around IOUs like that. I'll hold you to them and you'll find yourself forced to help me move my couch. Or worse, house hunt." He pulled out of the lot as soon as she clicked her seat belt, charting a course for the first caterer they were auditioning this morning with Caitlyn and Will. "What's wrong with your car? Or was this all an elaborate ploy to spend more time with me?"

"The battery died," she said, ignoring his over-the-top teasing—just another ploy from his playbook to put distance between them. "I must have left the door cracked and the dome light ran it out."

"Then it's as much my fault as yours. I should have noticed it was on when I left last night." He frowned, eyes on the road as he turned up the Pacific Coast Highway. "Doesn't it automatically shut off after a certain amount of time?"

Her hair began to fly wildly in the wind and she reached up to contain it in her fist, kicking herself for failing to bring a hair tie. "I'm sure automatic shut off is standard in shiny new BMW convertibles, but my lovely little SUV has the double whammy of being old and cheap."

"You take good care of it. It still looks new."

Unsure what to say to the small talk, she changed the

subject. "Why are you house-hunting? Time to upgrade your palace?"

"Actually, Marissa got the palace in the divorce. Or at least she got the beach house in Malibu. I've been living in the world's most depressing bachelor apartment in Studio City, but I've decided it's time to get out of there. Divorce Guy lives there and since I'm not going to be Divorce Guy anymore I need a new place to live. Thought I'd talk to a real estate agent tomorrow. Get the ball rolling."

"Good for you."

"Don't worry," he said, flashing white teeth in a grin as the GPS murmured directions and he took the turn toward the first caterer. "I won't really make you house hunt with me. I'm not that cruel."

She shouldn't be disappointed by that, but something about house hunting with Josh was all too appealing.

As friends, she reminded herself. Just as friends.

CHAPTER TWENTY-TWO

The house was magnificent. A sprawling estate looking out over the Pacific Ocean, it was everything a newly single celebrity could wish for. And with an asking price of seventeen point eight million dollars, it was also seventeen million over his budget, but his new realtor had taken one look at his famous name and taken him straight to a mansion right out of Lifestyles of the Rich and Famous, completely ignoring the fact that even before the divorce Josh had never had that kind of money to throw around.

He couldn't blame the guy for trying. The commission on this place would support a family of five for years. And it was incredible. If he ever had an unlimited budget, this was exactly the kind of place he'd be buying. It reeked of luxury, but still had a beachy warmth that made it feel almost cozy—if a fifteen acre estate looking out over the ocean could be cozy.

It was the kind of place *Marrying Mister Perfect* would rent out to shoot—

Josh went still, an idea crystallizing in his mind. Fifteen minutes and a conversation with the realtor later, he was standing poolside at the lavish estate, his cell phone pressed to his ear as he waited impatiently for Sidney to pick up.

It was a Wednesday afternoon. She couldn't be at a

wedding. "Come on," he muttered into the phone, impatient with the need to share his brilliance with her.

It was getting to the point where he expected voicemail to kick in when she picked up with a breathless, "Hello?"

"I have solved our venue problems," he announced, triumphant.

Her groan was not appropriately appreciative of his genius. "Tell me you didn't get the names of the couples with the Memorial Day bookings at Paradise."

"Actually, I did," he admitted, "but wait until you hear—"

"Oh God. Tell me you didn't bribe them."

"I didn't," he obliged. "Though it turns out the bride with the Saturday slot is a huge fan of the show."

"You're kidding. Don't tell me they agreed to change their dates just because they like you."

"Tell you, don't tell you. You're awfully bossy today."

"Josh."

"She laughed in my face."

Sidney laughed as well, the sound breathy and appealing.

"But she loves the show," he reiterated, in case she had missed the part where he was beloved by one and all.

"So we're back to square one." Sidney groaned.

"Weren't you listening when I said I have solved all our venue woes?"

"I tend to zone out when you speak," she teased. "Force of habit from all those years tuning you out on the show."

"Cute." Though he was relieved she was giving him shit. He hated when she tip-toed around him like she did whenever he screwed up and kissed her. "But trust me, you're going to want to see this. How soon can you get here?"

Forty minutes later, Sidney climbed out of her SUV, dubiously eyeing the for sale sign at the edge of the driveway. "Buying a replacement palace?" she asked as she approached.

Josh waited on the wide stone steps leading up to the double doors that could admit a guest riding on a elephant. "I wish. I can't even afford the gate house on a place like this, but my realtor was fixated on my name and forgot to take my budgetary limitations into account. Which may have been a stroke of luck."

Said realtor was inside, locked in a conference call with the production team of *Marrying Mister Perfect* and the seller's agent, hammering out terms.

"How so?"

"Turns out there's a limited market for seventeen million dollar estates and they can linger on the market for months or even years before finding the right buyer. Real estate agents are always looking for creative ways to raise the profile of their high-end listings. Ways like a television special about the wedding of the year being held here."

"You were serious? You really have found us a venue?"

"Wait until you see the view from the back." He grinned and reached for the massive front door to hold it for her. "Trust me. This is the place."

It was heaven.

From the giant stone patio for the reception to the small private beach for the ceremony, every detail was flawless. The only downside was that it didn't come with a small army of event staff, but she could bring in her own people to set up. Or *Marrying Mister Perfect* would provide a battalion of interns to do her bidding.

After a quick video call with Caitlyn and Will, Sidney had given Josh the thumbs up and he was now deep in discussion with the realtor, working out all the details. They'd already established that they would book the estate for the week prior to the wedding and host all the various wedding events on site. There were fifteen bedrooms—enough for the wedding party and most of the in-laws to stay here for the duration.

They'd have to work out parking alternatives and the restrooms would be tight, but she could make it work.

There was even a fence around the perimeter and a security gate at the front—which would make keeping out uninvited press a lot easier on Max, since her brother had already agreed to provide extra security.

Everything was falling into place. All thanks to Josh.

He shook the realtor's hand, wrapping up their conversation, and strolled over to where Sidney waited, his hands thrust deep into his pockets in a casual habit that she realized he only employed when he wasn't on camera. "Does it pass muster?" he asked, nodding toward the water view.

"It's exquisite," she said. "You found me the perfect venue. Now I really owe you."

"Remember that when I ask you to help me move my couch."

She knew he wasn't serious. Josh Pendleton wasn't the sort of man who moved his own furniture. And she was beginning to realize he was a hard man to thank. He teased and deflected whenever she tried to even the scales between them—which only made her want to pay him back more, because he never expected it.

Recalling what he'd said at Mama's, her next words were an impulse. "Let me make you dinner tonight. As a thank you."

"Is that a reward or a punishment?" he teased.

Her smile matched his. "You'll have to show up to find out."

Sidney felt good about issuing the challenge that Josh join her for dinner until she got home and panic set in. Thirty minutes of frantic cleaning and a light-speed trip to the grocery later, she had all the makings for homemade spaghetti carbonara—and was still on the verge of hyperventilating at the thought of Josh Pendleton here. In her space. Touching her things.

Yes, she'd gotten comfortable with him over the last couple weeks, but that had been on neutral territory. This was different. This was home.

But it was more than that. It was the undeniable date-ness of cooking a man dinner. Alone. Where no one would chaperone them.

She had genuinely meant it as a gesture of goodwill when she invited him, but now she was in her kitchen, staring down a bottle of red wine and trying to decide if opening it so it had time to breathe before he got here sent the wrong message.

Or the right message.

She wanted him. She'd wanted him from the second she met him.

Of course there was still Olga, but not fifteen minutes ago at the supermarket she'd seen a magazine cover with a small corner picture of Olga cuddling up to one of her *American Dance Star* costars with the caption *"Are Josh and Olga on the outs?"*

Even if they were, and Josh was available, he still wasn't available to her. Especially not if she wanted to continue to work with him on the MMP Wedding Special.

So no funny business. None. Dinner as friends. That's all this was.

Except...

No one would see them. No one would know.

She could have her cake and eat it too... as long as no one found out about it.

She'd never thought of herself as the kind of woman who had torrid secret affairs, but maybe it was high time she stopped worrying about what she should be doing and did what she wanted for a change.

She needed to take a run, clear her head, but there wasn't time before he was due to come over.

She reached for the bottle of wine... and her hand changed route of its own accord, grabbing her cell phone instead. She dialed Parvati—which was as good as admitting she was going to sleep with him tonight. If she'd wanted sense talked into her, she would have called Victoria. Parvati had a much looser moral compass.

"Yo, Sid!"

"Would you still respect me if I had a torrid secret affair?" she asked without preamble.

Parvati hesitated far too long for her peace of mind before asking for clarification. "You mean like with a married man?"

"No. Of course not."

"They why is it secret? Is he ashamed of you?

Because any guy who won't man up and be the boyfriend isn't good enough for you."

"It's not that. Let's just say for reasons I can't go into right now, we can't officially be together."

Parv groaned into the phone. "It's not Daniel, is it? Because I gotta say, Sid, he turned out to be kind of a douche in the end."

"It's not Daniel."

"But you can't be seen together in public."

"Exactly."

This time the pause lasted only a fraction of a second. "Holy crap! You're having a steamy secret affair with Josh Pendleton! I want all the details! Is he as good as I think he is?"

"I'm not having an affair with Josh Pendleton." She propped the phone against her shoulder and reached for the wine and the corkscrew. "Yet."

Parvati squealed and Sidney winced, wishing she had a hand free to move the phone away from her ear.

"I take it you approve."

"Hell, yes. But since when do you need my approval?"

The cork came free with a jerk and Sidney nearly dropped the phone. She hastily set down the wine and corkscrew, wondering if she had anything stronger in the apartment to take the edge off.

She ignored Parvati's question, explaining instead. "He's coming over here. I'm making him dinner. We've been playing at just friends, but I do not feel just friendly toward him and I'm pretty sure he feels something for me and now I'm making him carbonara."

"Ooh, bringing out the big guns. I love your carbonara. Save me some?"

"I'll make you some on Tuesday." It was their

traditional Girls' Night In with Victoria and Lorelei—reserved for gossip and watching *Marrying Mister Perfect* or whatever other television addiction was in season. "Just tell me I'm not a bad person for engaging in an illicit affair."

"Is anyone going to be hurt by you two being together?"

"I don't know. Last time we talked about it, he was still with Olga."

"Okay, so maybe that's something to get out of the way up front. Find out if those two are exclusive."

"Right. But even if they aren't, he could lose his job if they find out he's with me. And it would kill my reputation. Everyone would think I only got the MMP Wedding because I was banging the host."

"Which is why no one can find out. But it isn't a reason you shouldn't be together," Parv said. "The way I see it, it all boils down to one question—assuming he and Olga aren't an exclusive item."

"What's that?"

"Will keeping this secret make you crazy? And if it will, is he worth it?"

Sidney had a feeling the answer to the first question was yes. But so was the second.

Sometimes you just had to go a little crazy.

"Do you have any of today's tiramisu left?"

Parvati squealed. "I'll bring it right over."

CHAPTER TWENTY-THREE

"That," Josh declared, leaning back in his chair and lacing his hands over his stomach, "was transcendent. We should have had you cook for Daniel. He would have never let you leave."

Sidney stood to clear their empty plates. Daniel was about the last person she wanted to talk about tonight, but when she flailed blindly for another response, the one that came out of her mouth was the one topic she wanted to talk about less. "My mother is a firm believer in being the best. If Dewitts want to cook, we have to be gourmands or stay out of the kitchen—lest we sully the family name."

"No pressure," he said with a light laugh, rising to help her bring the dishes the three feet from her small, round dining table to the narrow galley kitchen. "I keep forgetting you're one of *the* Dewitts."

"Sometimes I wish I could," she said dryly.

"Silver spoon didn't taste so good?" He refilled their wine glasses, emptying the bottle, as she rinsed the dishes and slid them into the dishwasher. "Don't take this the wrong way, but I'm surprised one of *the* Dewitts drives a cheap SUV and lives in a tiny attic apartment—not that this place isn't charming, but growing up the way you must have grown up…"

She closed the dishwasher and he handed over her

wine glass. He reclined against the opposite counter in the narrow kitchen, watching her as he idly swirled his own wine. Sadly there was nothing seductive about the look in his eyes. Ever since he'd arrived things had been friendly and comfortable, with none of the electric sexual tension she had half-hoped would saturate her apartment the second he crossed the threshold. All her soul searching about whether or not she could be a secret mistress had apparently been nothing more than wishful thinking.

"My parents are big into standing on your own feet," she said, by way of explanation for her less-than-palatial living arrangements. "No hand-outs or hands-up allowed. My father even refused to invest in Once Upon a Bride. Didn't think our business plan was strong enough. What about you? What's your family like?" she asked, in part because she was curious and in part because she would rather talk about anything but her failure as a Dewitt.

"My folks are pretty much the middle class American cliché. They let me buy them a cruise when I landed my first big contract, but only because Marissa and I went with them. They have a nice little place in Washington, not far from Seattle."

"That's where you're from?"

He hummed an affirmative, sipping his wine. "I have one little sister, a high school English teacher, and she still lives up there, right down the street from where we grew up."

"While you ran off to Hollywood the first chance you got?"

"Actually, the Hollywood thing just sort of happened—not that I'm not thankful for it, I know I'm a lucky bastard to work in this business—but it wasn't really the plan. I came down to USC with dreams of being an architect, but I wound up majoring in partying instead." A self-deprecating shrug. "My frat had a drunken quiz bowl fundraiser and I played host. I was just screwing around, but someone taped it and, don't ask me how, but somehow it got into the right hands and the producers of *Brainiac* decided I had the perfect balance of class and smartass to make a good game show host."

"It doesn't hurt that you're pretty."

"Yeah, that's pretty much exactly what my first agent said, but I can't help it if the camera loves me."

She grabbed a handy dishtowel and chucked it at his head. He dodged with a grin, snatching it out of the air with his free hand. "What about you? Did you take classes on fairy godmothering in college?"

"No, I was taking business classes like a good little Dewitt—and pretty much hating every second of it—when my college roommate got engaged. I started helping her plan her wedding, trying to figure out ways to make it magical on a shoestring, and I realized that planning the wedding was the only part of my day I looked forward to. I'd always sort of wanted to do it, but it wasn't until that summer that I rebelled by giving up my summer internship in favor of working for a wedding planner. Victoria was also on staff there and we hit it off. After I graduated I began working there full time, and eventually we saved up enough to start our own place."

"Your parents must be proud, working your way up like that."

"My mother still calls me a party planner. I don't think my business is what they had in mind when they said I was born to succeed. My childhood bedroom was like a Successories storeroom."

"I can't imagine growing up like that," he said. "My family was pretty much the Cleavers."

"And you were the Beav?"

"Nah. I'm Wally. Obviously."

"You know I don't think I've ever actually seen that show," she admitted, draining the last of her wine.

"You're kidding. You're missing a vital part of our cultural history here."

She shrugged. "I guess I was just too busy watching *Marrying Mister Perfect* and *Brainiac*."

"You actually watched the quiz show?"

"Every episode. I had the biggest crush on you." Belatedly realizing what she'd just confessed, Sidney's face flamed as she shot an accusatory glare at the empty wine glass. "There's dessert," she said hurriedly, before Josh could comment on her crush. "Do you like tiramisu?"

"Love it." He set his own empty glass beside hers as she hurried to the fridge to pull out the dessert. "Is this homemade as well?"

"Of course. Well, homemade across the street. My friend Parvati runs the coffee shop in town and she has a serious baking addiction—especially desserts, though her savory muffins are to die for. The gruyere-and-bacon muffin is my favorite, but she won an award for the Brie Apple one last year. And recently she decided to try making tiramisu and—well, suffice it to say her brilliance is not limited to muffins. You'll never look at tiramisu the same way again." She was babbling, but even knowing she was babbling, she couldn't seem to shut off the flow of words. Sidney set the dessert on the counter, reaching for plates and a knife to serve it. "She tests out new recipes on me and Tori—and shares the leftovers sometimes."

She slid tiramisu onto a plate for him and thrust it toward him with a fork, turning back to serve herself when her mouth developed a fatal lack of restraint.

"Are you really dating Olga?" she blurted. "Because if you are, I won't say another word, but all the photos I see of the two of you together look so staged. You never look like *you* with her. But if you're happy, I'll shut up. It's none of my business. Obviously." Too late, she managed to put the brakes on her runaway mouth.

He hesitated, frozen holding a plate of tiramisu. "Sidney... even supposing you're right and Olga and I just have a business relationship—"

"Supposing?"

He shrugged, setting his plate down on the counter. "It's a convenient lie. We certainly aren't the first public figures to have a relationship for show."

She wet her lips. "So you're unattached."

"I can't date a former Suitorette."

"I know."

"I like you, Sidney," he said in a let-her-down-easy tone. "I'd like nothing more than to... see where this goes." His gaze flicked over her shoulder toward the bedroom. "But I can't."

"I understand," she murmured. And she really did. She knew exactly how much it could cost him, but she just needed to say one last thing. Just in case. Reckless desire inside her had her peeking up at him through her lashes. "No one would have to know."

CHAPTER TWENTY-FOUR

Josh went still.

He was unprepared for exactly how badly he wanted her in that moment. It had been easy to keep Olga at arm's length, easy to tell himself he simply didn't want the complication of a woman in his life, and that was true enough, but it wasn't the whole truth. He wanted Sidney with a magnitude that overrode his reservations, even as he knew he should excuse himself and walk out the door.

"Josh?"

She was exquisite—all temptation and vulnerable hope. She deserved better than to be any man's secret, but Sidney drew him in like a gravitational force and he knew he wouldn't say no. Not when she stepped closer and whispered his name again, the sound of it an erotic invitation—

An invitation he took from her lips with a kiss that burned sweet and fast.

He pulled away only long enough to whisper, "Are you sure?" and then she was back in his arms, tangled around him so urgently there was no question of her certainty. He boosted her onto the counter and her legs immediately twined around his waist. His hands plunged beneath her skirt, stroking up the smooth skin of her outer thighs. When he kissed his way down her throat, her head thunked back against the upper cupboards.

He cursed softly. "We aren't doing this here." Scooping her off the counter, he pointed toward the bedroom, stumbling slightly because for all she was lean, she was almost as tall as he was and she was no featherweight.

"I can walk." She squirmed, trying to drop her legs.

Not for long, if I have anything to say about it.

"I've got you." He hitched her higher, fueled by the masculine need to get his woman to the bedroom.

She gave up struggling, twining her arms around his neck and murmuring, "So macho" in a teasing undertone as he kicked open the door.

The bedroom was a tiny little cubby off the main room, the double bed with the curling wrought iron headboard taking up almost all of the available floor space, but the lack of footage did nothing to diminish the comfort and personality Sidney had infused into the décor. It was warm and elegant, feminine without being overpowering—and he barely registered any of it as he sat on the bed so she was kneeling astride him.

She leaned back in his arms, shaking her head dazedly. "Josh Pendleton is in my bed."

With anyone else, he would have taken the words as a warning sign, a red flag that the woman he was with only wanted him for his celebrity, but this was Sidney. She knew him—better perhaps than he wanted to admit—and her teal eyes glinted with humor, teasing him with his own self-importance. "*On* your bed at the moment, but give me five minutes."

"In a hurry, are you?"

"Oh, trust me, darling, I'm planning to take my time."

She shook her head with mock sadness, a smile flirting with her pink lips. "Some men are all talk."

"Luckily, I'm not one of them." Then he stopped any further talk with a kiss and got down to the business of taking his time.

Some men were all talk, but Josh was better than his word.

Sidney lay sprawled and satisfied beneath her covers as he snored beside her—who knew perfect Josh Pendleton sawed logs like a sputtering chainsaw? She lay in the dark, kept awake more by her own restless energy and the stirrings of her mind than the impressive noise he was producing, and waited for the guilt to creep in.

She was having an illicit affair. She really was supposed to feel guilty, wasn't she? But all she felt was… smug. The man knew what he was doing and then some. But her satisfaction went beyond the physical. Things just felt right with him. Easy. That clicking into place feeling she'd always imagined had finally clicked.

Unfortunately it had clicked with a man who was completely off limits and who, even if he had somehow magically become able to date her, probably wouldn't want to because he was still rebounding from his divorce.

No, this wasn't a love connection—and she wasn't going to let herself get all sappy about him just because he was a maestro between the sheets. She would keep her infatuation ruthlessly in check with the knowledge that they were going nowhere. He was just a temporary affliction, but one she was going to enjoy for as long as it lasted.

They would never be able to have a future together, but for right now she was exactly where she was supposed to be.

Next to him.

"Did you go for it? How was it? Is he as good as I imagine?"

Parvati was lying in wait and bombarded her with questions the next morning as soon as she descended the stairs into Once Upon a Bride. Josh had slipped out early enough to avoid Victoria and Lorelei on the stairs—and get his car out of the Once Upon a Bride back parking lot before it raised any eyebrows—but they were going to have to be more careful in the future if they wanted this secret affair to stay secret.

That was assuming there would be a future. As soon as he had left that morning, Sidney's euphoria had dimmed three notches and now she couldn't help second guessing all the things that had been left unspecified.

Had he thought they were having a one night stand while she thought they were embarking on an affair? Did he have regrets? When would she see him again?

With all those questions rattling around in her head, the last thing she wanted to do was answer Parvati's. Especially when Victoria came out of the office with a frown wrinkling her brow.

"What's she on about? She's been waiting here for half an hour."

Sidney ignored Victoria's question, aiming her response at Parv. "Don't you have a coffee house to run?"

"My highly trained minions are manning the espresso machine. They'll survive without me for an hour. Now dish. What happened with Josh Pendleton?"

Victoria's frown deepened. "When did you see Josh Pendleton?"

"He found us a venue yesterday for the MMP Wedding," Sidney explained, focusing on the innocent, professional reason.

"And then she made him dinner," Parvati ratted her out. "Complete with my panty-dropping tiramisu."

"You should call it that on the menu," Sidney advised. "You'd sell thousands."

"I just might," Parv said archly. "Now stop stalling and tell me what happened! I'm dying here."

"I don't think you can actually asphyxiate from lack of gossip."

"Sidney! Was there or was there not boot knocking last night?"

A giddy little smile curled her lips of its own accord and Parvati squealed delightedly.

"I knew it!"

"You didn't." Victoria groaned, dropping onto one of the chairs set up around a place setting display.

Sidney ignored the waves of disapproval radiating off Tori, focusing instead on Parv and her giddy delight, trying to recapture her own euphoria from the night before, when she'd been so sure she was exactly where she needed to be. "We never got to the tiramisu," she said with a wicked grin that sent Parvati into an exaggerated swoon.

"I'm dying. I'm actually dying of envy right now. *Josh Pendleton*. Be still my ovaries." She fanned herself with a brochure for a florist. "Quick, give me details."

"A lady never kisses and tells."

"Especially when said lady isn't allowed to tell anyone about the man she was kissing," Tori chimed in dourly.

"Could you let me enjoy this for five minutes?" Sidney moved to one of the displays and began tidying the already immaculate sample binders. "I'm living in the moment. So sue me. I know it's not something you ever do, but that doesn't mean I can't."

"You're a planner," Victoria said, as if that was all the counter-argument she needed.

"I know."

Tori flicked a manicured hand, impatient. "I'm not just talking about your job title. It's your personality to look into the future and plan for every eventuality, to constantly reassess and reevaluate, and to always be looking forward, working toward some goal. And now you're putting yourself on hold for some guy."

"Maybe I don't want to be a planner all the time. Could you at least consider that before you start trying to make me feel guilty? Maybe I'm going through a phase."

"Can I have a banging Josh Pendleton phase?" Parvati interjected, lightening the mood.

"No. He's mine."

Tori stood, moving to toss her empty coffee cup in the trash. "You're awfully possessive for someone who can't be seen in public with him."

"Just because we aren't public doesn't mean I'm willing to share."

"Does he know that?" Tori asked archly.

Sidney glared at her partner. "Why do you have to be the voice of doom? Can't you be happy for me?"

"I'm not the voice of doom; I'm the voice of reason. And I'll be happy for you when you're with someone who is good enough for you."

"Who's better than Josh Pendleton?" she asked, more seriously than she might have meant to, because at the moment she couldn't picture such a man existing.

"A man who loves you."

Sidney flinched. "Ouch."

"And on that note, I think I should get back to Common Grounds." Parvati stood, hugging Sidney and whispering, "Don't listen to her. You're allowed to cut loose and let your hair down. Especially with Josh Pendleton."

Then she was gone, leaving Sidney alone with her partner.

"Now that we have a venue, I'm on schedule with the MMP Wedding, if you'd like me to take any of your appointments this morning," she offered as an olive branch

Tori had been standing with her back to the room, fussing with one of the displays, but now she turned back. "I know you think I'm being the wicked witch, but I've been swept away by my emotions with a guy who wasn't in it for the long run and I wound up pregnant and alone when he decided he cared more about his career than he did about me and our baby. I don't want that for you."

"That isn't what this is," she insisted, but there was less certainty in the words. Tori did only want her to be happy—but she was biased by her own issues. There was no reason to suspect Josh was anything like He Who Must Not Be Named. She would not get paranoid.

"Just use protection," Victoria intoned direly.

"Don't worry, Mom. We are."

"You joke, but I'll be the one buying the ice cream and wine when you're heartbroken."

"I won't be heartbroken because my heart isn't going to get involved," she promised. "It's just chemistry. It'll run its course."

At least that's what she kept telling herself.

If only she didn't already feel like she was lying.

CHAPTER TWENTY-FIVE

"You can't actually be thinking of living here."

Josh couldn't help but grin at the undisguised horror in Sidney's voice. Inviting her to come house hunting with him had been an impulse. He'd told her he needed a second opinion, but the truth was he'd wanted an excuse to see her again.

Things with the wedding were rolling along smoothly. Releases were being signed and filming dates scheduled. The production team was happy, but he had no professional reason to seek her out and they hadn't exactly left things on any certain terms as far as their non-professional interactions went.

It hadn't seemed appropriate to call her for a booty call, but dragging her around southern California looking at condos and bedraggled shacks was another thing entirely.

"There are cracks in all the walls," she pointed out. "The foundation's probably shot. One good earthquake and you'll be crushed when your house collapses around you. And that's assuming you don't contract some rare flesh-eating disease from the bacteria growing in the bathroom."

She had a point. The bungalow was small, old, dingy and depressing. However... "I asked for a beach view within a reasonable drive of LA for when I need to get down there for filming. Apparently this is what exists in my budget."

"That's terrifying. I feel like I need a tetanus shot just standing in this kitchen."

He shrugged, nodding toward the grimy window over the sink. "It has a view."

"It should be condemned. Maybe you can tear it down and put something decent on the land."

"Tear-downs cost money." He propped a hip against the counter and it lurched beneath him. Jumping clear before it could collapse entirely, he ignored her dubious look.

"Are your finances really this tight? I thought you were supposed to be rich and famous."

"One out of two isn't bad, eh?" When she didn't return his grin, he explained, "I don't like loans."

"You don't like loans?"

"When they cancelled *Brainiac*, we didn't have any warning. One day we're filming as usual and the next I arrived at the studio and was told to go home because I was unemployed. Just like that." He flicked on a faucet, relieved that there was actually water pressure, though the pipes groaned ominously. "I was terrified I was going to have to declare bankruptcy. We'd just bought the beach house and a pair of fancy cars based on what I had expected to be making for the next five years. Then suddenly I was making nothing. We'd tapped out what savings we had on the wedding and honeymoon and now we had a house we couldn't afford and Marissa was still spending like I was made of money—and I felt like I couldn't tell her the money was going to run out because I was supposed to be the bread-winner. That was the deal. So when I got the MMP offer, I jumped at it so fast I probably lost several grand in negotiations, but I was so desperate for a steady paycheck I probably would have worked for less."

Marissa had been happy for him, happy that he was working again, but she never seemed to realize how tight it had been for a while there.

"I paid off the house and the cars and the loan I'd had to ask my parents for when some of the wedding checks bounced—Marissa's mom couldn't afford the kind of wedding she wanted—" Sidney winced and he slammed on the brakes—how did he always end up telling her these things? "What?"

Sidney cleared her expression, but her eyes were dark with sympathy and understanding. "I'm not surprised you started lying to your wife about your financial stability. You know how you're always asking me if I really believe every couple is going to make it? And I say I always hope they will but there are signs? Wedding loans can be a big red flag. The one thing almost every couple fights about is money and if you're putting yourself in debt before you even say I Do, it doesn't always bode well."

"You tell me that now. Where were you seven years ago?"

"College."

He grinned. "Long story short, this is my budget because this is how much cash I have on hand right now, the maximum amount I can spend and still feed myself for a couple years if MMP is cancelled tomorrow and I never get another residuals check."

"I thought celebrities never worried about money."

"Everyone worries about money. Especially when you have an image to maintain if you want to be able to keep working. Project an image of success, be seen in the right places, date the right people—"

"Do you like all of that? The trappings of fame?"

"I don't get off on it like I did when it was new, but I know how to manage it. It doesn't bother me. I'm never going to be one of those celebrities who fought to get famous and now bitches about how everyone wants a piece of them. That's the job."

"And you still want the job?"

He shrugged, wishing he hadn't confessed his misgivings about MMP to her. "It's pretty much the only thing I'm good at. I'd starve if I wasn't the host of MMP."

"I don't believe that for a second. I bet you're one of those guys who could do anything he set his mind to."

"I should hang out with you more often. I like the way you think of me."

"Are we exclusive?"

The sudden question startled him to silence but he rallied quickly with the oh-so-eloquent, "What?"

"I mean I know we can't be seen together in public," she rushed out. "I just want to know where we stand. We haven't talked about whether we would, you know, *again* and... Obviously we aren't a normal couple or even a couple, but sleeping around is a safety issue and if you're sleeping with a bunch of other women, I feel like I have a right to at least know that."

"I'm not," he said bluntly. "And I don't plan to."

"Good." She nodded, blushing fiercely. "Neither do I."

"So we're agreed. We'll tell one another if anyone else enters our lives in that way."

"Yes. Good. That's good." She met his eyes, her cheeks still blazing with a rosy flush. "So we're still..."

"If you'd like to be. I would."

"Right." She swayed back, putting one hand on the

counter to catch herself before she seemed to realize exactly what she was touching and snatched her hand back, snapping to attention. "Do you think we can get out of this kitchen now?"

"Trying to lure me back to your place?" he teased.

"Can you be seen there? The other night your car... Won't someone notice?"

"We're working together on the wedding. Who's to say we aren't working late? I'll just be careful not to leave it parked there overnight." He realized he was getting ahead of himself and pulled back. "That is, if that's okay with you."

"Definitely okay," she said, the breathless edge to her words sending his blood rushing south.

"Okay." He grinned, barely stopping himself from touching her as he waved toward the front of the house where his realtor waited. "Shall we?"

Sidney was officially having a tawdry affair—and loving every second of it.

For three weeks now she'd been seeing Josh in secret, and even though she'd never seen herself as the kind of girl who would be any man's dirty little secret, she had no complaints. If he had to sneak away in the middle of the night, he never left her unsatisfied. And when he dropped in for an afternoon visit... well, it was a good thing planning was going so smoothly for the MMP Wedding and all the others she was working at the moment, because she wasn't spending nearly as many of her afternoons working as she normally did.

He was the best kind of bad influence.

But tonight was Girls' Night In—and no matter how much she might wish she could cancel and call up Josh for their own night in, Girls' Night was sacred.

She just hoped she wasn't going to take any shit for sneaking around with Josh. At least she could use Lorelei as a human shield until her bedtime at nine.

Sidney tromped down the stairs. She was braced for Tori's scorn and Parvati's gossip-hungry glee. What she wasn't prepared for was the sight that greeted her when she opened the door to the apartment.

But then she was never prepared for the sight of her favorite ten-year-old in tears.

Lorelei sat on the couch, sandwiched between Parvati and Victoria, who each had an arm curled around her slim shoulders. They looked helpless and miserable as Lore sobbed with heartbroken wretchedness.

Sidney froze in the doorway, caught between wanting to ask what was wrong and not wanting to make the situation worse if talking about it would only stir it up again. Tori saved her by catching her eye and giving a soft shake of her head before hugging Lore and saying, "Aunt Sidney's here now. Why don't we pick out a suitably male bashing movie for tonight while she and Aunt Parv make us ice cream sundaes rich enough to make us all sick to our stomachs?"

Lore sniffled and wailed something that sounded almost like, "With cookie dough ice cream?" and let herself be led to the cabinet that housed the Jackson family DVD collection as Parv rose and met Sidney en route to the kitchen for sundae duty.

"What happened?" Sidney whispered under her breath as they pillaged the freezer for frozen dairy salvation.

Parvati grimaced. "One of Lore's friends sent around a little note, polling the girls in her class about which boys they thought were the cutest—"

"Oh God, tell me the teacher didn't find it and read it aloud."

"Worse. Her friend's brother took it out of her bag, took a picture of it and shared it on one of those photo-sharing websites where people can like and comment on it. Their parents found out pretty quickly and it's been taken down now, but not before all the boys in Lorelei's class saw it—including Hunter, the one she admitted she has a huge crush on."

Sidney winced in sympathy. "Ouch."

"It gets worse. Apparently he commented."

"Do I want to know?"

"Probably not," Parv admitted as she scooped diabetes-inducing quantities of ice cream into the bowls Sidney had laid out. When Sidney arched her brows in silent question, needing to know exactly what they were dealing with so she didn't imagine things even worse than they were, Parv whispered, "He just said, 'As if.'"

"Oh God." She squirted a liberal layer of chocolate syrup onto the mounds of ice cream.

"Yeah. He's ten and he's an idiot male trying to save face—apparently he's been seen on the swings with Lore and some of the other comments were teasing him about marrying her and having lots of babies, so he was probably reacting to that, but it still sucks for the kiddo. She was at swimming practice when it all went down, so the shit only hit the fan about a half hour ago."

"Poor baby." Sidney sprayed an extra layer of whipped cream on top of Lorelei's already towering sundae.

"Tori's keeping it together, but you can tell she wants to murder anyone who made her baby cry—even if the kid is only ten himself."

"I'd want to go after the brat who posted it."

"I already offered to help hide the body, if it comes to that." Parv held up a banana. "Splits?"

"Definitely."

"Apparently he's already being punished. Tori talked to the parents and they are not taking it lightly. And the school's already heard about it—he might get suspended or even expelled because the new anti-bullying policy is so strict, but either way he's not going to get to go to his basketball camp—or maybe it was hockey? All I know is body burying is probably not going to be necessary to make sure he never does something like this again. But that isn't making Lore feel any better. I think she's partially upset that everyone saw she likes Hunter, but even more crushed that he rejected her so publicly when she thought he was almost her boyfriend. Which he probably was, even though he's scared to admit it. Typical boy."

Sidney resisted the urge to draw a parallel to her own boy who refused to admit he was almost her boyfriend. Lore's crisis trumped everything going on in her life. She busied her hands putting away the sundae makings.

"We've decided on explosions," Tori announced, holding up a special-effects-laden action-fest with little-to-no plot and absolutely no romantic tendencies.

"Perfect," Sidney agreed, before meeting Lore's red eyes with a sympathetic gaze. "You coping, hon?"

"Boys are jerks," Lore said with a sniffle.

"I enthusiastically agree," Parvati declared, sliding a bowl across the counter toward Lore. "Have a banana split."

Lore managed a smile—albeit a weak one—and accepted the sundae which was roughly the size of her head. Sidney collected her own bowl, meeting Tori's gaze with another kind of sympathy as they carried their sugar rushes back to the couch and settled down to watch two hours of pyrotechnics and fight scenes.

Lore stared at the screen, only sniffling once or twice, distracted by the unchecked violence she wasn't normally allowed to watch. When the movie ended, Lorelei headed off to bed and Tori went with her to tuck her in, both of them moving carefully, like their pain was physical.

Parvati and Sidney washed the ice cream bowls in silence, not even speaking when they returned to the couch to wait for Tori, both lost in their own thoughts.

When Tori returned, she collapsed onto the loveseat perpendicular to the couch, her gaze distant, locked on the hallway that led to Lorelei's room. "I'm not ready for this," she murmured softly. "She's a baby. I'm not ready for her to get her heart broken."

"Maybe she won't. Maybe this is just a bump in the road," Sidney said, striving for the optimism that usually came so easily to her.

"She never wants to go to school again and I have to make her." Tori rubbed a hand across her eyes.

Parvati went to sit next to Tori, lacing their fingers together. "She'll be stronger for it."

"She'll have a scar on her heart," Tori murmured. "I wanted her to go through life blissfully untouched by any sort of pain or disappointment, but I should have guessed she'd inherit my taste in men. If there's a man who's going to leave you when the going gets tough, a Jackson woman will fall for him every time."

"He's ten," Parvati argued.

"And so is she," Sidney added. "You don't know what kind of guys she's going to fall for when she grows up."

"It wasn't supposed to happen to her," Tori

sniffled—not crying, Tori never let herself cry, but not far from it. "My father left. Her father left. But she was supposed to be the one to get the happily ever after."

"She's *ten*," Sidney repeated. "Her love life isn't over. And yours doesn't have to be either. You could still get your happily-ever-after. You have to believe that. You plan weddings, for crying out loud."

"I'm organized and I'm good at managing bridezillas. Not all of us got into this business because we see hearts and flowers everywhere we look."

"You're jaded, but deep down you're a romantic just like me," Sidney said with absolute faith. "And so is Lorelei. She's going to bounce back from this. Kids are resilient."

"Even their hearts? I don't want hers so scarred over no one can penetrate it anymore." *Like mine* remained unspoken. "Did I do this to her? Turn her into a mini-me?"

"Hey, you're the best mom I've ever met." Sidney got up and squeezed in beside Parv and Tori on the loveseat, taking Tori's other hand.

"She'd be lucky to be a mini-you," Parvati agreed. "You're smart, you're savvy, you love her to pieces, and you've shown her every day that you don't *need* a man to be happy. That's a lot more than most of us can hope for."

"I just want her to have everything. Even the things I missed out on."

"And she will. But just because we aren't there yet doesn't mean we missed out," Sidney insisted. "We're all going to get our happily-ever-afters. Whether that involves men or not. Especially Lorelei." She squeezed Tori's hand. "We'll accept nothing less. Deal?"

"Yeah." Tori squeezed back. "Deal."

CHAPTER TWENTY-SIX

On a Tuesday night in April, TV's Josh Pendleton sat in his Divorce Guy apartment and decided he was officially done being pathetic.

Admittedly, he'd been pathetic for a long time, but now instead of wallowing self-indulgently in the depths of his own patheticness, he found himself itching with the urge to fish himself out of the mire of lameness he'd fallen into.

It was Sidney's Girls' Night In that threw his life into sharp relief.

He hadn't seen her every day—though he found himself texting her constantly for the most inane reasons—but whenever he had wanted to see her she'd been available. Until tonight.

She'd begged off, citing a prior commitment to her Girls' Night, and he'd been totally cool with it, utterly unbothered—okay, fine he'd still wanted to see her, was more tempted than he cared to admit to try to talk her into seeing him instead, but that seemed like a screaming red flag that he was getting too invested so he kept his mouth shut and wished her a good night. She wasn't his life. He was fine with not seeing her. Fine, damn it.

Until he'd arrived home, sat down in his depressing apartment, realized he'd already caught up on the entire new season of *House of Cards* and was forced to confront exactly how pathetic his life had become.

He didn't have friends.

He used to have friends before he became TV's Josh Pendleton. His frat brothers had been more than just drinking buddies. They really had been more like brothers. And in his early twenties he would spend three or four nights a week hanging out with the guys.

But then he'd met Marissa and his career had taken off and being seen at the right places with the right people had become more important than grabbing a beer with the same guys he saw all the time. Until gradually he wasn't seeing them all the time. And then not at all.

It hadn't bothered him at the time. He'd been growing up. Maturing. That was what people did. He couldn't stay a frat boy forever. So of course he'd spent more time at industry parties, playing the role of TV's Josh Pendleton. He'd loved being that guy. That first shot of fame had been heady and he'd wanted more.

It was only recently that it had begun to taste a little bitter. Only recently that he'd started to be exhausted by the need to play that part all the time. He kind of missed hanging out with the guys and just being Josh.

That part of his life was lost. He wouldn't know how to reconnect with his brothers if he wanted to. He could hardly expect them to still be hanging around the same clubs. Going to the same pub trivia night at Flannigan's every Tuesday night.

For all he knew Flannigan's had probably closed years ago. Although they'd had the best damn burgers within a twenty mile radius and plentiful cheap beer, so the odds were good they were still hanging in there.

Struck by a sudden jolt of nostalgia, Josh grabbed his

car keys and headed out the door, headed back to his old stomping grounds to see if the burgers were still as good and the beer still as cheap as he remembered.

Thirty minutes later he walked through the oh-so-familiar doors of Flannigan's Pub and realized even less had changed than he thought. The lighting was still dark to conceal the stains, the floors were still sticky with spilled beer—and his frat brother Brian, who had been known as High Ball for as long as anyone could remember, was still holding a microphone, hosting the pub trivia contest Flannigan's held every Tuesday night.

High Ball spotted him as soon as he stepped through the door and immediately broke off mid-trivia question with a disbelieving laugh. "Ladies and gentlemen, I'm sorry to interrupt our regularly scheduled programming, but we appear to have a celebrity in our midst. If my eyes do not deceive me, we have been graced by the illustrious presence of Mr. Almost Perfect himself!"

Josh crossed to the podium where High Ball held court, stepping behind it to slap him on the back and receive a bro-hug in return. Only then did he register the cheers and jeers from a nearby table and realize High Ball wasn't the only familiar face on site.

Three of his frat brothers had laid claim to the large corner booth that was considered premium territory during Flannigan's trivia night due to its proximity to both the bar and High Ball's podium where all answers had to be delivered on little slips of paper.

Josh approached, smiling even as he felt a stirring of nerves in his stomach. He wouldn't blame them if they were bitter about his defection. He'd vanished on them, choosing his career over his friendships, and they'd be within their rights to hate him. But the same you're-not-such-hot-shit grins and "How are you, you asshole?" greetings met him when he reached their table.

Tate and Surrey hadn't changed much, but Short Stack had gone entirely bald and looked like he'd aged fifteen years in the last seven—but still no one had ever looked better to Josh as all three of them rose, slapping him on the arm, asking him where the fuck he'd been, and welcoming him home like the freaking prodigal son.

"Hey Carly!" Tate called out to the waitress weaving between the tables. "We need another round. The good stuff this time. Our boy made good. Gotta buy this son of a bitch a beer."

"I should be the one buying the beers," Josh said as he slid into the giant corner booth. "I've got a lot of years to make up for."

"Don't worry, Pretty Boy," Surrey said, using his old college nickname. "The next round's on you."

And so it began.

They didn't pay much attention to the trivia questions High Ball was dishing out—though they heckled him whenever possible in true brotherly fashion. Tate got on his phone and within the hour two more of their brothers had arrived.

Round after round slid down his throat until he knew he'd be taking a cab back to his apartment. It was like coming home again, catching up with these guys he used to know better than he knew his own family. Tate was married for the second time, Short Stack divorced with two kids, while Surrey remained a tom cat with at least five girls on speed dial. Rodriguez—when he arrived after Tate's text—explained that he hadn't been to trivia much lately because he and his wife had just had twin daughters. Homer traveled for business most weeks, but he video chatted with them from Tokyo for a few minutes before he had to go board a plane. Lucas was out of touch, deployed overseas, but they snapped a picture of the rest of them together and emailed it to him in whatever Middle Eastern nation was his current residence.

Everyone had grown up and moved on, but stayed together somehow, and they welcomed him back with open arms. It was a smaller group than the dozen or so that had once made it a weekly tradition, but everyone tried to make it when they could and there were usually three or four guys there every week—even with jobs and families and other obligations pulling at them.

When the pub quiz ended, High Ball joined their table and they grabbed another round before migrating to the dart boards. The bar had cleared out now that the pub quiz was over and they had the area entirely to themselves. Sadly, Josh was still just as shitty at darts as he had always been and the six beers he'd already had weren't helping his aim.

He and High Ball were dueling it out to see who could get the least pathetic score at one of the dart boards. His old buddy rocked back to throw, tossing out an idle comment along with the dart, "We had a bet going, some of us, if you were going to show back up again now that you're divorced."

Josh frowned, running his fingers along his own darts as he waited for his turn. "Do a lot of guys come back to the fold after a divorce?"

High Ball shrugged. "One or two. You just seemed the type."

"What type is that?" Josh asked, unoffended.

"You know. The kind of guy who drops his entire life when he meets a girl to try to be whatever she wants you to be. It was pretty obvious when you met Marissa that she wanted you to be TV Guy, so you became TV Guy. No surprise there. A bunch of us were just betting on whether you'd still be TV Guy now that you aren't with her anymore."

"I'm still TV Guy," he said.

"Yeah, but you're only here with us now because you aren't seeing anyone."

It was on the tip of his tongue to argue that he was seeing someone, but he bit back the words just in time. "Maybe," he admitted, though it bugged him to say it. He wanted to defend himself—and Sidney. He wanted to brag that while he'd tried to become whatever Marissa wanted him to be, he was still himself with Sidney.

He wasn't sure if that had ever been true of any other woman he'd dated. He did have a habit of making himself into whatever his girlfriend wanted him to be— the perfect project boyfriend—but with Sidney he wasn't hiding anything.

And that was scary as hell—but he didn't want to give it up.

Not yet.

CHAPTER TWENTY-SEVEN

"Sidney!"

She opened her eyes, squinting into the dark, wondering if she'd imagined the hoarse call coming from what sounded like the stairwell. She lay in bed, listening in case it came again, and within seconds it did. An odd whispered shout of her name from the stairwell.

In a familiar made-for-television voice.

"Josh?"

She scrambled out of bed, grabbing her wrap and tugging it around her automatically as she rushed to the door before he could increase his volume and alert Victoria and Lorelei to his presence. She peeked through the peep hole and sure enough, there was Josh Pendleton, slanted against the wall on her landing, looking like he was one unruly sway from tumbling headfirst down the stairs.

She opened the door and he lurched away from the wall, his face lighting. "Sidney!"

"Sh!" She caught his arm and steadied him before he could take a header down two flights, pulling him inside before he woke the apartment below.

"I missed you," he declared, slurring in a manner that was entirely too adorable. A man who was staggering drunk should not be attractive in any way, but trust Josh to make it charming somehow. "But 's not cuz I need you to tell me who I am. See!" He spread the lapels of his jacket showing off his chest. "I'm me again."

"Good for you." If by him again he meant falling down drunk. He stumbled against the back of the sofa, barely catching himself before he face-planted into the cushions. "Tell me you didn't drive here in that state."

"O' course not." He drew himself up to his full height, dripping dignified outrage. "I'm *drunk*."

"I noticed."

"Missed you."

"You said that, but drunken booty calls are harder to explain away as wedding planning meetings. This isn't exactly stealthy."

He held up a finger, visibly proud of his own masculine brilliance. "Ah, but this way my car isn't here. So we can spend the night together."

"What about the taxi that drove you here? How can you be sure he won't sell the story to the tabloids?"

"Wasn' a taxi. And high ball can be trusted."

"You realize you aren't making any sense."

He snorted, lurching away from the couch and prowling toward her in a way he probably thought made him look like a panther, but instead made him look like a clown still learning how to walk in the floppy shoes. "*I* am making perfect sense," he declared, stopping inches away from her and tapping her on the nose. "*You* are the one who's..."

He trailed off, seeming to forget the rest of his sentence, and Sidney bit her lip on the urge to laugh, failing to completely contain her grin. "What are you doing here, Josh?"

"I wanted to see you," he said, brown eyes liquid with sincerity and the concentration required to stay on topic. "Marissa makes me TV Guy, but you make me

Josh. I like being Josh."

"I'm glad," she said, completely giving up on making sense of his babble tonight.

He nodded decisively, then his thoughts seemed to slide sideways again and his gaze went blank for a moment.

"Josh? You feeling okay?"

He focused on her again and a little boy grin about melted her heart. "I like you. Even though your eyes are impossible."

"I like you too."

"No, I *like* you."

"I'm glad to hear it."

"You're so *you*. That's what I love..." Her heart fluttered stupidly at the word and he swayed toward her, clearly intending to steal a kiss, but his coordination was a distant memory and he wound up landing a glancing buss on her cheek before lurching to the side and nearly taking them both down, his arms tangled around her.

Sidney choked off a laugh, stabilizing him as best she could. "Okay, Romeo, let's get you to bed before you break something."

Or say something you'll regret.

He twisted in her grip, pointing himself toward the bedroom, and began to sing an off-tune rendition of a song about breaking hearts. Sidney smothered another laugh, wishing she had a video camera to capture this moment for all time. Always cool, always together, always poised Josh Pendleton was a very cute drunk.

She had to wonder how he'd gotten in such a state—even that first night when they'd met, he hadn't approached this level of inebriation—but that was a question that would have to wait until the morning.

There was no way she'd get a sensible answer out of him tonight.

With one of his arms slung over her shoulder, she managed to steer him on an almost steady path to the bedroom. When they reached the small space, he spun toward her—the rapid movement proving too much and he went down onto his side on the bed with a grunt.

"Careful, cowboy. You'd better take it easy." She managed to get his shoes off while he was wrestling with his suit jacket—and losing. He had somehow pinned both of his arms behind his back by the time she had his feet bare.

Wishing again for a video camera, she helped him free his arms and folded his jacket on top of her dresser. When she turned back around, he was battling his belt with more enthusiasm than success. She helped him get the belt off, but then had to stop him before he could strip entirely. "I think you need to sleep it off, hot shot."

"Hey." He caught her around the waist, hauling her down onto the bed with him before she knew what he was about and curling himself around her until she was wrapped in a warm cocoon that smelled of man and beer. "I'm not a hot shot, or a cowboy, or a Romeo," he insisted, with the careful concentration of the deeply drunk. "I'm a Josh. And I like it when you call me Josh. Cuz you make me me." He rolled so they were lying side by side, face to face on the pillows. "You, Sidney Dewitt, are the only woman who makes me me when I'm in love. So do that."

Her heart hitched, seeming to stop for a second before drumming hard. He hadn't just said it. The L word. Twice now. She closed her eyes, reminding herself that he was drunk. Telling herself to keep it together and not get carried away. When she opened her eyes, his face was inches away—

And slack with the sleep of the dead.

Wasn't that just like a man?

Josh's first thought on waking was that this must be what seasickness felt like. Combined with a mild case of plague. The room was spinning and his entire body ached with the kind of fatigue that should only come from running marathons.

And it wasn't his room.

Sidney's bedroom.

He had no memory of how he'd gotten here.

Which was why his second thought on waking was that he was too damn old to be getting blackout drunk.

Then coffee hit his olfactory receptors and Josh groaned with undiluted lust.

"You have to sit up to drink."

Her voice was from right next to the bed and he belatedly realized he'd closed his eyes in self-defense against the spinning. When he cautiously opened them again, the rocky room seemed to have settled down at least enough for him to lever himself up the few inches required to be rewarded with the cup of heaven Sidney held out for him.

It probably wasn't the best coffee in the history of mankind. It just tasted like it.

"You are a goddess," he groaned into the cup.

"Are you talking to me or the coffee?"

"Can it be both?"

She chuckled and sat down on the bed, which bounced his stomach, and Josh cringed as it kept on bouncing around inside him for several uncomfortable seconds until he placated it with another careful sip of java heaven.

"What happened to you last night? I've never seen you that hammered and that includes the night we met. Wild bachelor party?"

"I didn't tell you?" he asked, stalling for time to try to remember himself.

"You were pretty incoherent. Though you did keep telling me you were Josh, so that was reassuring in a way."

He told her what he remembered. "In my quest to overcome my Divorce Guy persona, I reconnected with some old college buddies. We had a few beers... then I seem to remember shots... and very little else." He managed to sit up all the way, cradling the coffee like the nirvana in a cup it was. "I didn't drive here, did I?"

"I don't think so. You were pretty insistent that your car wasn't here. Then you started babbling about drinking high balls and I stopped trying to make sense of it."

"High Ball. That's Brian's nickname. He's not much of a drinker and tends to wind up as our de facto designated driver. I must have given him your address instead of mine." A decision he wasn't going to examine until he was fully sober. If ever. "I don't suppose I can persuade you to give me a ride back to my car? I can call a taxi, but being picked up at dawn at your place is exactly the kind of thing the tabloids would love if someone recognized me."

"I can make time this morning. Cowboy."

There was a certain emphasis to the last word that had him wincing. "God, I didn't do some sort of rodeo act, did I?"

Something that might have been disappointment moved behind her eyes, but it was gone so fast he was certain it was a fabrication of his incoherent mind.

"No," she said. "Nothing like that." She stood, moving to the dresser. "I'll just get dressed and then we can return you to your own world."

"You're a life saver."

If she was bothered by his casual tone, she didn't show it as she gathered up some clothes and moved to the bathroom to change. He'd seen her naked dozens of times, but he was glad she didn't do anything as intimate as dress in front of him this morning. That was too relationshipy.

He hadn't intentionally used the coffee as a shield, but it had been a convenient prop. The lack of kissing had been intentional. In part because he probably had the world's most revolting hangover breath and in part because waking up in her bed, after she saw him at his worst the night before, he needed to put some boundaries back up.

Friends with benefits was one thing, but they were crossing all sorts of lines lately until he wasn't sure where they were anymore. Distance was best. At least in the harsh light of the morning after.

He had no idea what he'd said or done the night before—and he wasn't going to ask. This was fun and chemistry. Nothing more. And it was past time he remembered that.

Sidney frowned at Josh's gorgeous muscular back until it disappeared inside his Beamer, trying to figure out exactly why she felt simultaneously better and worse about being his secret mistress than she had just twenty-four hours before.

She pulled out of the parking lot on auto-pilot,

headed back north toward Eden as Josh headed back to the apartment she'd never seen and whatever he had planned for the rest of the day. He didn't share his life with her. He wasn't opening up. If anything, this morning he'd been even more distant and standoffish than ever.

But last night...

Last night he'd said the L word. Twice. Admittedly he hadn't said it quite the way a girl dreamed of hearing it. As in preceded by I and followed by you. But it was a start. A step. Some little indication that told her she wasn't alone in getting caught up in whatever it was they were doing together.

She'd liked having him wake up in her bed far too much. She'd liked everything he said to her the night before—when he was rambling incoherently. But was it *in vino veritas*? Or had he not been himself?

If this morning was anything to go by, it was the latter.

He didn't seem to remember anything he'd said the night before. Or if he did remember, he was doing an excellent job of pretending he didn't.

But a man didn't just throw around the L word if he wasn't feeling *something*. Even if he was drunk out of his mind.

Did he?

She needed to stop thinking about it. She needed to forget the L word accidents and remember how cool and businesslike he'd been this morning. And most of all she needed to remember that regardless of his feelings or hers, he would still lose his job and she would lose her reputation if anyone found out they were sneaking around together.

Secrecy might be exciting, but it wasn't true love.

Those words became her mantra as she drove home to start her day.

CHAPTER TWENTY-EIGHT

The road to hell was paved with high-end travertine pavers, Sidney thought as she pulled into her parents' driveway, pausing at the gate to punch in the code. She'd originally planned to spend this Saturday—a rare non-wedding weekend—with Josh.

Two days after The Incident, as she'd started thinking of the night he showed up at her place drunk, he'd called her and asked her to meet him on the weekend to look at more houses in his seemingly never-ending quest for someplace livable with a killer view, but fate had intervened in the form of a contract issue for *Marrying Mister Perfect*. So she still hadn't seen him since That Night and now he was down in Los Angeles negotiating terms while she prepared for an even more arduous experience—having lunch with her mother at the Dewitt Estate.

Thank God her brother Max would be there to take some of her mother's microscopic focus off her, though her father was once again traveling for business. No surprise there.

Sidney pulled past the gate and up the long winding drive, parking her SUV beside the latest in her brother's ever-changing sequence of muscle cars. She let herself into the house, unsurprised to find her brother alone in the sunroom when she arrived—their mother doubtless delayed by some urgent work matter, even though it was Saturday.

"Ahoy, Maximus."

He looked up from his phone, pocketing it as he stood. "Well, if it isn't little Sidney. I hear you're poised to become the next big thing in reality television wedding planners."

She went in for a hug, swallowed up by his massive frame. "Where did you hear that?"

"Oh, I have my sources."

She didn't doubt that. For the last couple years her brother had been making his living providing specialized bodyguards for celebrity clients. And celebrities loved to gossip. They traded in hearsay like it was currency.

Her brother released her and flopped back down on the overstuffed sofa, his muscular bulk taking up most of the space. Sidney perched on a chair opposite, keeping her back straight in case her mother appeared unannounced.

It should have been easy to hate Max. He was her opposite in every way. Favoring their father with his darker coloring and slate colored eyes, he also favored their father in that success seemed to follow him wherever he went.

Where Sidney struggled and flailed, Max moved through life with easy purpose, achieving anything he wanted. While she worried about what others thought, Max was blithely unconcerned with the opinions of others—not that he had anything to worry about. Everyone adored him. Especially Parvati, who liked to offer herself up to Max as an egg-donor if he should ever decide to reproduce. Not that he would lack for volunteers. Even as his sister, she could acknowledge—

in a purely platonic way—that he was a handsome devil.

Max was the golden boy. And she would have been bitterly jealous if he hadn't also been the best brother on the planet, staunchly taking her side without question and loving her without condition. He never made her feel judged, even when she'd felt like the rest of the world looked down on her for her size.

They approached life in opposite directions, but somehow he always managed to find her in the middle. If only things were so easy with her mother.

"How's the business?" she asked him, offering the typical Dewitt greeting.

"Busy." Max beamed, flashing bright white teeth offset by his tan. He launched into a description of his two most recent hires, glowing with pride that his business was expanding yet again, and waxing poetic on the joys of success until a voice sharp with disapproval heralded their mother's arrival.

"That isn't how a gentleman sits, Maximus."

Max rolled to his feet, grinning his charming get-away-with-everything grin, and went to the doorway to hug their mother. "What's for lunch?" he asked her, completely unfazed by her scowl—which was already fading into an indulgent smile.

"Lamb," she replied. "A specialty of my new chef. She's a treasure."

Sidney stood to greet her mother, standing straight for her perusal. "Mother."

"Sidney, you're looking slim. It must be a relief to have that whole *Marrying Mister Perfect* business behind you."

Sidney held onto her brittle smile and hummed something noncommittal as she followed her mother toward the formal dining room, Max trailing in their wake. She'd avoided her parents since the show began airing—which had proved easy to do since they both worked eighty-hour weeks and traveled constantly—but she should have known she couldn't avoid it today. Of course it would be her mother's first topic of conversation. Or interrogation, as tended to be the case when they had lunch.

The pretty new chef had barely set the soup course in front of them before her mother asked in her coolly judgmental way, "Have you seen an increase in traffic through your little shop since you put yourself on display on national television?"

"Some," Sidney admitted. "And I expect there will be even more after the wedding special airs."

Her mother looked up from her bisque. "What's this? You're not going back on television, are you?"

"Actually we start filming in a couple days. It's a special about the planning of Caitlyn's wedding. I'll be front and center, advertising Once Upon a Bride. You can't buy exposure like that."

"I can't imagine why anyone would want to," Marguerite said dryly. "Those shows are the lowest common denominator of entertainment. Are those viewers really your target demographic?"

"Romantics who might be looking for ideas for their own weddings? Yes. That's exactly my demographic, Mother."

"It just doesn't seem very dignified."

"Well, your company's erectile dysfunction commercials aren't very dignified either, but they get the job done."

"Sidney." Disapproval saturated her mother's tone.

Sidney found herself ducking her head and staring at her bisque contritely. The silence lasted only a few seconds before her mother embarked on another delightful conversational foray.

"Did that show at least help your romantic life as you'd hoped it would?" her mother prodded. "Are you seeing anyone?"

The show had certainly helped her love life—or at least her sex life—but she couldn't tell her mother that. And she didn't even want to hint vaguely at someone special when things with Josh were so unsettled. "No one serious."

"I am entirely single. If anyone was wondering," Max chimed in helpfully. Her mother's personal chef had returned to clear their bowls and Max winked at her as she took his, earning a glare from their mother.

"Don't flirt with my new chef, Maximus."

He dimpled for their mother, completely lacking contrition. "I can't help it if I'm irresistible."

"You'd better help it if you ever want to dine here again," Marguerite threatened.

Max's reply was typically unrepentant, but at least it took the conversation away from Sidney and her lack of love life, among other shortcomings.

Somehow with Max running interference they made it through the rest of lunch without a reappearance of the Spanish Inquisition. After they polished off the raspberry tarts, their mother excused herself with a brisk apology, retreating back to her home office, and Max walked Sidney out.

"Thanks for heading off the interrogation in there," she said as they stepped out into the sunny afternoon. "I couldn't handle her judgment today."

Max frowned, hesitating on his way over to his Mustang. "I know it's none of my business and I try to stay out of it, but has it occurred to you that maybe she isn't judging you when she asks you all those questions? That maybe she's just curious about your life?"

"She has a funny way of showing it."

"She doesn't know how to talk to you. And you aren't exactly forthcoming. How else is she supposed to find out about what you're up to if she doesn't ask? And yes, I know she sucks at asking tactfully," he said before Sidney could complain about her mother's manner. "But she's used to being the boss of everyone and demanding answers. That's just who she is. But at least she's trying."

"Easy for you to say. You're the golden boy. They never interrogate you."

"I talk to them," he said flatly, leaning against the side of his car and folding his arms. "I know this might shock you, but they don't need to grill me because I actually like telling them what's going on in my life. I like asking them for advice about the business and running things by them when I want to make a big decision like where to live or what to do with my life. You just spring things on them after the fact and get defensive when they ask questions."

"So you're saying it's my fault I have a shitty relationship with my parents."

"Don't be a brat," Max said with typical older brother bluntness. "I didn't say that. And it isn't all your fault. Mom doesn't understand you at all and has no freaking idea how to talk to you without coming across as a disappointed dictator—that's on her. But you aren't making it any easier for her and that's on you."

"So I'm supposed to just smile and nod when she says I'm pandering to the lowest common denominator by trying to promote my business on national television? I'm supposed to ignore the fact that the only compliment she ever gives me is that I look thin—which just makes me angry because her love is conditional on my size."

"Her love isn't conditional—"

"Of course not. That's why she was always trying to fix me. Always putting me on another diet and heaping on another helping of guilt."

"I know that was awful for you, growing up. And you're right, she is always trying to fix everyone and everything. But she's also proud of you for losing the weight. And she wants to talk about the things that are important to you, but she doesn't know how. So she says stupid shit because she's trying to help. She knows you want to get married, so she asks about your love life and you get prickly. She worries about you. She worried about you going on the show because she didn't want you to get hurt."

"Then why was she so disappointed when I quit?"

"Because she doesn't understand why you would. I think you mistake her confusion for disappointment."

"And I think you're assigning shiny happy motives to everything she says out of wishful thinking. She treats me like I'm a failure in everything I do, Max. Like I will always be the pudgy girl who wasn't worth showing off to her friends. That isn't in my head."

"Do you think you are?"

"What? Of course not."

"No one can make you feel inferior without your consent. So are you?"

"Are you quoting Eleanor Roosevelt at me?"

"If the shoe fits."

She glared at her brother. "It's easy for you to talk about failure and inferiority. You've never failed at anything in your life. Some of us aren't perfect, Max."

He laughed. "You seriously think I'm perfect? I fail all the time, Sid. But I don't define myself by the mistakes I've made."

"And I do?"

"You tell me."

She locked her jaw. Not wanting to examine whether or not he was right.

She hated when he was right. But this was more than that. She didn't want to admit that all of her fear of failing her parents stemmed from a feeling that *she* thought she wasn't good enough. And she never had. She'd lost the weight, but she was still the disappointment.

So who was she trying to prove herself to? Them? Or herself?

Max seemed to realize he'd pushed her as far as she was willing to go today. His easygoing demeanor returned as he rocked back against his car. "Hey, what do I know? I'm just the hired muscle."

She lunged for the change in topic with undignified speed. "You'll be at the MMP wedding, right? Like we talked about?"

"Of course. We've gotta make sure you're a paparazzi free zone." He straightened, pulling his keychain out of his pocket and jangling it. "Don't worry. I'm bringing two of my guys and the MMP people are letting me boss around their guys too. It'll be Fort Knox."

He turned to get into the car and she stopped him. "Max. Thanks." She wasn't even sure what she was thanking him for—the security? Telling her to get her head out of her ass and stop feeling inferior all the time?

He shrugged, hauling open the door to his car. "What are brothers for?"

CHAPTER TWENTY-NINE

Her brother's words—and Eleanor Roosevelt's—haunted her for the rest of the weekend. It had always been convenient to blame her mother for her feelings of inadequacy—she was such a handy target—but it wasn't her mother's goals that she was failing to achieve now. Her mother didn't care if she was married. Her mother didn't care if Once Upon a Bride made some list. Sidney did. Her mother cared about success in general, but those particular metrics, the ones that always made Sidney feel like she had come up short in life—she'd come up with those all on her own.

But the trouble with coming up with your own definition of success was that when you failed you had no one to blame but yourself.

She should have made being on television one of her life goals. Then at least she'd be succeeding in that.

Today was the first day of filming for the Wedding Special. Which meant she would see Josh, but with camera crews present she wouldn't be able to clear the air about any residual weirdness lingering after That Night.

She was due at the estate at nine, when she and Josh would be filming their "first look" at the venue. Later in the week they would be filming a few less suitable venue options, which would be edited into a Goldilocksesque montage before they found the one that was just right. But today her job was to guide Josh through the beach house, explaining her vision for the wedding—flowers here, altar there, reception here, band there—with Josh providing color commentary.

The producers and camera crews would already be on site when she got there. This afternoon they'd film at Once Upon a Bride. Victoria had elected to make herself scarce rather than sign the waivers to appear in the special. She seemed convinced she would say something she shouldn't on national television and she didn't want Lore on television, so the two of them would be avoiding the main showroom at Once Upon a Bride for the next few days while Sidney and Josh shot all the preliminary interior footage—essentially explaining to the cameras over and over again where they would be going and what they would be doing.

And throughout the week they had appointments to revisit all of the vendors hired for the wedding. Eager for the free publicity, the caterer and bakery had both agreed to do a special round of tastings just for the benefit of the camera crews. Then they would visit the florist, make a show of picking up the invitations and designing the programs, and even pretend to audition a handful of bands before "finding" the one they had already booked.

The work of two months would be filmed in one marathon week.

All part of the magic of television.

She pulled through the gate of the estate at a quarter to nine, following the gate guard's directions to park beside a trio of cargo and passenger vans. She climbed out of her SUV, smoothing the wrinkles out of her skirt nervously as she headed toward the front door—which had been propped open.

Part of her—stupidly—hoped that she'd be able to catch Josh alone, but when she stepped inside the first person she saw was a slim, dark-haired woman with the intense, slightly-manic air of a producer.

"Sidney! You're early! Aren't you a champ? Let's get you into hair and makeup." The producer caught her arm and began to steer her rapidly through the massive main house, power-walking alongside. "I'm Dani. We spoke on the phone and I'm the one sending you all those emails. I'm very thorough." She laughed abruptly, as if she'd made a joke and Sidney smiled awkwardly. "I'll be playing EP this week—sort of my little audition—so we're just going to keep everything running smoothly, aren't we? Okay? And here's Eunice."

Dani handed her off to the hair and makeup people, who fussed over her cheerfully for the next half hour while the chair beside hers remained conspicuously empty. Where was Josh?

The maestros of hair and makeup released her, pointing her toward another room where she obediently changed out of her own pastel skirt suit and into the pastel skirt suit they had chosen for her. She emerged, received nods of approval from the wardrobe consultants—and still Josh was nowhere to be seen.

She returned to the front of the house, where camera crews were setting up the first shot, and there he was.

He looked entirely too good—and his eyes passed over her without even pausing as he called out a cheerful, "Hey, Sidney."

"Hey."

She joined him at a craft services table behind the cameras, but before she could grab a coffee Dani appeared and directed them to the front door.

"Remember, this is your first time seeing the place. We just need you to verbalize all the reasons why it's perfect as you walk in. Remember that the other places were too small or too ostentatious…"

"Or smelled of fish," Sidney muttered under her breath.

"What was that?" Dani chirped.

"Nothing. I'm all set."

"Great! And just remember Josh is here for you, so really use him. Play off him. Really let a natural rapport develop. Flirty, argumentative—feel free to play around with different dynamics and we'll see what works. Okay? Okay!"

Dani hustled back out of the shot and Josh moved up to stand beside her.

"You ready for this?" he asked with his trademark perfect TV smile. But again his gaze passed right over her. *TV's Josh Pendleton, ladies and gentlemen.*

Sidney slapped on a smile. This wasn't about Josh. This was about Once Upon a Bride and she was a professional, damn it. "I was born ready."

"Mmm, that is positively orgasmic."

"And I think we have a winner, folks." Josh's deep chuckle dripped with sensual promise.

Sidney opened eyes she had closed to truly savor the raspberry Chantilly cake. "I *know* this one will be Caitlyn's favorite," she said with absolute confidence fueled by the fact that Caitlyn had tasted this exact cake last month and declared it beyond heavenly. "We'll do alternating tiers of this one and that decadent gluten-free chocolate."

"Perfect. Now we may have made our decision, but we can't let the rest of these cakes go to waste," Josh said, his eyes glinting. He scooped up a giant forkful of the lemon chiffon and wagged it in front of her face.

"Nice try, but I'm immune to your temptation," she teased. "My heart belongs to the raspberry Chantilly."

"You don't know what you're missing." That wicked spark glittered in his eyes—so much naughtier than he usually employed with his flawless made-for-TV smile—and he shoveled the heaping bite into his mouth, groaning contentedly. "Delicious," he declared after he made a show of slowly chewing and swallowing. He licked the last of the buttercream from the fork—and Sidney stared, envying the fork.

"Cut! That's perfect. I love the bit with the temptation. Sidney, Josh, we're done with you two for the day if you want to take off." Dani dismissed them, turning to the cameramen to instruct them to get some nice panning shots over the display cases at Sweet Indulgences.

Sidney set down her fork without tasting the light raspberries and cream cake, her appetite vanishing as Josh's expression went from charmingly wicked to blank and distant in point two seconds.

Sweet Indulgences Specialty Bakery was their last stop on the fourth day of filming and the producers were in raptures—especially Dani. Apparently she and Josh had electric chemistry, the kind of natural rapport that money couldn't buy. He made it easy—she was never awkward in front of the camera with him, or even aware of them. Dani practically clapped with glee every time they flirted and bantered for the cameras. She teased them, asking them if they were *sure* they weren't attracted to one another—and Sidney would have been worried that the jig was up, except all that lovely chemistry evaporated every time the cameras stopped rolling.

Josh's expression just died, going flat and blank, and he still seemed incapable of looking at her when they weren't on camera. She would think it was all an act for the crew's benefit—but he hadn't called her once and she kept getting his voicemail, he never dropped by after hours, and even when it would have been convenient for them to drive between locations together, he had avoided being alone with her.

And it was getting harder and harder to tell herself that everything was okay.

The cameras began to move, filming the cakes on display and Sidney got out of the way, moving to the far side of the small tasting room to collect her purse. If it happened to be near where Josh was standing—well, that was just a convenient coincidence.

"Any big plans for tonight, Pendleton?" she asked, mindful of the fact that half the crew could hear them.

"Just a movie premiere and few after parties," he said, the same way another man might say *sitting on the couch, watching a game and drinking a beer*. "Olga keeps me busy."

Sidney managed not to cringe, reminding herself it was all an act. He wasn't really *with* Olga. Or at least he hadn't been. Was he throwing his imaginary girlfriend in her face now for a reason?

No one can make you feel inferior without your consent. So why was she giving it to him?

But before she could find a way to get him alone and have it out with him, an authoritative voice cut across the low mumblings of the crew at work.

"Don't tell me I missed all the fun."

Miranda Pierce stood in the doorway—and Dani jumped as if she'd been tazed. "No, no, we're just finishing up here. Right on schedule and under budget. Everything is great. Have you seen the footage? Fun stuff, really fun!"

"I saw," Miranda drawled, her eagle-sharp gaze finding Josh and Sidney in the corner. "That's why I wanted to come see for myself."

"Well, as you can see, everything's under control!" Dani enthused.

Sidney sidled closer to Josh, asking under her breath, "Why does Dani look like she's about to puke on Miranda's Jimmy Choos?"

"She wants Miranda's job," he said, meeting Miranda's gaze across the room, a frown tangling his brow. "This is her audition and Miranda's vote will count for a lot—all of the junior producers are sucking up hardcore in the hope of getting her recommendation."

"I'm surprised no one is sucking up to you. Doesn't your recommendation mean anything?"

"Me? I'm just the talent. They fawn all over the talent, but your opinion doesn't actually mean anything."

"I thought you were producing."

"Which just meant I followed you around and said, 'Let's shoot here' and 'The network will approve this.' Everyone's a producer in this town. And now my job is to go where they tell me and be charming on cue—beyond that they don't really care what I think. And speaking of being charming on cue, I have a premiere to get ready for. See ya tomorrow, Sidney."

"I'll walk out with you," she said, louder than necessary.

The tiny parking lot of Sweet Indulgences overflowed with crew vans, so Sidney had parked down the street at Once Upon a Bride and walked, but Josh's silver convertible was sandwiched between two of the large white vans. He didn't react when she followed him into the small lot.

She waited until they were hidden by the vans before speaking, keeping her voice low because there was still a crew not thirty feet away, filming exteriors. "Are we okay?"

"We?" He turned to face her, his eyes blank. "We're fine. Why?"

She knew he couldn't show his feelings in front of the crew, but they were alone now and the least he could do was look her in the eye. But even facing her he seemed to look through her.

She was done playing games. "Because you've been fake with me all week and you can't seem to look me in the eye since you woke up at my place."

His gaze darted to the left and the right as he stepped closer, bending his head and lowering his voice. "I know I should apologize again for showing up at your place drunk like that—"

"I'm not looking for an apology. But I wouldn't mind an explanation as to why we're suddenly back to where we were two months ago."

"Sidney, we're filming. We can't be—"

"I know. I know. We have to be careful in front of the crew, but is it more than that? Did I do something?"

"No, of course not. It's only..." He hesitated. "I don't know. I guess I thought we'd pretty much run our course anyway."

Ouch. "So you vanished and that was it. Is that why you canceled on Saturday?"

"No. I was busy Saturday. I haven't lied to you. Things are just—work is fucked up right now with Miranda leaving the show and no one willing to sign on as Miss Right. We were supposed to start filming in a couple weeks, but everything's been pushed back now. And when we do start filming, I'll be gone, so I didn't figure a few weeks one direction or another really mattered."

"And I don't get a say?"

"What was there to say? We were never really official to begin with."

Double ouch. He'd practically said he loved her just a week ago and now he was acting like she was a convenient booty call. *No one can make you feel inferior...*

"You could have at least done me the courtesy of sending me a brush-off text message to let me know we were done," she snapped.

"You're right. I'm sorry. I was waiting for things to fade away naturally, but I should have said something."

He'd expected them to fade away. She'd been falling in love and he'd been fading. She swallowed around the thickness in her throat, fighting to keep her composure. "You're probably right. You have the new season coming up and I'll be crazy busy as soon as the special airs. And the *Veil* list comes out in a few weeks. If we're on it, you know how nuts things will get."

"Exactly." He smiled, but his relief seemed false. "Though if you decide you'd like some extra exposure and want to be the next Miss Right, we'd still love to have you."

She felt like she'd been sucker punched. "You're asking me if I'll be Miss Right?"

"Well, we need one and your name keeps coming up. And you don't seem as uncomfortable on camera anymore."

His words buzzed in her ears, incomprehensible. "Do you want me to be Miss Right?"

"I'm not going to stand in your way if that's what you want. It could be a great opportunity for you—"

He kept talking and she wondered how the producers would react if he showed up for filming the next day with a fat lip because she had punched him to get him to shut up. "It doesn't matter to you? You'd be totally fine if your job was to help me find my dream guy?"

He shrugged. "It's what I'm good at."

She didn't think he was trying to hurt her—but somehow that made it that much worse. If he'd been a malicious prick, that was one thing, but he was getting out of the way of her happiness—which would have been great if she wasn't realizing with shattering certainty that she was in love with the idiot.

"I have to go."

Hugging her arms tight to her body, she walked away before he could stop her—but he didn't even try. She'd known from the start that he wasn't a forever guy, but her heart had tricked her into forgetting. Just another case of seeing Prince Charming when all along she'd been kissing a frog.

But why did kissing frogs have to hurt so much?

CHAPTER THIRTY

That had not gone well. But it had gotten the job done.

Josh stared after Sidney, his chest aching, waiting for the certainty that he'd done the right thing to take hold. But for some reason what he felt when he watched her walk away felt a lot more like regret. All week he'd been off. He knew putting distance between them was the right thing to do, but it had felt so wrong.

"Josh, you idiot. How long have you been sleeping together?"

Somehow he wasn't surprised to see Miranda standing at the front bumper of his car when he turned around. "I don't know what you're talking about."

"Nice try," she said, though the tone said *Don't insult my intelligence.*

"Is it obvious?"

"It's in the footage. Though I think I'm the only one who's noticed."

"You always did see more than anyone else. The Suitorette Whisperer." And now she was leaving, just another thing making his life feel wrong and off-balance. "You sure you wanna leave all this?"

"Sure? Never. But certainty's overrated." Miranda cocked her head, her gaze intent and direct behind her glasses. "You sure you wanna stay? Because if you do, you might want to look into having that morality clause rewritten before you sign anything."

"It doesn't matter anymore. It's over."

Miranda snorted. "The way you looked at her when she was walking away? That isn't over. I don't know what that is, but it isn't over."

Josh fished his keys out of his pocket. "I should go. I've got a thing to get to."

"Do you love her?"

His head snapped around. "Of course not."

"Does she love you?"

"It's over, Miranda."

"She looked upset. Were you a dick? Never mind. Of course you were."

"Aren't you supposed to forbid me from seeing her?"

"Is that what you want me to do? So you don't have to man up and own your feelings?" She held up a hand as if to stop him, but he wasn't speaking. "Never mind. I'll just leave you with this. I've known you for a lot of years and I never once saw you look at Marissa with half the feeling you had watching Sidney walk away. I have been in this business for a long time. Long enough to see a *lot* of people trying to force themselves into feelings they don't have—talking themselves both into and out of love—and the one thing I've learned is that the real deal is rare. But you don't mock the fates when they see fit to give it to you, because they don't give many second chances."

"I'll keep that in mind. Now if you'll excuse me, I have a date with Olga."

"Excellent. Try to act surprised when she breaks up with you."

Josh froze in the act of getting into his car. "What?"

"That role she landed because you helped rehab her image? Turns out she's started having an affair with the director and they think it will help the box office down the road if they go public with it—so she needs to be well clear of you before all that comes out, strategically timed around the premiere."

Josh stared. "Do you ever think this business is insane?"

"All the time." Miranda grinned. "Isn't it great?"

He'd used to think so. Now he wasn't as sure.

Josh climbed in his car, fired it up and looked at the clock. He'd have to hurry if he was going to have time to get cleaned up before the premiere. He had a break-up to get to—and since the pictures were likely to be in every tabloid in America, he'd better look good.

Sidney took it as a personal victory that she didn't shed a single tear in her march down Main Street toward Once Upon a Bride.

She opened the door and called out, "It's just me!" toward the back office—hoping that Victoria would be so engrossed in whatever she was doing that she wouldn't emerge from her lair and Sidney could slip upstairs unnoticed.

But her luck was consistent, if nothing else. Victoria appeared seconds later and her face instantly tightened with concern, proving Sidney wasn't keeping it together nearly as well as she'd hoped.

"What's wrong?"

"I don't want to talk about it." She headed toward the back stairs, already regretting that she hadn't snuck around the building to come in through the parking lot and avoided Victoria entirely. She loved her friend, but right now she could do without the reminder that she'd been an idiot and Victoria had seen it coming.

Tori trailed behind her, keeping pace. "It's Josh, isn't it? What did he do?"

"I really don't want to talk about it, Tori."

Victoria blocked the way when she would have started up the stairs. "Sidney."

Sidney stopped trying to evade her. "You were right, okay? Get your I-told-you-sos ready."

There was no satisfaction on Tori's face. Only understanding and sympathy that made Sidney feel like even more of a brat for snapping at her. "What was I right about?" she asked gently.

"Me. Josh. Getting hurt."

Her voice broke on the last word and Tori stepped forward to envelop her in a lavender-scented hug. "Oh honey, I didn't want to be right."

As soon as Tori's arms closed around her, the last of her resistance broke and Sidney sank onto the steps in a defeated heap, half-dragging Tori down with her.

"I wasn't supposed to fall for him." She propped her elbows on her knees and dropped her forehead onto her palms. "I knew it was a fling. Impossible for it to be more. So why can't I make myself feel as little for him as I'm supposed to? So we're done. Why does it matter?" Pressing on her temples felt good, so she did it harder, trying to push all the hurt back inside, as if she could cram the unwieldy feeling bursting out of her brain back into place.

"Should I break out the ice cream?" Tori offered. "We don't have any more appointments today. We can close up early and watch *The Expendables* until our eyeballs burn."

"I don't need ice cream or action movies," Sidney insisted, lifting her head and turning to face one of her very best friends in the whole wide world. "Why aren't you gloating?"

"You're my sister," Tori said simply, ignoring the obstacle of basic genetics. "I'd rather be wrong and have you be happy."

"I let myself believe he was my Prince Charming, but he was just using me and I was letting him. I can't even blame him because I knew exactly what I was getting myself into. I was his accomplice."

He couldn't be with her because of the show, but when he'd said he wasn't sure he liked his job anymore, a tiny part of her had hoped that he would leave MMP for her. She'd spun that dream out of thin air, telling herself it was possible, but she'd just been fooling herself.

"Don't blame yourself. At least you followed your heart. That's more than I ever do."

"A lot of good it did me."

"Hey." Tori nudged her shoulder with hers. "This is a bump in the road to your happily ever after, right? Isn't that what you're always telling Parv when she meets another dud? You'll find someone who deserves you. Someone who is crazy about you and treats you right."

"That's the problem. I can't even look at someone who might deserve me because all I want is him. That's what happened on *Marrying Mister Perfect*."

"Well, the first step is ending it. Now you just need to get over it and then you can get down to the business of picking the right guy."

"He asked me if I wanted to be the next Miss Right. Can you believe that?"

"He's a dick."

"He didn't mean it like that."

"I don't care how he meant it. He's a dick." Then Tori

paused, her ivy eyes going distant. "Are you going to?"

"No." But then the idea rolled through her brain. "Maybe. No. Only if he isn't the host."

"You could make that a stipulation—"

Before Sidney could explain that she hadn't meant it, the back door burst open and Lorelei bolted inside. "Mom!" she shouted, her backpack bouncing on her shoulders as she sprinted to where they sat at the foot of the stairs. Sidney swiped quickly at her cheeks, relieved to find them dry.

"He kissed me!" Lorelei squealed with unchecked glee.

Tori visibly paled. "What?"

"Hunter! Hunter Fraser! He kissed me by the swings in front of everyone! *And* he held my hand on the way back from recess!"

"My baby has a boyfriend," Tori moaned under her breath before rising to hug Lorelei. "That's great, sweetie. But if he tries to get more than a kiss, you just tell him I have a shot gun and I'm not afraid to use it."

"*Mo-om*," Lore groaned, embarrassed as only a preteen daughter could be.

Sidney stood to offer her congratulations as well—shoving down the stupid pang of envy that wanted to rise up. A ten-year-old boy wasn't afraid to show his affection in public. He was proud to be Lorelei's boyfriend—and why shouldn't he be?

Didn't she deserve as much?

"Josh, you know I love you, but why do you insist on making my life difficult?"

"Hey, Harry." Josh panted into his hands-free headset, not slowing his pace on the treadmill as his agent bitched in his ear. "What have I done now to damage your zen?"

"It's what you haven't done. Would you like to explain to me why you're still dragging your feet on signing the extension contracts?"

"I'm not dragging my feet. I just haven't gotten around to it." He had a month before the contractual deadline to sign them and the next season of *Romancing Miss Right* looked like it was going to be pushed back anyway, so it had been easy to put off. "What's the big hurry all of a sudden?"

"The big hurry is they're talking about replacing you and we don't have a signed contract in hand."

"What?" Josh stumbled, catching himself on the side bars of the treadmill before he did a facer onto the spinning belt. He braced his feet on the side panels and slapped the emergency stop. "Are you screwing with me? Since when are they looking at someone else?"

"They aren't talking to anyone yet, but apparently the new Suitorette they're considering for the next Miss Right is asking for a different host. Did you do something to piss her off?"

Dread tightened his gut. "Which Suitorette is it now?"

"That Sidney girl."

He was glad he wasn't still running because the words hit him hard enough to knock him down if he had been. Even though he'd been half-expecting them. "I thought she wasn't interested in doing the show."

He'd meant it when he told her she'd be great as Miss Right—but the thought of coaching her through her romance with thirty other men still went down like acid. He didn't want her dating anyone else, but he didn't have any right to be possessive. He couldn't have her and he wanted her to be happy, so he'd man up and host her fairy tale romance if that was what she wanted.

Except apparently she didn't want him anywhere near her.

"All I know is she's talking to them," his agent said. "And they're talking to me about why you haven't signed. So what's the hold up?"

"There's no hold up."

"Good. Then sign. And make peace with the Suitorette. You're the most likeable man in show business. I don't want the producers to start questioning that because you ruffled some reality diva's feathers."

"She isn't a reality diva."

"It doesn't matter who she is," Harry said with his usual tact. "All that matters is that we get you locked in for four more years before the network starts asking questions about why little Miss Right doesn't want you hosting her season. So work it out."

"I will," Josh promised. But when he disconnected the call, he just stabbed the button to resume his workout on the treadmill, the pounding rhythm of his feet doing little to erase his tension like it usually did.

The contract would keep for another few hours. And Sidney?

He couldn't call her. There was nothing he could say that would magically make the situation better. They'd both let their off-the-books relationship get a little too real. It was time to get back to reality and talking about it more wasn't going to make it any easier for either of them.

And if she wanted to be Miss Right…and she didn't want him anywhere near her while she was doing it… he wasn't going to fight her on it.

It had been a week since they'd wrapped shooting on

the special. After the wedding they would add in some still photos of the final product and some voice-over descriptions of the event, but all the work they had to do together was done. He didn't have any reason to see her again until the big day.

Josh put his head down and ran, sweating through the miles on his treadmill. Better that he stayed away. A clean break.

It didn't matter if he missed her.

CHAPTER THIRTY-ONE

The day the *Veil* list would be published dawned sunny and clear—which considering it was Southern California wasn't much of a shock but Sidney decided to take it as a good omen anyway. She would take good signs anywhere she could get them today.

The issue would be posted online any minute, but she and Victoria had made a pact that they were going to look together and somehow Sidney resisted the urge to sneak a peek on her tablet as she got dressed, barely aware of what she put on.

They had to have made the list. Everything they'd done in the last year to raise the profile of Once Upon a Bride must have paid off.

She hit the showroom at seven-forty—nearly two hours before their usual nine-thirty opening time—and Victoria was already there, rearranging a plastic floral display in the front window.

"How long have you been down here?" Sidney asked.

Victoria jumped, whirling toward her with a hand pressed over her heart. "Sidney! I didn't hear you."

"I figured. You okay?"

"Couldn't sleep," Tori admitted. Her eyes flicked toward the office where the computer—and its access to the *Veil* website beckoned. "Are you ready for this?"

"No changing it now. We might as well know."

Together they made their way back to the office and perched side by side in front of the computer. Tori selected the *Veil* website from their favorites list. As they waited for it to load, Sidney clasped Tori's hand, squeezing tight. "We've got this," she murmured.

The website's banner popped up, the rest of the page rapidly filling. The Top Twelve List was the featured article, a huge Best of the Best graphic filling the top half of the page. Tori clicked on it and they both rapidly skimmed through the introductory paragraphs—which told them nothing about the planners who had been chosen other than that they were the best of the best. They advanced to the next page—and the first selectee splashed large across the screen.

Tyson Scott Weddings.

"Of course," Victoria muttered, already scrolling down to click ahead to the second selection.

The Atlanta based wedding planner catered to high profile athletes, rock royalty, and in some cases actual royalty. He'd been a perennial feature on the list for the last four years, so it was no surprise to see him there again.

The second and third choices were also repeats, but the fourth splashy graphic had both Tori and Sidney leaning toward the screen and frowning. "Who are *I Do, I Do Weddings*?" Sidney asked.

"Never heard of them," Tori admitted. "Do you want to read the details or skip ahead?"

"Go," Sidney ordered, too impatient to check out the new competition. "We can come back to them."

After they knew.

Five through eight were familiar. Nine and ten unheard of. And eleven was so obvious Sidney was surprised they hadn't been listed first—they did weddings for Khardashians, after all.

Victoria paused with her hand hovering over the mouse. "Last one."

"We've got this," Sidney said again, though her voice was weaker this time and a sick feeling had begun to coil and churn in her stomach. *Please, please, please.*

Tori clicked the mouse.

Sidney couldn't speak. All the air felt like it had been sucked out of the room, leaving only a vacuum pressure on her lungs. Right. Okay then.

"Dream Weddings, Inc.," Victoria read, as if to reassure herself that she wasn't seeing things.

They hadn't made the list.

It wasn't the only reason Sidney had gone on MMP, or planned Caitlyn's wedding, or gone to the bridal expo. There was more to a successful business than one little list—which was probably all politics and who you knew anyway. But she couldn't seem to wrap her brain around it. They'd failed.

Only one phrase repeated in her head and she said it aloud to Tori. "I'm sorry."

"What?" Tori jerked out of her own haze. "Honey, no. If anyone should be sorry, it's me. I practically forced you to go on that show and for what?"

"No one forced me. I wanted to. Promoting Once Upon a Bride was a convenient excuse, but I wanted to get swept away in my own fairy tale romance so badly I probably would have gone on the show even if it would have hurt the business—God, you don't think it hurt our chances, did it? My mother said something about the lowest common denominator of the viewing public—"

"Stop. Business has almost doubled since the show began airing and it will do even better once the Wedding

Special plays. We don't *need* this stupid list to make rent—not anymore anyway and that's thanks to you."

"I really thought we had it in the bag." Sidney couldn't stop staring at the screen. Dream Weddings, Inc. from Manhattan. They had a good reputation. Professional.

"It's just a list," Tori said, though she sounded more like she was trying to talk herself into it than like she actually believed her own words. "There will be others."

"They'll look like idiots for not including us when Caitlyn's wedding is the event of the summer," Sidney said—though she had no more conviction in her voice than Tori had in hers.

"It's arbitrary," Tori murmured.

"Favoritism and name recognition," Sidney agreed.

"Lots of people are successful who never get these random accolades," Tori said. "It doesn't mean we aren't the best wedding planners for our brides."

"Happy clients are the best advertisements," Sidney repeated the mantra they had lived by when she first started at Once Upon a Bride. "Who needs a list telling us we're the best?"

Tori didn't reply, but they both heard the words hanging unspoken in the air. *They did.* They both wanted the validation—each for their own reasons—and they'd both fallen short this year.

A firm knock rattled the frosted panes of the front door. Tori and Sidney exchanged a glance. "Parv," Sidney predicted. "I'll get it."

Parvati had been almost as excited about the release of the list as they'd been. Sidney only hoped she'd brought some of her muffins to go along with the sympathy.

But when she stepped into the main room of Once

Upon a Bride and looked through the glass front door, it wasn't Parvati waiting impatiently on the front step, but Marguerite Dewitt in all her glory.

"Shit."

Her mother's laser-like eyes had already locked onto Sidney. She couldn't pretend she hadn't heard the door and disappear upstairs to mope until her first appointment of the day. No, she had to deal with her mother.

Her mother never visited Once Upon a Bride. Trust her to pick the absolute worst morning to start.

Or God, what if it was worse than that? What if her mother knew about the list and her failure to get on it? What if she was here to tell Sidney to give up her failing wedding planning career and go into corporate boredom?

Sidney forced herself to keep trudging toward the front door. If she worked the locks more slowly than usual, could anyone really blame her? The chimes overhead jangled cheerfully as she pulled open the engraved door.

"Mother. To what do I owe the honor?"

"I needed to speak to you," Marguerite said, as if the answer should be obvious—ignoring the fact that she had never once, in all of Sidney's twenty-eight years, dropped by to chat.

"Is everything all right?" Sidney stepped back to let her mother inside, closing and locking the door again behind her.

"Of course," she said, since to Marguerite every other option was an impossibility. "Can we go up to your apartment? I prefer not to have my conversations standing around in public if it's all the same to you."

Sidney ground her molars, biting back the urge to tell

her mother that Once Upon a Bride before they opened was hardly *public,* where only Victoria could possibly overhear them.

It wasn't worth the effort. "By all means. Let's go upstairs."

She led her mother to the back stairs. Victoria popped her head out of the office long enough to wince sympathetically when Marguerite's back was turned before retreating back inside. She was probably obsessively researching the twelve wedding planners who had been picked and why. That's what Sidney would have been doing if she hadn't had an unexpected visit from her mother to contend with.

She opened the door to the apartment—silently thanking the fates that she'd been obsessively cleaning since the last time she'd seen Josh and her apartment was now a shrine to cleanliness. Though of course her mother still studied her shabby-chic furniture dubiously, as if wondering if any of it was safe to sit on.

"Would you like some coffee?" Sidney offered, leading the way to the small table near the kitchen so her mother wouldn't have to make the Sophie's choice between the worn-out couch and the over-stuffed recliner.

"Strong and black," her mother instructed, taking one of the chairs at the café table.

Since coffee was one of the few things she and her mother shared a passion for, Sidney knew exactly how to make it and busied herself with the familiar task to avoid thinking about the fact that her mother was here—right when she had failed again with that damn list.

"Your brother told me you didn't make that list you were hoping for."

And she would be sure to kill him next time she saw

him. "I see good news travels fast." *Thank you, internet.*

"Was it an important list?" her mother inquired. "A requirement for doing business?"

"It's good exposure, but we're doing fine on our own," Sidney said, sounding more defensive than she wanted. The words were one hundred percent true—thank goodness—so why did she feel like she was lying when she said them to her mother?

"You'll be on it next year, of course."

Sidney decided she officially hated her mother's *of courses*. As if the option of not making the list for another year was unthinkable. But then, Sidney excelled at failing when her mother saw failure as absurd.

She handed her mother her coffee before taking her own seat across the table, somehow managing not to slam her cup onto the wood. Maybe it was the disappointment, maybe it was the stress of the last few months piling up on her, maybe it was anger at herself for the fact that the one person whose shoulder she wanted to cry on right now was Josh—but whatever the reason, she said exactly what she was thinking.

"*Of course*, we'll be on it next year. Anything less wouldn't be fitting for a Dewitt."

Her mother frowned. "That wasn't what I meant and I don't think I've done anything to deserve that tone."

"How else could you mean it?" Sidney asked.

Her mother set down her coffee, glowering across the table. "I only meant that you've been working very hard lately to increase the profile of your business in a way these magazine people would take notice of, but that those kinds of efforts take time to reap rewards and by this time next year you'll be seeing the benefits of your efforts in a more concrete way."

Sidney froze—the glower and the icy tone were

familiar, but she couldn't seem to process the words. "What?"

"Magazines work months in advance. In order to ensure they could get the photos and quotes they need for the spread, they would have set their list ages ago—probably before they even saw you on that show of yours and you began to be known on a more national level. Certainly before they had any awareness of this TV wedding you're planning. When they see what you've done with it, they'll put you on the list for next year. Probably feature you prominently, if they have any sense."

Sidney's brain moved sluggishly. Her mother sounded certain. Far more certain than either she or Tori had when they were giving themselves pep talks downstairs. She sounded as if the *fact* of Sidney's talent was obvious and the magazine people would be idiots to ignore it. Her mother sounded *proud*. "Thank you?"

"I'm not complimenting you," her mother said, in her usual frank way. "Compliments are for people who need to be told they are good at what they do. You should know without being told."

Sidney frowned, trying to make sense of her mother's unique logic. "Are you telling me you never tell me I do a good job because I should just *know* I've done a good job and I should be insulted if you thought I needed to be told?"

"Exactly."

Sidney tried not to be annoyed with her mother's approach to—well, to everything. She didn't have the energy to make sense of it today. But for the first time, she looked at her mother, really *looked* at her since she'd arrived. There was extra gray in her hair that she hadn't bothered to cover up with dye and the lines around her mouth were more pronounced, her shoulders tight with tension, her grip around her coffee cup white-knuckled.

Whatever she'd come over here to say, she hadn't spit it out yet.

"Mom, why are you here? You never come to Once Upon a Bride and I think this is the third time since I moved in here that you've been to my apartment. Is something wrong? Are you sick?"

"Of course not." Again that tone—as if insulted by the mere thought that she might allow disease into her body. She cleared her throat and adjusted the angle of her coffee mug handle. Then she looked up, meeting Sidney's gaze with matching eyes. "I would like things to change. Between us."

Sidney blinked and then brilliantly said, "Oh."

CHAPTER THIRTY-TWO

Marguerite pursed her lips, seeming to radiate disapproval, but now Sidney was beginning to wonder if she was reading something that wasn't really there.

"Your brother had to tell me about that list of yours because you hate talking to me and if not for Max I would never know about this man you're seeing—"

"I'm not seeing anyone," Sidney interrupted. At her mother's single raised eyebrow, she admitted, "Not anymore."

"I don't want that to be our relationship, Sidney. I know I'm not a normal mother. I've never been good at the maternal things and I don't like to focus on things at which I can't excel, so I've undoubtedly shortchanged you in the mothering department—for which you have my apology—but I do want... that is to say, I want us to talk about things."

Sidney shifted uncomfortably in her chair, not even knowing where to begin. "Don't take this the wrong way, but... what brought this on?"

Her mother's lips pursed again—disapproval or defensiveness? "Your father and I are separated and I'm realizing I don't really know my family."

"Mom! That's the kind of news you lead with. When did that happen?"

Her mother flapped a hand. "It was months ago. We

decided not to publicize it to avoid destabilizing our companies with rumors of a messy divorce."

"I'm not the public, Mom. I'm your daughter. How long has Max known?"

"I spoke with him yesterday, but I think he may have suspected. He didn't seem surprised."

Sidney was surprised enough for both of them. "You've lied to both of us for months?"

Her mother's lips pursed yet again—definitely defensive, Sidney realized. "I didn't know how to tell you. It's not something I'm proud of."

Sidney felt a stab of sympathy. With her mother's obsession with success, a failed marriage had to burn like a son of a bitch.

"You adore love—your entire business is about matrimony. How was I supposed to tell you that your father and I have decided to go our separate ways?"

Sidney didn't have an answer for that, so she stalled for time by drinking her coffee. She'd always felt so uncomfortable around her mother. So ashamed. Was it really possible that her mother felt exactly the same way? "I'm sorry you felt like you couldn't talk to me."

"Yes, well, I've made mistakes in our interactions and I want to rectify them." Trust her mother to be businesslike even when she was trying to mend mother-daughter bonds. "I don't know how to be other than I am, Sidney. I don't know if I was a good wife and I'm fairly certain I wasn't a very good mother, but I do love you."

"I love you too."

Her mother's tense face softened. "Thank you. And that's a start. But I'm hoping that perhaps you and I can get to the point of *liking* one another as well. If you'd be interested in that."

Sidney felt her own defensiveness softening. "I think we can both be better about some things."

Maybe there was hope for them after all.

By the time her mother left and Sidney went back downstairs for her first appointment, everything was not magically solved in her relationship in her mother, but she was—rather surprisingly—in a better mood than she had been before Marguerite's unexpected appearance.

They'd talked some about her parents' separation and Sidney found herself remarkably unfazed by the event which pop culture had taught her ought to be traumatic. But it had been so long since she'd seen her parents actually physically in the same room with one another, and even before then they'd never had the Leave It To Beaver style marriage Josh had ascribed to his parents—her parents were more the board room merger types—so it was hard to work up much more emotion than she would feel at the dissolution of a long-standing business partnership. The fact that they had both contributed DNA to her existence didn't change that.

Sidney met with her ten o'clock prospective client—a nervous young bride down from Santa Barbara who didn't want her socialite mother-in-law to know she wasn't capable of planning the entire wedding herself while also studying for her MCAT exams. She walked the girl out after her appointment and then walked back to the office in search of Victoria.

She found her partner still staring at the *Veil* magazine website.

"Please tell me you haven't been obsessing over that list for the last three hours."

Tori looked up. "I'm not obsessing. I'm researching. I just want to know what they're doing that we aren't." She spun her chair away so her back was to the screen. "What did your mom want?"

"To tell me that she wants to be friends. And she's positive Once Upon a Bride is going to make the list next year. Oh, and just to slip into the conversation that she and my father have been separated for six months."

"Holy shit."

"Yup."

"How are you feeling about all that?" Tori asked cautiously.

"Surprisingly okay."

The chimes over the front door rang.

"Are you expecting a client?" Sidney asked, automatically moving in that direction.

"No." Tori rose to follow her, so they were both nearly knocked off their feet when they stepped into the main room of Once Upon a Bride and literally ran into Parvati.

The stack of magazines she'd been carrying slid from her hands to splat on the floor. A shiny print edition of *The Veil* splayed open beside an *Us Weekly* and a pair of other entertainment tabloids—all three of which featured splashy pictures of Josh and Olga with the words *Splitsville!* and *Dumping Mister Perfect?* in giant yellow letters.

"Sorry!" Parv dropped to her knees, hurriedly shoving the Josh and Olga covers underneath *The Veil* magazine and picking up the stack. "I have the list! I got the first one as soon as they put them on the display at the market, but I haven't looked yet. I came straight here—"

"We've seen it," Tori interrupted as Parv clambered

to her feet. "It's online."

"Oh." Parv's bright-eyed expression fell a notch. "Of course it is. Everything is these days, isn't it? Stupid me." She read the truth on Tori's face and her own fell farther. "You aren't...?"

Sidney shook her head. "No."

Parv rallied quickly. "Well it doesn't mean you aren't the best. What do they know?"

"Maybe we don't need to be the best," Sidney said, and Parv and Tori both looked at her like she'd grown a second head. "What?"

"Are you feeling okay?" Tori asked. "You're the only person I know who is more obsessed with wedding perfection than I am."

Sidney shrugged and moved to the sample table to grab a chair. "I still want the weddings to be perfect for our brides, but maybe the list isn't the most important thing as long as we're making our brides' dreams come true."

"Who are you and what have you done with Sidney Dewitt?" Parvati teased, grabbing another chair at the table as Tori came over to join them as well.

"Are we happier now than we were when we started trying to be on the list?" Sidney asked her partner.

"We have more clients," Tori said carefully. "That's a good thing."

"Remember a few months ago when you tried to remind me that we started this business to help every bride get her dream wedding? Do you still want that?"

"Yeah," Tori said, the answer eloquent in its simplicity.

"Me too. And I want to figure out how to make my dreams come true too."

"I like that plan." Parvati reached across the table to

squeeze her hand.

"What does that entail?" Tori asked—she who had always been nervous about change.

"I'm not going to be Miss Right. If I want to date, maybe I'll join eHarmony to look for a nice guy—"

"Fair warning: internet dating is weird," Parvati announced.

"I'll take my chances. It can't be any stranger than reality television."

Parv snorted. "Wanna bet?"

"Either way, I'm going to stop letting the things I can't have get in the way of my happy ending."

Tori stood abruptly. "Hold that thought." She darted out of the room, returning moments later carrying a bottle of champagne, shiny with condensation. "I had this on hand just in case we made the list, but this is even better." Parvati grabbed glasses off one of the display tables and Tori popped the cork. When they each had a brimming glass of bubbly, Victoria lifted her glass high. "To true friendship, *true* happiness, and to each and every bride getting a dream wedding on her budget. To Once Upon a Bride."

Sidney clinked her glass against Tori's echoing the last words—and for the first time in a long time, feeling like herself again.

CHAPTER THIRTY-THREE

It was strange, standing in front of the beach house and feeling like it was his, but knowing it was only Marissa's now. Marissa's and her new fiancé's.

He'd told himself when he moved out that he would never be back, but it turned out his health insurance didn't care about his vows to himself. They kept sending his mail to the beach house. Marissa had offered to drop them by his apartment, along with a crystal vase his mother had given them for their first anniversary, but he'd balked at the idea of having her see his depressing Divorce Guy apartment—and since he hadn't been house-hunting since things went sideways with Sidney, he was still living the crappy life.

He'd thought this would be better, salvaging what was left of his pride, but seeing his old place might be worse.

He missed it.

Not just the house, but the life. The way living here had made him feel.

Pulling into this driveway had always made him feel like he had it all. He'd loved his life—far more than he'd loved Marissa, if he was honest.

He walked up to the front door and pressed the doorbell, a sense of disorientation swamping him as waited, listening for footsteps on the other side of the door. Instead he heard the sound of the surf and got caught up remembering a thousand nights standing on the back deck, listening to the waves and feeling like he had the world on a string.

He knew she was expecting him, but he was so caught in nostalgia he was surprised when the door popped open suddenly and there she was. Marissa.

Still petite and gorgeous, with her hair flowing over her shoulders in dark brown waves.

He struggled for something to say. "Hi." *TV's Josh Pendleton, ladies and gentleman. Always smooth and suave.*

"Hi." She smiled tentatively up at him. "Come in." She waved him into the foyer, radiating the same discomfort he felt. "I'll just, ah, get the box with your stuff."

She disappeared through the arch toward his den while he hovered awkwardly in the foyer, trying not to feel a sense of possession for the house that still felt like *his* down to his bones. He'd thought he was going to raise his children here, that they would have their thirtieth wedding anniversary party down on the beach. He'd been wrong about a lot of things.

"Here it is," she announced as she reentered the room, carrying a small cardboard box with the logo of an online retailer on the side. "Everything should be in there. The letters look important, so..."

He took the box from her. "Thanks. I appreciate it."

"Of course! It's the least I could... you know."

He nodded, hitching the box up uncomfortably, even though it wasn't heavy or awkwardly shaped. "You doing okay?"

"Yeah!" she said, lunging a little too enthusiastically at the pathetic conversational gambit. Then calming herself down several notches she repeated, "Yeah. You?"

"Good," he confirmed, nodding. "Place looks nice. Different."

She'd redecorated since he moved out. Nothing major. Things that only the two of them would have noticed, but he realized almost instantly that he shouldn't have commented on it. What little comfort she'd gained during their chit-chat vanished and she grimaced uneasily.

"Sorry," he said.

"No, don't apologize. I'm sorry this is so weird."

It could have been a lot worse, he realized. A few months ago, it probably would have been. He wasn't sure what had changed. He still missed his old life, missed it hard, but the grief wasn't so fresh anymore and he felt like he could actually mean what he was about to say.

"I am sorry. About the way things turned out." He hadn't handled the divorce well. Hadn't handled much of the marriage well, if he was being honest. "Did you hate me?"

"No. It would have been easier if I did." She grimaced. "Do you hate me?"

"No. I was mad at you for a long time though." Not anymore, he realized. He wasn't sure when that had stopped. Or maybe it had just receded for a while, like the tide, held at bay by his current bout of nostalgia.

"I didn't sleep with him until we were officially separated, if that makes any difference."

Maybe it should have made it better, but it didn't. Somehow knowing that she hadn't been technically unfaithful when she met and fell in love with another guy while still married to him didn't change a damn thing about how he felt about it. He still hated it.

But he was having a harder time blaming her than he

used to. Strange that being back here at the house he had loved more than his wife made him wonder if he'd ever been any good as a husband.

"Was I a bad husband all along?"

Marissa looked pained by the question. "No. You were great... and horrible."

She didn't need to explain more. He knew exactly what she meant. He'd loved the idea of being married, just like he loved the idea of his perfect life, but he hadn't been good at being there for her. He'd excelled at the big romantic gestures—the MMP-style stuff—but when it came to the minutia of the day to day, he'd mentally checked out.

"We were just wrong for each other," Marissa said, giving him a free pass he wasn't sure he deserved. Though she wasn't entirely innocent either.

He stopped that thought before it could veer into bitterness. At least they weren't snarling at each other anymore. They were never going to be one of those couples who became friends after their divorce. Seeing her was always going to be awkward and complicated—but it wasn't as bad as he'd imagined it might be.

"I should get going."

"Right," she agreed, a little too quickly. "I really hope things go well for you, Josh."

"Yeah. You too."

Autopilot took Josh halfway to Eden before he realized he was on his way to see Sidney—and she probably wouldn't want to see him. His convertible was almost on empty, so he pulled into a gas station to fill up and get his head clear.

It was Tuesday. He should head down to Flannigan's

and meet the guys. He should sign his contracts and drop them at Harry's place so his agent would stop calling him. He *should* do any number of things, but all he wanted was to see her. Or at least talk to her on the phone.

He wanted to tell her about his elaborately staged break-up with Olga—just to see if he could make her laugh. She was the only one with whom he wanted to talk about seeing Marissa again—and see the understanding in her teal eyes. He needed to make sure she was okay after the *Veil* list skipped over Once Upon a Bride—he'd stalked that damn website for weeks, waiting to see if she would hit the list.

He just wanted to hear her voice—and if he wasn't supposed to be seeing her and he wasn't supposed to have feelings for her—well, fuck that.

Josh pulled out his cell phone. Harry answered on the third ring.

"Josh! Did you sign yet?"

"I can't sign them, Harry."

"I don't think we're going to get more money by waiting—"

"I need them to rewrite the morality clause."

That shut Harry up. "What?"

"I'm going to date a former Suitorette—" If she would have him. "—and I'd like you to make it so I'm not in breach of contract by doing so. Have a good night, Harry."

He hung up before his agent could argue and immediately dialed another number.

Sidney's phone connected on the first ring—but it wasn't Sidney's voice saying icily, "She doesn't want to talk to you."

The line was dead before could say a word.

Girls Night In.

She was with her friends and using them as a shield. But the wedding festivities began on Friday. She'd have to see him then. He could wait three days, but then they were going to talk.

He didn't know if he could be any woman's Prince Charming, but Sidney made him want to try. He wasn't giving up yet.

CHAPTER THIRTY-FOUR

Sidney's primary job in the last hours leading up to a wedding was to take all of the bride's worries and concerns onto herself and make them vanish. She was excellent at her job—but in this case it was easy.

Caitlyn was remarkably relaxed for a bride—only freaking out twice about her family and Will's clashing like oil and water, and only having one minor moment of panic over the weather. She had virtually no worries—which left Sidney plenty of time to obsess about her own.

She didn't want time to think about Josh officiating the ceremony tomorrow, or the fact that she would have to talk to him at the rehearsal tonight. She wanted to be consumed with the last minute details, but unfortunately with a small army of MMP staff at her disposal all details had already been seen to.

The wedding party had arrived and were all settled into the bedrooms. Security was already patrolling the grounds—augmented by her brother's specialists. The trellis arch that Caitlyn and Will had selected instead of an altar was set up on the beach, waiting for the rehearsal tonight, and the patio was set with tables for the rehearsal dinner to follow. The centerpieces were lovely, the tablecloths crisp, and the photographer had already been through to take stills for the wedding special.

Everything was set, but Caitlyn scrolled through to-do lists on her tablet, desperately seeking some untended detail to take her mind off the fact that in exactly two hours she would see Josh again.

She wasn't doing a very good job of getting over him so far.

Maybe it was the wedding, maybe it was her innate romanticism, but she couldn't escape the feeling that things weren't quite over between them. They had a final act yet to play out. She felt it in her gut. She just wished she had some hunch what that final act would look like.

When no convenient catastrophe arose to take her mind off him, she tucked her tablet inside her attaché case and wandered down the path to the beach. She kicked off her shoes when the path gave way to sand, leaving them at the edge of the path as she headed down to inspect the trellis arch.

It would be decked out with flowers in the morning—so the delicate blooms wouldn't get damaged by the wind that was expected to kick up along the coast overnight, and so the bride and groom could see the full effect for the first time during the ceremony. Though they would probably have eyes only for one another. Caitlyn and Will had been making goo-goo eyes at one another ever since they arrived. If ever Sidney had to bet on a couple going the distance, she would bet on them.

And to think six months ago, Caitlyn had agreed to marry Daniel.

Sidney walked down the aisle between the white chairs that had been squished into the sand. A light breeze ruffled the ribbons looping between the rows, the sun glinting off the crystal blue water as the surf added its own music to the scene. If tomorrow was half as gorgeous as today, the wedding would be perfect.

Sidney stopped under the trellis arch, trailing a hand over the white painted surface that had finally finished drying.

"Surveying your handiwork?"

Sidney froze at the sound of that voice, taking time to school her features before she turned.

Josh stood a couple feet away, where Will's best man would be tomorrow. Her eyes ate up the sight of him. He wore a pair of khaki trousers and a pastel button down, the casual, beachy look complementing his golden tan. Did he have to look so damn good?

"You're early," she said inanely.

"I was hoping to talk to you."

Her heart rate accelerated in an unruly rush at his words, but she forced herself to stay calm. "Did you have questions about your part in the ceremony?"

"No, I'm good on that front." He thrust his hands into his pockets and she recognized the nervous gesture. "I was hoping we could talk about us."

"Of course." Sidney nodded, clasping her hands in front of her so she wouldn't fidget. This was good. Their final act. She'd known it was coming and it was good to get it out of the way now so it wouldn't be hanging over her during the wedding festivities.

They'd never really had a break-up fight because they'd never really been together, but now if they were going to talk about things she could get the closure she needed. And then she'd finally be able to move on.

There were things she hadn't said the last time she saw him. Things she hadn't felt like she was allowed to say because he hadn't made her any promises. But now she could get it all out.

She would be strong and put a period on their relationship so she could open another chapter in her life.

Sidney glanced back toward the house. They weren't in sight from the patio, but anyone coming down the path would see them long before they knew they were observed. Unsure how this was going to go, she waved down the beach to a more secluded area. "Shall we walk?"

Josh nodded, falling into step beside her. And together they walked down the beach and toward the end of their relationship.

The setting couldn't have been more perfect. It had been picked for the wedding because it reeked of romance and Josh had every intention of using that to his advantage. He'd kicked off his shoes beside hers and they walked barefoot down the beach, the waves washing over their feet and ankles. She kept her hands clasped in front of her, not looking at him or touching him as Josh tried to find the right words to begin.

He had so much to tell her—that he was demanding a contract change so they could be together, that he would do whatever it took to make her not want to go on *Romancing Miss Right* ever again, that he'd officially broken up with Olga and about the strange revelations of seeing Marissa and revisiting his old life.

All the words piled up on his tongue, crowding for space in his mouth, until all he could think to do was what he always told the Suitors and Suitorettes to do— speak from the heart.

"I miss you, Sidney. I want things back the way they were between us."

Her head snapped around and her feet rooted in the sand. *"What?"*

Josh stopped as well, hoping it wasn't a bad sign that she was so shocked. "I love how it felt to be with you. I don't want to lose that. Do you?"

"No."

Relief surged at that single word. She didn't want to lose it either. "There's no reason we have to—"

"No, that's not what I meant."

He frowned. "Sorry?"

"I didn't love how it felt to be with you." She shook her head, struggling for words. "No, that's a lie. I did love it. Until I fell in love with you."

Hope surged. "Sidney—"

"Stop. I didn't say that so you'd feel like you have to parrot the words back to me. I wouldn't believe them now anyway. And it wouldn't matter. How I feel about you and however you feel about me… it's not enough. I'm not going to be the secret mistress forever just because you like how I make you feel."

"I wouldn't ask you to be—"

"No, you don't have to ask, because I'll volunteer for duty, right? Because it's all about the contract and out of your control. But that's bullshit. It's a pretty excuse, but that's all it is. You used me to remind yourself who you could be without Marissa, and even if your job wasn't there as this giant obstacle between us, casting looming shadows of morality clauses and lawsuits, you still wouldn't man up and become the guy I need you to be. Because you're too scared of being hurt again. And too damn cynical to believe that I could be the love of your life. And I'm not going to waste my life hoping you'll suddenly figure out how to be brave."

The sand seemed to be sliding beneath his feet,

everything he wanted slipping away and he couldn't find a single thing to say.

But she wasn't done.

"You know what I think is the only reason you let yourself even look at me? Because you knew I was safely off limits. You couldn't get hurt because I couldn't reject you because you couldn't want me. Well that's great for you, but now I'm the one getting hurt and I don't want to do it anymore."

"I never meant to—"

"No, of course not. No one can blame you because you didn't *want* to hurt me. It just happened. A nasty side effect of letting myself fall for you—which was my own fault. I own that. But I'm planning all these weddings, all day every day, and I *love* what they say. I love the promise to love someone forever. I love being brave enough to say you're going to hold on through thick and thin. But I am never going to have that with you. You want a secret mistress, that's your right. But I'm not that woman. I can't go back to what we had, Josh. I can't get caught up in chemistry and forget everything else. I need to pick the right guy, not just the one who makes me feel dizzy and free and forget everything that really matters to me. Because commitment? That matters to me. Proclaiming yourself in public and belonging to another person till death do you part? I want that. And I'm not going to settle. Not even for you. I deserve better."

He needed to say something. He needed to be brilliant. This was his moment. He was good at big moments. At grand gestures. At speeches. He was TV's Josh Pendleton.

So there was no excuse for what happened next.

He choked.

All the smooth words piled up on his tongue and he couldn't get a single one out of his mouth. He wanted her back—no doubt about that, but this...

He didn't know if he could be what she needed. He didn't want to let her down again. He'd sucked as a husband. He wasn't sure he believed in marriage.

She was right. He was scared shitless. Scared to try again. Scared because when he lost Marissa he lost everything—including his sense of who he was—but with Sidney it would be even worse, because he would lose his whole heart. But living without her...

Unimaginable.

It wasn't just about how she made him feel. It was her. How he wanted to make her feel. He wanted to be good enough for her, but the idea of jumping into commitment again scared the shit out of him and he didn't do scared.

He was good at cocky and arrogant and smoothing over the rough emotional stuff with charm to put the audience back at ease, but he wasn't sure he'd ever really had to be brave before. He was good at taking the easy way, but now that he had to walk the walk, he was balking.

Sidney's name echoed down the beach and she turned back toward the house. "That's Caitlyn. I should get back. Make sure everything's okay."

"Sidney." He caught her wrist, still at a loss for words but needing her to stay, just a little longer, just until he could find the right thing to say.

She tugged away. "We're done here, Josh. I'll see you at the rehearsal."

Josh watched her walk away, his thoughts swimming with everything he hadn't managed to say. Whoever had said it was better to have loved and lost than never to have loved at all had clearly never loved Sidney.

CHAPTER THIRTY-FIVE

Sidney hadn't known it was possible to feel righteous and strong while simultaneously depressed and cranky. Josh was teaching her all sorts of things.

Caitlyn met her halfway up the beach as she headed back toward the house. "How's the bride?" she called as she approached.

Caitlyn frowned, studying her. "Are you okay? Your face looks funny."

"I'm fine," Sidney assured her.

Caitlyn glanced over her shoulder—and Sidney could tell the moment she recognized Josh. "Oh."

"Did you need something?" She would almost have hoped for a wedding crisis to take her mind off things, except she wanted everything to flow smoothly for Caitlyn.

"I was actually hoping you could lie to my mother for me."

It was certainly not the strangest request Sidney had ever gotten from a bride—and she knew Caitlyn's relationship with her mother was as complicated as her own. "About anything in particular?"

"She wants me to play at the reception," Caitlyn explained as Sidney bent to collect the shoes she'd left at the side of the path—pointedly ignoring the large male loafers beside her wedges. "I'm hoping you can tell her that the piano is off-limits according to the owner's orders. Or wildly out of tune. Anything so I don't have to perform at my own wedding. I'm going to play some of *our* songs for Will on our honeymoon, but I don't want my reception to turn into a concert with my mother as the conductor."

"I'll take care of it," Sidney promised. "Overbearing mothers are my specialty."

Together they climbed the steps to the patio, where the tables were set for the rehearsal dinner. Caitlyn stopped, looking over the tastefully decorated area with a little smile. "I'm getting married tomorrow."

"I heard a rumor to that effect," Sidney said with a grin.

Caitlyn looked at her sideways. "Are you sure you're okay?"

"Of course. I'm thrilled for you," Sidney said, intentionally misunderstanding.

"I didn't see it before, but he's the reason you left *Marrying Mister Perfect* early, isn't he?"

If Caitlyn had been just another bride, Sidney might have lied, but she was also a friend—and one of the few people in the world who understood how completely bizarre the experience of reality television dating could be. "Yeah. He is. But it's nothing. There's no future there."

"Do you love him?"

"Maybe. But since when is that enough?" She waved a hand, dismissing the topic. "Let's not talk about my drama. Let's talk about you and Will." Caitlyn beamed and Sidney's own lips curved in automatic response. "You look amazing, Caitlyn. So happy."

"I'm just glad I'm not puking as much anymore. If I can just get through the wedding without morning sickness—or all day sickness, as seems to be my case—then I'll be happy."

She wasn't showing yet. Her modest curves might be a little fuller, but other than that the only symptom of her pregnancy was a distinct glow. Or maybe that was just the euphoria that came with marrying the man of her dreams.

Caitlyn had it. The life Sidney had always wanted. Adoring fiancé. Baby on the way. She'd taken a detour through Daniel to get there, but she'd found her happily-ever-after.

"I envy you," Sidney admitted, linking arms with Caitlyn as they headed back inside. "Will looks at you like you're a princess."

"Not a princess," Caitlyn corrected. "Daniel tried to put me on a pedestal, but Will wants to hold my hand as we go through every adventure in life. That's a thousand times better. Not that he's perfect—he's grumpy in the mornings and he holds grudges like you wouldn't believe, but he's mine. And I think he's going to be a great dad, which is good because I'm terrified of becoming a mom."

"You're going to be amazing."

"So are you, Sid." Caitlyn squeezed their linked arms. "It's going to happen for you. What is it you're always saying? Just a bump on the road to your happily-ever-after?"

"My road might need some serious maintenance."

"Just dodge the potholes the best you can. You'll get there." Caitlyn paused, looking out the bay window with the view out over the ocean. "Did I ever tell you Will was engaged before?"

"No, you never mentioned it."

"Broke his heart. Took him ages to get to where he

could even see past it, but when he did, do you know what he saw?"

"You?"

"Yeah, well, he heard me first. Playing the piano. So just keep your heart open and keep listening, okay? It'll be your turn soon."

Sidney knew Caitlyn was trying to help, but it was hard to believe her today. She knew she'd made the right choice by turning down Josh's offer to go back to being his secret mistress. She needed more than he could give her—and the look of terror in his eyes when she'd mentioned marriage had proved that. But how was she supposed to forget the way he made her feel?

Her heart had been open and he'd snuck right in—and now she didn't know how to get him out again.

The rehearsal had gone well—as long as Josh didn't mind the fact that Sidney was avoiding him as if he were contagious.

He knew she was busy, so he tried to stay inconspicuous as the rehearsal dinner devolved into an endless series of toasts by the groom's very enthusiastic sisters. Or at least that's why he told himself he was lurking in shadows. It had nothing to do with the fact that he still didn't know what to say to her.

Silver-tongued Josh Pendleton at a loss for words.

If his friends could see him now.

His cell phone vibrated in his pocket as another of the groom's sisters got up and began speaking in an attempt to outdo her siblings. He withdrew it and, seeing the caller-ID, almost let it go to voicemail, but he must be a glutton for punishment today, because he connected the call, moving into the yard away from the celebration as he answered.

"Hey, Harry. Did you get that morality clause revised?"

"No, but we don't have to worry about that anymore. The show's been canceled."

Josh froze, an oily mess of déjà vu called up by the words. "That isn't funny."

"Believe me, I know," Harry grumbled. "The network has decided to use the time slot for one of those dark scripted dramas that are so trendy right now. Something political and edgy that will get people screaming at one another on Twitter."

"But I thought our ratings have never been better." The feeling was familiar—solid ground sliding out from beneath his feet, but it felt different this time than when *Brainiac* had been cancelled. Like a graze of panic rather than a direct hit.

"Reality shows like MMP are blowing up on cable, but the network thinks a wrongful imprisonment drama is going to get them more viewers. There's a chance *Marrying Mister Perfect* might get picked up by Bravo or OWN, but they're going to be doing a stripped down version—less exotic travel and they aren't going to have the budget to pay your salary. They'll bring in a younger, cheaper host unless you're willing to take a huge pay cut."

Josh cursed.

"Hey, don't worry," Harry said. "This is a temporary setback. How do you feel about *Dancing with the Stars*?"

"Hosting?"

"No, they love Tom. But can you dance?"

"No."

"That's okay. They teach you."

"Harry, I'm not going on *Dancing With The Stars*."

"Don't decide anything right now. Just think about it," Harry insisted. "We need to keep you current and get something else lined up before the entire town knows MMP is going to basic cable."

"How big a pay cut are we talking if I stay with the show?"

"Let's not go there yet. Stay positive, Josh. They're still planning to air the Wedding Special when they need to fill a slot. Be grateful for that."

But as Josh signed off and disconnected the call, there was only one thing he was grateful for—no more morality clauses. He could date whoever the hell he wanted.

He waited for the dread and what-the-hell-do-I do-now panic to hit like it had last time his show had been cancelled, but instead all he felt as he replayed the conversation again in his mind was a subtle whisper of relief.

It was over. That chapter of his life was closed. And for once he wasn't freaking out about that.

He needed to find Sidney.

He moved quickly back to the rehearsal dinner to find that the party was winding down—and a familiar figure with long blonde hair was nowhere in sight. He did bump into the bride—who was surrounded by her bridesmaids and giggling just as enthusiastically as the heavy drinkers even though she hadn't had a drop thanks to the baby.

"Have you seen Sidney?" he asked.

"I'm pretty sure she went home," Caitlyn told him. "Big day tomorrow!" The bridesmaids—most of whom he recognized as the groom's sisters—cheered.

He thanked Caitlyn, swearing internally. He could go to Sidney's apartment—it wasn't far—but he wasn't sure how well that would go over. And he knew how important this wedding was to her. He didn't want to throw her off her game.

But if he could just see her, just get the damn words out—

"Hey Josh."

He turned back to the blushing bride, who was no longer surrounded by a horde of bridesmaids.

"Are you in love with her?" the redhead asked, gazing up at him calmly—as if she hadn't just asked him the biggest question of his entire freaking life.

"Yes."

And for the first time, he admitted—to himself, to Caitlyn, to the world—that it was true.

Caitlyn smiled. "Good."

She turned to head into the house and he called after her, "That's it?"

Caitlyn turned back. "Does there need to be more?"

"I guess not."

She grinned. "Good answer. Now try not to screw it up."

She vanished inside.

But he'd already screwed it up. And he didn't have the words to put it right again. Not tonight.

CHAPTER THIRTY-SIX

The wedding was perfection. Even when Will got so choked up he stumbled over his vows. Or perhaps especially then. Sidney had sniffled sentimentally along with the rest of the guests as the groom struggled for words.

Josh had been the ideal officiate—but she shouldn't have been surprised by that. He excelled at setting the perfect tone of weighty importance and celebratory joy.

Sidney had managed to avoid him all through the afternoon wedding and well into the evening reception—grateful that her job kept her busy. Nothing was going wrong, but there were always dozens of micro-issues which could snowball into disasters if they weren't caught and managed before they could explode. So she stayed on top of them, making sure Will and Caitlyn had nothing to worry about but one another and how euphoric they were.

Sidney ducked inside the house, retreating from the glow of the fairy lights that illuminated the patio now that the sun had set and into the quasi-dark of the house—kept dim enough to discourage the party from spilling inside but still bright enough that none of the guests crashed into walls on their way to the restrooms.

"Hey, Max." She approached the form of her brother, lurking in one of the shadows provided by the low lighting as he watched over the party. "Have any of your guys seen Elena? She looked upset when she was talking to Daniel earlier and now she's missing."

"She didn't come this way, but maybe someone else saw her." Max took a moment to murmur over his comms with the rest of his team while Sidney fidgeted.

When Caitlyn had said she was inviting Daniel, Sidney had been surprised, but Josh had been supportive of the idea of including the former Mister Perfect—and Caitlyn's former fiancé—in the festivities. He'd said it would give the tabloids fewer opportunities to make up stories about bad blood and MMP feuds. Caitlyn had just wanted Daniel there because she saw him as an integral bump in her road to love, so Sidney had swallowed her reservations.

But now that Daniel was drunk and making an ass of himself with all the other Suitorette guests, she was wishing she'd been a little firmer when she aired her concerns. Daniel had even cornered her at one point, asking if there was still a chance for them to reclaim what they had lost—as if there had ever been anything to lose. She could only imagine what he was saying to Samantha and Elena—the last two girls he had dumped before proposing to Caitlyn.

Samantha had looked annoyed, but it was Elena— tough as nails and sexy as sin Elena—who had looked distraught after speaking with Daniel. Elena who never shied away from making a scene—not that Sidney expected her to do so at Caitlyn's wedding, but she'd feel better if she knew where the tempestuous Latina was hiding.

"Dylan saw her head through the side door and upstairs a few minutes ago," Max reported. "You want me to have him check up on her?"

"Do you mind? I'll feel better if I know where she is, but I don't want to compromise your security."

"It would take more than that to compromise our security," Max said, sounding slightly offended. "I'll have Dylan take a look and let you know if anything's wrong."

"Thanks."

She stepped back out onto the patio—and nearly ran into a tall figure in a dark suit. Josh.

"Sidney. I've been looking for you."

"Oh?" she feigned nonchalance. "I've been so busy I haven't had a second to spare. In fact, right now, I really should be—" Her mind went blank. A blackboard totally erased of all excuses. "Um…"

"Dance with me?"

"No, the cake. I need to check on the cake—"

"The one we already ate?"

"Leftovers. Make sure everyone got enough. Freeze the top tier for Caitlyn and Will's first anniversary. A wedding planner's job is never done."

"Everything is perfect. You can take five minutes to dance with me."

"In public? Doesn't that violate your morality clause?"

"Not anymore. The network is dropping MMP."

"You're joking." Shock ricocheted through her system. "But it's so popular."

"Not compared to scripted crime dramas, apparently. The show might be picked up for basic cable, but either way I'm out."

"Oh Josh. I'm so sorry."

"I'm not sure I am."

"What?" she asked, in the height of eloquence.

"I'm still figuring out what I want to do next, but

right now I just want to dance with you. Please, Sidney? After I choked yesterday, I went home and wrote a whole speech. Rehearsed it in front of the mirror for hours and I really think it has more impact if we're dancing."

"You wrote a speech?"

"Sort of a romantic manifesto. Though maybe it's better if I deliver it here. No bells and whistles. No big, dramatic *Marrying Mister Perfect* staging."

"A manifesto?" she repeated dazedly.

"You said your piece yesterday. Now it's my turn."

She swallowed nervously, trying to smother the tendrils of hope that tried to twine around her heart. He just wanted the same closure she'd gotten. That was all this was. "That seems fair."

He nodded. "Right. So I guess here it is." He took her hands and his were clammy. She noticed the sweat beading his brow. No smooth TV host here. He was more nervous than she'd ever seen him. His Adam's apple bobbed as he swallowed. "The night we met, you promised not to fall in love with me—"

"You remember that?"

"I remember everything about you, but don't interrupt."

"Sorry."

He nodded. "The night we met, you promised not to fall in love with me, but you never promised not to make me fall in love with you."

Her mouth fell open. "Oh."

"I know you said you won't believe me if I say it now, but I have to. Because it's true. I love you. And I am scared—scared shitless—but not for the reasons you think. I was a bad husband—I didn't love her like I should have. I was great at the big romantic MMP bullshit, the greeting card, social-media version of love, but I sucked at the day to day business of being there for someone—and I don't want to screw it up with you. Because you know me in a way no one else does. You see through my bullshit and you still love me anyway. Or you did, before I screwed it up."

"Can I say something?"

"There's more."

"We were never about big romantic gestures," she told him. "House hunting and wedding planning and cooking dinner at home or sharing Mama's cannoli—those aren't big MMP moments. That was just us. The question is whether that's what you want. That regular, non-glamorous life."

"I cover that in my speech."

"Then by all means, continue."

He nodded, resuming his rehearsed speech. "I thought I had the picture perfect marriage before, but it was all surface and no substance. I'm not looking for the picture perfect life anymore, but I don't know how to be anything else. I'm not sure I can be the kind of husband you deserve, but you make me feel like I'm not pretending. Like I'm not an actor playing at being Josh Pendleton. I want to be real with you. And you make me want to be what you need. You said, that first night we met, that you want to believe in love. So believe in mine. Where's that crazy optimist who hid in my room that first night? Because I know she's still in there. Please let her believe in us."

She caught her lip between her teeth, her own nerves spiking with a surge of hope and uncertainty. "Are you sure this is what you want, Josh?"

"Sidney, I want you. However I can have you."

Her heart galloped.

"I want us," he continued. "I don't know what the future holds, but I want to figure out the next step with you. And someday—though it still scares the shit out of me to say it—I want you to be the one I come home to every night. I want kids. I want cheesy vacations at Disney World. And I want to be a television host who knows how to go home and be a real person. Because none of it will mean anything without you. So what do *you* want, Sidney?"

A year ago she would have said a spread in *The Veil* magazine and Mister Perfect—but that was the picture perfect life Josh had been talking about. She'd been just as seduced by it as he was, in her own way. And now... what did she really want?

"I want to keep planning weddings, giving every bride her dream—even if it isn't always high profile or glamorous. I want to stop counting my failures and successes and just enjoy where I am in the moment. I want to look in the mirror and be proud of who I am now without any bitterness about how the world sees me. And I want..."

"Yes?"

She met brown eyes as rich and warm as chocolate. "I want you."

"So I didn't screw everything up already?"

"Can you repeat that thing you said before?"

"The whole speech?"

"No, just the part I said I wouldn't believe."

He grinned, perfect white teeth flashing. "I love you."

She'd told herself that it took more than love, that she needed more than a feeling, that she would never let her heart overrule her head. But... "That was a pretty good speech." She hooked a finger in his lapel.

"I practiced it." He looked down at her, brown eyes intent—his nerves shining through his debonair shell. "So what do you say, Sidney? Will you take a chance on me?"

She pulled his mouth down to hers, brushing it with a kiss. "I think I'll take that dance now."

CHAPTER THIRTY-SEVEN

The cans Will's sisters had tied to the back of the limo rattled off into the night as it carried Caitlyn and Will off to their honeymoon. Josh tucked Sidney tighter against his side as they turned and headed back into the mansion with the remaining guests. The reception was winding down, but there were still a few die hards on the dance floor.

It was strange, his life had never been more up in the air, the future such a complete unknown, but he'd also never felt so settled and so *right* as he did just swaying on the dance floor with Sidney, enjoying each moment and waiting to see what the next would hold.

He'd been caught up in making life happen in the last decade and it had gotten him where he wanted to go, but it wasn't until he got there that he was left to wonder if the journey had been any fun. He may not know what his destination was with Sidney, but he was going to enjoy every second of the journey. And maybe the destination would turn out to be the one he'd thought he wanted all along. Or maybe not. Only time would tell.

He bent his head close to her ear. "Do you need to stick around to supervise clean up or can we take off?"

"I have a crew coming in the morning to clean up. We can call it a night."

"Thank God," he groaned, not bothering to hide his relief. He hadn't had Sidney alone in far longer than he wanted to think about. "Did you valet your car?"

"Max gave me a lift. I'll just grab my bag and text him that I have a ride home and we can get out of here."

She tugged him toward the small room where the staff had stored their belongings, but before they got two feet a strident voice stopped them.

"Josh Pendleton. I hear you're unemployed."

He turned toward Miranda, surprised to find her dressed in a flowing scarlet dress with her arm around Bennett Lang—the King of Reality Television. It looked like they were definitely on again.

Josh joined Miranda and Bennett as Sidney slipped away to grab her things. "You know this business," he said with a shrug.

"I do," Miranda agreed, her signature note of arrogance touching the words. "Which is why I think they're morons for not keeping you attached to the MMP brand when they move to a new network. But their loss is my gain."

"Are you looking for a new host of *American Dance Star*?"

"Actually, lately I've been toying with an idea for a new show. Ah, Sidney. Good. This concerns you too," Miranda said as Sidney joined them. She waved to the patio where the last of the wedding celebration was winding down. "All this was fabulous. How would you feel about doing it again?"

Sidney frowned, confused. "That is my job. I plan weddings."

"I meant on television. I've seen the footage from the wedding special. You two are dynamic together. And a happily-ever-after every week would certainly fit right into both of your brands. I was thinking sort of an Extreme Makeover: Wedding Edition, where you swoop in to give deserving brides the wedding of their dreams. Cancer survivors. Military vets. Real feel good stuff. Everyday Cinderellas and the wedding fairy godmother. We could even call it *Once Upon a Bride*."

Sidney blinked. "Are you serious?"

Josh knew Miranda too well to ask that. "You already have a network interested, don't you?"

"We're still working out the details." Miranda glanced toward Bennett Lang. "Just think about it. We can talk more on Monday."

Having dropped her bombshell, Miranda and Bennett retreated in a cloud of importance. Sidney and Josh walked in silence toward where he'd parked his car—having claimed one of the few driveway spaces not occupied by the bridal party.

"We don't have to do it," Josh said, dying to know what was going on in her head as he opened the passenger door of his convertible for her. "I know you weren't comfortable in front of the cameras and you never wanted to be famous—"

"It's different with you," she interrupted, climbing in. "I never felt like I had to hide from the cameras when you were there. I could just be me. And this wouldn't be *Mister Perfect*. I could be the fairy godmother." He rounded the hood and when he slid behind the wheel, she smiled at him. "You do make a good wedding planner."

"We make a good team."

"True." She nodded. "Though maybe we shouldn't work together *and* date all at once right from the start. Are you sure you don't want me to go on the new cable version of *Romancing Miss Right*?"

"Don't even joke about it." He put the car in gear, carefully backing out of the drive.

"This was fun," she said, cautious and slow. "Planning the wedding on television. It could be fun to give it another go. We'd be doing something good. Don't you think?"

"I've wanted to do it from the second she mentioned it," he admitted. "But that might just be because I can't imagine anything better than being paid to argue with you about floral arrangements."

"*Once Upon a Bride*... It could be pretty awesome. And if it fails..."

"Where's the fun in life if we don't crash and burn every now and then? Besides, it's about the journey, not the destination, right?"

She groaned. "New rule. If we do this, no *journey* talk. I had enough of that on *Marrying Mister Perfect* to last a lifetime."

"Deal. We'll just make sure we talk about how all our brides and grooms are there for the *Right Reasons* and they want to make the most of this *amazing experience* with their *hearts open* and—"

"Josh."

"Yes, my love?"

"Shut up and drive."

"Yes, my angel."

She might not want to hear the word journey, but he had a feeling their life together was going to be an amazing one. Wherever it took them. Perfection not required.

ABOUT THE AUTHOR

Winner of the Romance Writers of America's prestigious Golden Heart Award, Lizzie Shane lives in Alaska where she uses the long winter months to cook up happily-ever-afters (and indulge her fascination with the world of reality television). She also writes paranormal romance under the pen name Vivi Andrews. Find more about Lizzie or sign up to receive her Newsletter for updates on upcoming Reality Romance books at www.lizzieshane.com

DID YOU ENJOY
PLANNING ON PRINCE CHARMING?

Sign up to receive Lizzie's Newsletter at www.lizzieshane.com or support the series by leaving a review on Amazon or Goodreads.

AND DON'T MISS THE REST OF THE REALITY ROAMNCE SERIES:

MARRYING MISTER PERFECT
(Reality Romance, Book 1)

ROMANCING MISS RIGHT
(Reality Romance, Book 2)

FALLING FOR MISTER WRONG
(Reality Romance, Book 3)

PLANNING ON PRINCE CHARMING
(Reality Romance, Book 4)

COURTING TROUBLE
(Reality Romance, Book 5)
Coming in 2016

CPSIA information can be obtained
at www.ICGtesting.com
Printed in the USA
LVHW101148220422
PP17295200002B/1

9 781516 906727